D1486593

C334252047

AN UNWANTED GUEST

Shari Lapena

BANTAM PRESS

LONDON · NEW YORK · TORONTO · SYDNEY · AUCKLAND

TRANSWORLD PUBLISHERS
61–63 Uxbridge Road, London W5 5SA
www.penguin.co.uk

Transworld is part of the Penguin Random House group of companies
whose addresses can be found at global.penguinrandomhouse.com

First published in Great Britain in 2018 by Bantam Press
an imprint of Transworld Publishers

Copyright © 1742145 Ontario Limited 2018

Shari Lapena has asserted her right under the Copyright,
Designs and Patents Act 1988 to be identified as the author of this work.

This book is a work of fiction and, except in the case of historical fact,
any resemblance to actual persons, living or dead, is purely coincidental.

Every effort has been made to obtain the necessary permissions with
reference to copyright material, both illustrative and quoted. We apologize
for any omissions in this respect and will be pleased to make the
appropriate acknowledgements in any future edition.

A CIP catalogue record for this book is available from the British Library.

ISBN 9780593079645 (hb)
9780593079652 (tpb)

Typeset in 11.5/16 pt Sabon by Jouve (UK), Milton Keynes
Printed and bound in Great Britain by Clays Ltd, Elcograf S.p.A.

Penguin Random House is committed to a sustainable
future for our business, our readers and our planet. This book
is made from Forest Stewardship Council® certified paper.

1 3 5 7 9 10 8 6 4 2

To Mum

Acknowledgements

I continue to be hugely grateful that I work with some of the best people in the business. To my publishers in the US – Brian Tart, Pamela Dorman, and the fantastic team at Viking Penguin – thank you, once again, for doing a terrific job. To Larry Finlay and Frankie Gray at Transworld UK and the fabulous team there – thank you – you are all outstanding. To Kristin Cochrane, Amy Black, Bhavna Chauhan, and the superb team at Doubleday Canada – thank you, again, for everything. I'm extremely fortunate to have so many truly talented, committed, and enthusiastic people behind me. I could not do this without all of you.

Thank you, once again, to Helen Heller – I appreciate you more than I can ever say. Thank you also to everyone at the Marsh Agency for your continued excellent representation worldwide.

Special thanks to Jane Cavolina for being a super copyeditor.

Thanks, too, to Lieutenant Paul Pratti of the Sullivan County Sheriff's Office for his generous assistance.

ACKNOWLEDGEMENTS

I'd like to say that any mistakes in the manuscript are entirely mine.

Lastly, and always, thank you to my husband, Manuel, and to our kids, Christopher and Julia – your support and enthusiasm mean the world to me.

AN UNWANTED GUEST

Chapter One

THE ROAD CURVES and twists unexpectedly as it leads higher and deeper into the Catskill Mountains, as if the further you get from civilization, the more uncertain the path. The shadows are deepening, the weather worsening. The Hudson River is there, appearing and disappearing from view. The forest that rises on either side of the road has a lurking quality, as if it might swallow you whole; it is the forest of fairy tales. The softly falling snow, however, lends it all a certain postcard charm.

Gwen Delaney grips the steering wheel tightly and squints through the windscreen. She's more one for grim fairy tales than picture postcards. The light is going; it will soon be dark. The snow coming down makes driving more difficult, more tiring. The flakes hit the glass in such profusion that she feels as though she's stuck in some kind of relentless video game. And the road is definitely becoming more slippery. She's grateful that she has good tyres on her little Fiat. Everything is turning into a white blur; it's hard to tell where the road ends and the ditch begins. She'll be glad when they get there. She's beginning to wish they'd chosen an inn a little less remote; this one is miles from anywhere.

Riley Shuter is silent in the passenger seat beside her, a ball of quiet tension; it's impossible not to pick up on it. Just being with her in the small car puts Gwen on edge. She hopes she hasn't made a mistake bringing her up here.

The whole point of this little escape, Gwen thinks, is to get Riley to relax a little, to take her mind off things. Gwen bites her lip and stares hard at the road ahead. She's a city girl, born and bred; she's not used to country driving. It gets so dark up here. She's becoming anxious now – the drive has taken longer than planned. They shouldn't have stopped for coffee at that cute little antique place along the way.

She's not sure what she expected, suggesting this weekend getaway, other than a change of scenery, a chance to spend some quiet time together, with nothing to remind Riley that her life is in ruins. Perhaps that was naive.

Gwen has her own baggage, less recent, and she, too, carries it with her everywhere she goes. But she's decided she's going to put that behind her for this weekend at least. A small luxury hotel deep in the country, good food, no internet, pristine nature – it's exactly what they both need.

Riley watches nervously out of the car window, peering into the shadowy woods, trying not to imagine someone jumping in front of their car at any second, waving them down. She clenches her hands into fists inside the pockets of her down jacket. She reminds herself that she's not in Afghanistan any more. She's home, safe, in New York State. Nothing bad can happen to her here.

Her career has changed her. Seeing what she has seen, Riley is so different that she hardly recognizes herself any more. She glances furtively at Gwen. They'd been close once. She's not even sure why she agreed to come with her to this faraway country inn. She watches Gwen concentrating fiercely on the winding road up the slippery incline, heading into the mountains. 'Are you okay?' she asks suddenly.

'Me?' Gwen says. 'Yeah, I'm fine. We should be there soon.'

In journalism school, when they were both at NYU, Gwen had been the steady, pragmatic one. But Riley was ambitious – she wanted to be where it was happening. Gwen had no taste for adventure. She'd always preferred books, and quiet. Out of journalism school, unable to find a decent job at a newspaper, Gwen had quickly parlayed her skills into a good corporate communications position and had never seemed to regret it. But Riley had headed to the war zones. And she'd managed to keep it together for a long time.

Why does she do this? Why does she keep thinking about it? She can feel herself starting to come apart. She tries to slow her breathing, the way she's been taught. To stop the images from coming back, from taking over.

David Paley parks his car in the shovelled parking area to the right of the hotel. He gets out of the car and stretches. The weather made the drive from New York City longer than expected, and now his muscles are stiff – a reminder that he's not quite as young as he used to be. Before grabbing his overnight bag from the back seat of his Mercedes, he stands for a moment in the thickly falling snow, looking at Mitchell's Inn.

It's a three-storey, graceful-looking structure of red brick and gingerbread trim, encircled by nearby forest. The front of the small hotel is open to view, with what must be a rather grand lawn underneath all the snow. Tall evergreens and mature trees bereft of leaves but draped in white seem to encroach on the building from a short distance away. In the front, an enormous tree in the middle of the lawn extends its thick branches in every direction. All is covered in a pure, muffling white snow. It feels quiet here, peaceful, and he feels his shoulders begin to relax.

There are large, rectangular windows spaced regularly across all three floors. Wide steps lead up to a wooden porch and double front doors decorated with boughs of evergreens. Although it is still daylight – barely – the lamps on either side of the doors are lit, and soft yellow light also spills from the windows on the ground floor, giving the building a warm, welcoming appearance. David stands still, willing the stresses of the day – and the week, and the years – to recede as the snow falls gently on his hair and tickles his lips. He feels like he's walking into an earlier, more gracious, more innocent time.

He will try not to think about work for an entire forty-eight hours. Everyone, no matter how busy, needs to recharge once in a while, even – perhaps especially – a top criminal attorney. It's rare for him to be able to fit in any downtime at all, much less an entire weekend. He's determined to enjoy it.

Friday, 5:00 PM

Lauren Day glances at the man next to her, Ian Beeton. He's driving his car expertly in rather challenging conditions, and making it all look easy. He has a disarming smile, and he turns it on her now. She smiles back. He's nice-looking, too, tall and spare, but it's the smile that first attracted her to him, his laid-back charm that makes him so appealing. Lauren rummages through her handbag for her lipstick. She finds it – a nice shade of red that brightens her face – and applies it carefully while looking in the mirror on the visor in front of her. The car skids a bit and she stops what she's doing, but Ian straightens the vehicle skilfully. The road winds more steeply now, and the car has an increasing tendency to swerve as it loses traction.

'Getting slippery,' she says.

'No worries. Nothing I can't handle,' he says and grins at her. She smiles back. She likes his self-confidence, too.

'Whoa – what's that?' she says suddenly. There's a dark shape in front of them to the right. It's a dull day, and with the snow falling so heavily it's hard to see, but it looks like there's a car in the ditch.

She stares keenly out of the window as they pass the vehicle, and Ian looks for somewhere to stop. 'I think there's someone in that car,' she says.

'Why don't they have the hazard lights on?' he mutters. He pulls over slowly to the side of the road, careful not to slide off the road himself. Lauren gets out of the warmth of the car and plunges into several inches of virgin snow, which immediately falls inside her boots, stinging her ankles. She can hear Ian getting out of the car, too, slamming the door.

'Hey!' she cries down to the motionless car. The driver's door opens slowly.

Lauren clambers down the incline carefully, sliding as she goes. The ground is uneven and she finds it hard to keep her balance. She reaches the car and grabs on to the door with her left hand for support as she peers into the front seat. 'You okay?' she asks.

The driver is a woman close to her own age – around thirty. She appears a bit shaken up, but the windscreen isn't cracked and she's wearing a seat belt. Lauren looks beyond the driver to the woman in the passenger seat. Her face is pale and sweating, and she's staring straight ahead, as if Lauren isn't even there. She looks like she's had a dreadful shock.

The driver glances quickly at her companion, and then turns back to Lauren gratefully. 'Yes, we're fine. We went off the road just a few minutes ago. We were wondering what to do next. Lucky for us you came along.'

Lauren feels Ian come up behind her and peer over her shoulder at the two women inside the car. He smiles his charming smile at them. 'Looks like you're going to need a tow.'

'Great,' the driver says.

'Where you headed?' Lauren asks.

'Mitchell's Inn,' she answers.

'Well, isn't that lucky,' Ian says. 'That's where we're going, too. Although I don't think there's much else out here. Why don't we give you a lift, and you can arrange from the hotel for someone to come and get your car out?'

The woman smiles with relief and nods. She's obviously glad to be rescued. Lauren doesn't blame her. You could freeze to death out here all by yourself. But the woman with her doesn't react. She seems to be in her own world.

'You have any bags?' Lauren asks.

'Yes, in the back.' The driver gets out of the car and struggles through the deep snow to the back of the vehicle. Her passenger now seems to snap out of her trance and gets out on the other side. The driver opens the boot as the woman appears beside her. They each grab an overnight bag.

Ian reaches down and offers all three women a hand up to the road. Even with help, it's an awkward climb.

'Thanks so much,' the driver says. 'My name is Gwen, and this is Riley.'

'I'm Lauren and this is Ian,' she says. 'Let's get in the car. It's so cold.' She casts a furtive glance at the woman named Riley, who hasn't said a word. She wonders what's up with her. Something about her definitely seems off.

Chapter Two

BEVERLY SULLIVAN DROPS her overnight bag at her feet and lets her eyes sweep around the room. It's perfect. Just like the one in the brochure. There's an old-fashioned luxury here that she's not accustomed to, and she moves about the room, touching things. The antique, king-size bed is heaped with pillows. The carved wardrobe is gorgeous, and the thick Oriental carpet must have cost a fortune. She steps up to the windows, which face out over the front of the hotel. The snowfall has made everything indescribably beautiful. New-fallen snow always makes her feel hopeful.

She turns away from the windows and peeks into the en suite bathroom – a spotless oasis of white marble and fluffy white towels. She checks her appearance briefly in the elaborate mirror over the vanity unit and turns away. Sitting down on the bed, testing it, she begins to wonder what's taking her husband so long. Henry had stayed down at the front desk to inquire about

8

cross-country skis and God knows what else, and she'd come up to the room herself. He insisted that she not wait for him, although she'd been perfectly willing to sit in one of the deep-blue velvet chairs or sofas around the stone fireplace in the lobby while he fussed over the equipment. But she didn't want to make an issue of it. She tries not to feel disappointed. It will take time for him to begin to relax. But he seems to be looking for ways to fill their weekend with activities, when all she wants is to slow down and simply be together. It's almost as if he's avoiding being with her, as if he doesn't want to be here at all.

She knows her marriage is in . . . disrepair. She wouldn't say it's in trouble, exactly. But it needs work. They have drifted apart, begun to take each other for granted. She's guilty of it, too. How does a modern marriage survive all the forces that converge to tear it apart? Too much familiarity, the dreariness of domesticity, of paying bills, raising children. Of having full-time jobs and always too much to do. She doesn't know if a weekend away at a lovely and remote place in the country will make that much of a difference, but it could be a start. A start they certainly wouldn't get if they stayed at home. They desperately need a chance to reconnect, to remember what they like about each other. Away from squabbling, sullen teenagers who demand their attention and drain their energies. She sighs and slumps inwardly; she wishes they didn't argue so much about the kids. She's hoping that here they'll be able to talk about things without being interrupted, without that constant, wearying, underlying tension.

She wonders with a vague unease how the weekend will unfold, and if anything will be different by the time they return home.

*

Henry Sullivan lingers near the reception desk in the lobby to the left of the grand staircase. The smell of logs burning in the fireplace reminds him of Christmases as a boy. He looks at some glossy flyers advertising local restaurants and attractions. Although 'local' may be stretching it a bit. They're pretty far away from things up here. Unfortunately, with all the snow, it looks like it might be too difficult to go anywhere anyway, but the young man at the desk said the snowploughs would be running tomorrow, and the roads should be fine. Henry fingers the mobile phone in his trouser pocket. There's no reception up here, which is something he hadn't been expecting. Beverly hadn't mentioned that. He feels a twinge of annoyance.

He's not sure why he agreed to this weekend away, except perhaps out of guilt. He already regrets it; he just wants to go home. He fantasizes harmlessly for a moment about getting back in his car and leaving his wife here. How long would it be before she noticed he was gone? What would she do? Quickly, he squashes the fantasy.

His wife has been looking increasingly unhappy lately, but, he tells himself, it's not just because of him. It's the kids, too. Her job. Encroaching middle age. Her thickening waistline. It's everything. But one person can't be responsible for another person's happiness. She is responsible for her own. He can't make her happy.

Yet, he's not a complete heel. He knows it's not that simple. He loved her once. She's the mother of his children. He simply doesn't love her any more. And he has no idea what to do about it.

Dana Hart stamps the snow off her Stuart Weitzman boots at the front doorstep and looks around the lobby approvingly. The first thing that strikes her is the grand central staircase. The newel post and banisters are elaborately carved out of a burnished, dark wood. The stairs are wide, with a thick runner in a dark floral pattern. She can see the glint of the brass carpet rods holding the runner in place. It's very impressive, and these days Dana isn't easily impressed. The staircase makes her think of Scarlett O'Hara in *Gone with the Wind*, or perhaps Norma Desmond in *Sunset Boulevard*. It's the kind of staircase you put on your best long dress for, and make an entrance, she thinks. *I'm ready for my close-up.* Unfortunately, she didn't bring any evening gowns. What a shame for such a glorious staircase to go to waste, she thinks. Next she notices the large stone fireplace on the left side of the lobby; around it are arranged a lot of comfortable-looking sofas and chairs for lounging in, some in deep-blue velvet, others in dark brown leather, accompanied by little tables with lamps on them. The walls are panelled halfway up from the floor with dark wooden wainscoting. A gorgeous Persian carpet covers part of the dark wood floors and makes everything feel cosy but expensive, which is just what she likes. A chandelier sparkles overhead. The smell of the wood fire reminds her of blissful days spent at Matthew's family cottage. She breathes deeply and smiles. She's a very happy woman. Recently engaged, on a weekend tryst with the man she is going to marry. Everything is glorious, including this lovely hotel that Matthew has found for them.

He dropped her at the front and is parking the car. He'll be here in a minute with their bags. She sets off across the lobby past the fireplace to the old-fashioned reception desk to the left of the staircase. Everything here gleams with a patina of age and good furniture polish. There's a young man behind the desk, and another man, older – obviously a guest – leaning against it, leafing through some pamphlets. He glances up when he sees her. He stops for a second, stares, and then smiles in an embarrassed way and looks away. She's used to it. She has that effect on men. As if when they see her, they can't believe their eyes for a minute. She can't help that.

The younger man behind the desk does an almost imperceptible double take, but it's there. She's used to that, too.

'I'm Dana Hart. My fiancé and I have a reservation under the name Matthew Hutchinson?'

'Yes, of course,' the young man says smoothly and looks at the register. She notices that they use an old hotel register – how quaint – rather than a computer system for checking in guests. Behind the desk, against the wall, are wooden pigeon-holes for the room keys. 'You're in room 101. Up the stairs to the first floor and to the right,' the young man tells her.

The door opens behind her with a burst of cold air and she turns to see Matthew with a bag in each hand and a dusting of snow on his coat and on his dark hair. He comes up beside her and she brushes the snow off his shoulders; she enjoys these little demonstrations of ownership.

'Welcome to Mitchell's Inn,' the young man behind the desk says, smiling and handing over a heavy brass key. She notices now how attractive he is. 'Dinner is in the dining room from seven to nine pm. We offer drinks in the lobby before dinner. Enjoy your stay.'

'Thank you, I'm sure we will,' her fiancé says, giving her a look. She raises her perfectly shaped eyebrows at him, her way of telling him to behave himself in public.

*

12

Matthew picks up the bags again and follows Dana up the wide staircase. He notices that there's no lift. It's a small hotel. He chose carefully. He wanted somewhere quiet and intimate to spend some time with Dana before all the craziness of the wedding, which he would prefer to avoid altogether. He wishes they could elope to some delightful spot in the Caribbean. But the heir to a large fortune in New England does not elope. Such a thing would crush his mother, and all his aunts, and he's not prepared to do that. And he knows that Dana, despite her sometimes becoming overwhelmed with the stress of the planning, the appointments, the millions of details such a wedding entails, is actually quite thrilled about the whole thing. But she's been prone to emotional outbursts lately. This break will be good for both of them before the final push to their spring wedding.

The thick rug softens their footsteps so that it is almost perfectly quiet as they walk up the stairs to the first floor and a few steps along the hall to room 101. There's an oval brass plate on the door, engraved with the number, and an old-fashioned keyhole lock.

He unlocks the door and opens it for her. 'After you.'

She steps inside and smiles approvingly. 'It's lovely,' she says. She whirls to face him as he closes the door firmly behind them.

He puts his arms around her and says, '*You* are lovely.' He kisses her; eventually she pushes him away with a playful shove.

She shrugs out of her coat. He does the same and hangs them up in the wardrobe. They examine the room together. The bed is king-size, of course, and the linens, he notes, are first rate. There are chocolates wrapped in foil resting on the pillows. The bath is obviously intended for two, and a bucket of champagne on ice rests on a little table near the door, with a note of welcome. The windows look out onto the vast front lawn with snow-weighted trees, and the long, curving drive leading down to the main road, filling up fast now with snow. Half a dozen cars are in the car park to the side of the lawn. The two lovers stand together side by side, looking out.

'It's the honeymoon suite,' he tells her, 'if you haven't already guessed.'

'Isn't that bad luck?' she asks. 'To book the honeymoon suite when it's not really your honeymoon?'

'Oh, I don't think so.' They watch a car struggle bravely up the drive and pull slowly into the cark park. Four people get out. Three women and a man. He nuzzles her neck and says, 'How about a nap before dinner?'

Ian Beeton drops into one of the chairs next to the fireplace in the lobby while Lauren signs in and gets the key to their room. He wouldn't mind a drink. He wonders where the bar is. The dining room is to the right, off the lobby – the glass doors to the dining room are open and he can see tables with white linen tablecloths set up inside. The place is quite charming. Probably lots of little rooms and hallways and alcoves by the look of it; not like a typical modern hotel, built for efficiency and maximum returns.

He turns his attention to the two women they rescued. Gwen, the driver, is getting the key to their room. It looks like they're sharing. He watches them go up the stairs together. He lets his mind drift.

Lauren approaches and holds out her hand to him. 'Ready to go up?'

'Sure.'

'Dinner is from seven to nine in the dining room, but we can have cocktails down here,' she tells him.

'Good. What are we waiting for?'

'We're on the second floor.'

He gets up and lifts the bags, then follows Lauren up the stairs. The place seems so quiet. Maybe it's the snow, or the thick carpet, or the soft lighting, but everything seems muffled, subdued.

'Did you notice anything odd about that woman Riley?' Lauren whispers as they climb the elaborate staircase.

'She looked pretty rattled,' he admits.

'She didn't say a word the whole time. I mean, they only slid into a ditch. No actual harm done.'

'Maybe she's been in a car accident before.'

'Maybe.' When they reach the second floor she turns to him and says, 'She seemed awfully tense. I got a weird vibe off her.'

'Don't think about her,' Ian says, giving her a sudden kiss. 'Think about me.'

Chapter Three

GWEN SITS ON the bed furthest from the door – they have a room on the second floor with two double beds, as requested – and watches Riley anxiously. She could tell that woman, Lauren, had been wondering about her.

It dawns on Gwen for the first time that maybe she isn't what Riley needs right now. Gwen is becoming infected by Riley's quiet panic, rather than Riley being reassured by Gwen's calm pragmatism. Riley has always been the stronger personality; she probably should have realized that Riley would have an effect on her rather than the other way around. Already Gwen finds herself looking into dark corners, jumping at unexpected sounds, imagining bad things happening. Perhaps it's just being in a strange place, and the old-world atmosphere of this hotel.

'Maybe we should freshen up a bit and go down for a drink before dinner,' Gwen suggests.

'Sure,' Riley says unenthusiastically.

She's pale, and her long blonde hair hangs limply around her face. There is none of that liveliness she used to have. She was beautiful once, but now it's hard to think of her that way. What an awful thought, Gwen realizes. She hopes that beauty will return. Gwen looks imploringly at her. 'I know you're going through a tough time. But you have to try.'

Riley flashes a look at her; annoyance maybe, or resentment. Anger. Gwen feels a little flare of anger of her own and thinks suddenly that it's going to be a long weekend if she has to watch everything she says. But she immediately reminds herself that Riley is one of her best friends. She owes her. She wants to help her get back on her feet; she wants her gorgeous, vivacious friend back. She wants to be jealous of her again, she realizes, like she used to be.

'Let me brush your hair,' Gwen says. She gets up off her bed and rummages through Riley's handbag for her hairbrush. Then she sits down on the bed behind her and starts brushing her hair in long, soothing strokes. As she does, she sees Riley's shoulders begin to loosen a little. Finally she says, 'There. Put some lipstick on. I will, too. And we'll go down and get something to eat. Then we can come up here and have a quiet night and talk, just like we used to. Or read, if that's what you want.' She's brought a couple of books herself. She wouldn't mind escaping into a book. Her own life is far from perfect.

A corridor runs past the reception desk along the west side of the hotel, dividing the west wing of the hotel into front and back rooms. Down the hall is a bar, but when David Paley pops his head in, the room is empty. To the right of the door is the bar

17

itself, with an impressive array of bottles, but there is no one behind it to serve him. The room is panelled in the rich, dark wood of the lobby. Across from the bar, on the other side of the room, is a fireplace with a handsome mantel, and above the fireplace is an oil painting – a dark, moody study of a man holding a pheasant by the feet. The windows look out onto the front lawn. In front of the fireplace is a gathering of small tables and aged, comfortable leather chairs. It's a man's room. He wonders whether he should stay and hope a bartender shows up, or return to the lobby and have a drink brought out there. It's awkward, travelling alone. He sits in a leather armchair by the fireplace, even though there is as yet no fire burning in the grate, waits a few minutes, supposes that no one is coming, and wanders back out to the lobby. There's no one there either; the young man who was behind the desk earlier has vanished. David taps the old-fashioned bell on the front desk. The clear ring is louder than he expected and he starts a little. The same young man from before rushes up to the desk, appearing from the hall that runs behind it, beside the staircase.

'So sorry to keep you waiting,' he says. 'We're a bit short staffed because of the weather.' He smiles apologetically.

'I was wondering if I could get a drink.'

'Of course. We're going to be serving drinks here in the lobby. I'll be bringing out the bar trolley in a couple of minutes.'

'That's fine,' David says amicably. He just wants a drink, a comfortable chair, and a warm fire. And then a good dinner and a deep, undisturbed sleep.

He sits down and wonders who might join him. He soon hears the rumble of wheels and the sound of glasses and glances up and sees the young man pushing a well-stocked bar trolley into the lobby. The usual bar staples are there, as well as a cocktail shaker, a bucket of ice, several mixes and garnishes, good liqueurs, and assorted glasses. Underneath are wine bottles, as well as a champagne bucket filled with ice, with the foil-wrapped neck of a bottle sticking out.

'What will you have?' asks the young man.

He's just a kid, really, David thinks. He looks so young. Twenty-one, maybe. 'What's your name?' David asks.

'Bradley,' he answers.

'Are you old enough to serve alcohol in the state of New York, Bradley?' he quips.

'I'm older than I look,' Bradley grins. 'Twenty-two.'

'Then a gin and tonic, please,' David says, smiling back.

He prepares the drink expertly. As David watches him, he catches movement in the corner of his eye and looks up. There's a youngish couple coming down the stairs.

'Oh, look,' the man says, spying the trolley. He smiles and rubs his hands together for effect.

David can't help but notice his smile. It makes the man instantly likeable. He's tall and lanky, with rumpled brown hair and a five o'clock shadow – the casual type, in jeans and a plaid shirt, but David suspects he could carry that look off anywhere. David is pleased to see him; he could use some light, distracting conversation. The woman with him is attractive, but not as striking as the woman who passed him a while ago on the stairs. For a moment he wonders if everyone here is part of a couple.

'Mind if we join you?' the man says.

'Not at all,' David says.

'I'm Ian,' he says and extends a hand.

The woman beside him reaches out her hand in turn and says, 'I'm Lauren.'

'Pleased to meet you,' he says. 'David.'

'It seems a bit empty,' Lauren muses, looking around.

Bradley nods and says, 'The hotel isn't full. We have twelve guest rooms but only six are occupied this weekend. We had some cancellations because of the snow. And some of our staff – the bartender, for one, and the housekeeper, for another, weren't able to make it in. But I'm here, so we're good.' He clasps his hands together. 'I know a few things about mixing drinks,' he adds spontaneously. 'The bartender's been teaching me.'

'Excellent!' Ian says. 'Can you make me a whisky and soda?'

'Of course.'

'And I'll have a Manhattan,' Lauren says.

'Did the chef make it in okay?' Ian asks. 'Because I'm starving.'

Bradley cocks one eyebrow. 'Don't worry. My dad's the chef. It's a family-owned hotel. We live on-site – in an apartment at the end of the hall, past the bar.' He nods towards the hallway. 'He and I should be able to manage all right until the roads are cleared. Although dinner will be more of a buffet tonight.'

A blast of wind slams angrily against the windows. The guests turn instinctively towards the sound.

'We get some good storms up here,' Bradley says.

Now David notices an older man appear in the lobby. Judging by the apron he's wearing, he came from the kitchen, which must be behind the dining room. Bradley's father.

'Welcome,' he says. 'I'm James Harwood, the owner of the hotel. And the chef.' He adds, 'And don't worry, I promise we will take very good care of you, whatever the weather.'

David sizes him up. He has a confident air, someone who is certain he can make good on his promise. He's obviously been very successful with this hotel; he's proud of his establishment, and it shows. He chats with them for a moment and returns to his kitchen.

David settles back in his chair, once again looking forward to his weekend.

Lauren watches Ian charm the man sitting by the fire. Ian can get on with anyone. He's already discovered that David is a criminal defence attorney from New York City. Now he's trying to draw him out about some of his cases.

'What was the most interesting case you ever worked on?' Ian asks curiously.

'They're all interesting,' the attorney says, with a slightly evasive smile.

'Are there any we might have read about in the papers?' Lauren asks.

'Possibly.'

At that moment she senses someone coming down the staircase and glances upwards, over her shoulder. She sees that it's Gwen and Riley. She catches the attorney watching them as they descend. The two women make their way over to them and sit down together on a sofa across from the fire. Gwen gives them a tentative smile; Riley doesn't look at anyone. But Bradley is there with the drinks, creating a useful distraction. They each ask for a glass of merlot and fall silent.

Gwen looks quite different without her ski hat and puffy winter jacket, Lauren thinks. She's petite and slim, and her shiny black hair makes a striking contrast to her creamy white skin. Riley is taller, and her blonde hair falls limply to her shoulders. She looks unhealthy next to Gwen.

Ian won't let it go with David, the attorney. 'Have you defended any murderers?' he asks. His enthusiasm finally brings a reluctant smile to the attorney's face.

'Yes, I have.' He swirls his drink around in his glass. 'Many.'

'Come on, tell us!'

'Never mind him,' Lauren interjects. 'I think he watches too many crime shows.'

'It's not always like it is on TV,' the attorney says.

'What do you mean?' Lauren asks, noting his downturned mouth.

He shrugs. 'On TV, justice is usually served. It doesn't always work out that way in real life.'

'You mean – as a defence attorney – you're too good at your job?' Ian suggests, and they all laugh.

Lauren can hear the two women murmuring now, but she can't quite hear what they are saying. They're keeping their voices low.

'I do my best,' the attorney says.

'How do you do it?' Lauren asks him. 'How do you reconcile what you do with your conscience – defending someone you know might be guilty of something horrible?' Then she adds hastily, 'I'm sorry. I don't mean to judge.'

David Paley looks down at his almost empty glass and thinks about how to answer. It's a question he's been asked many times. He's been very successful as a defence attorney. As a human being – he's not so sure. His partners at the firm have gently suggested that he take some time off, perhaps travel. But he has no one to travel with. He no longer has a wife. And while travelling the world might distract him for a while, it won't mend the emptiness in his soul. Spending the better part of his career successfully defending murderers has definitely taken its toll. But he has his answer to Lauren's question ready. He knows what to say – he doesn't necessarily have to believe it.

'I have a job to do as a defence attorney. Under our legal system, everyone is presumed innocent until proven guilty. My job is to represent any accused to the best of my ability.' He adds, 'If attorneys could simply refuse to represent someone because of their own squeamishness, or conscience . . .'

She is listening to him intently.

He shrugs. 'Well, without the defence attorney, the system wouldn't work.' He takes a large swallow of his drink. It all sounds so good. 'You have to look at the bigger picture,' he adds. He doesn't tell them how difficult that can be.

He realizes now that the two women sitting a bit further away on the sofa are both watching him, listening. He finds the dark-haired one quietly attractive. She looks at him with intelligent, appraising eyes. He would like to talk to her. Perhaps the weekend will turn out to be distracting, after all.

Gwen looks at the attorney sitting by the fire. He's older than she is, perhaps forty or so; his short dark hair is beginning to grey at the temples. He has a good face – attractive and kind – and a sort of rueful smile that appeals to her. She likes the sound of his voice, its timbre – it carries without effort, probably from years of speaking in court. He has a confidence, an ease about himself that she finds attractive. She's a modern young woman. She considers herself a feminist. But she has never been particularly sure of herself; it's a quality that she admires – even envies – in others. She wants to be strong and independent, like Riley. Well, like Riley used to be. She glances at her friend. But just look where that got her.

Beside her, Riley guzzles her first glass of wine like water on a hot day. Or as if she were drinking shots with the boys. She was always an accomplished drinker. Gwen's own drink is barely touched, and now she takes a big gulp. Riley seems to emerge from her semi-catatonic state to motion to the young man with the bar cart and says, 'May I have another?'

'Of course,' he says, and pours her another glass.

'Thank you,' Riley says. And chugs it right back. Now everyone is silent, watching her, and Gwen is uneasy and embarrassed. She doesn't want Riley to draw attention to herself. She also doesn't want her to get drunk; she has no idea what she will do, what she will be like. Riley always used to be a fun drunk, a party girl, but now Gwen doesn't know what to expect. She's so different since she came back from Afghanistan this time. Sometimes she's withdrawn, and just stares at nothing. Other times she's irritable and even a bit aggressive. And her occasional displays of nervous energy – her fidgeting, the way her eyes dart around constantly – it's already beginning to get on Gwen's nerves. Inadvertently, she catches the attorney's eye and quickly looks away.

She's already regretting suggesting this weekend away. Her

car is sitting in a ditch miles from here. The tow company said they wouldn't be able to fetch it until the morning. By then it will probably be so buried that they won't be able to find it.

She leans in closer to Riley and whispers, 'Maybe you should slow down.'

Chapter Four

DANA SLIPS OUT from under the covers, slapping Matthew's hand away as he reaches for her. She smiles at him. 'We should go down. Aren't you hungry?'

'Now that you mention it,' he says cheerfully, and gets out of the bed.

She gets dressed quickly in a simple but elegantly cut dress. Everything she wears flatters her. Genetics has been kind to her, and she now has the money to make the most of what she's been given.

Matthew is a warm, generous man, and she's very much in love with him. Of course, the money doesn't hurt. She thinks often of how lucky she is, of how awful it must be for most women – to marry and have children on a budget.

She's well aware that she and Matthew have a charmed life. She's not going to apologize for it. But she's certainly not going to rub anyone's nose in it, either. She knows what it's like to want – to want desperately – things that you can't have. To anyone who doesn't know who Matthew is, they just come across as a well-heeled, successful couple. But Matthew is from money, and lots of it.

'Ready?' he asks, as she puts in her second earring. She's sitting at the antique dressing table, looking at him in the mirror as he stands behind her. It feels very romantic.

'Why don't ladies have dressing tables like this any more?' she asks.

'I don't know. They should,' he says, looking back at her in the mirror and gently touching a tendril of her long hair.

'After dinner we can sit in front of the fire here and drink the champagne they've left us,' she says. She thinks about how lovely it will be, just the two of them, here, in this perfect room, by the light of the fire, the snow still coming down, silencing the outside world. How far away from their everyday lives it feels.

Matthew closes their door behind them and shoves the key into his pocket.

When they come around the landing and view the lobby, he sees a small gathering of fellow guests. The young man who was at the front desk earlier is mixing drinks, chatting comfortably with the handful of people seated near the fireplace.

'Bar's closed this evening,' the young man says as they reach the bottom of the stairs and approach the group. 'We're missing a bartender and making do. I hope that's all right,' he says.

'No problem at all,' Matthew assures him, smiling, his hand on the small of Dana's back. It looks like a cosy enough arrangement. They sit down on a sofa across from a couple close to their age. There's a slightly older man who seems to be on his own, and a pair of women sharing a sofa across from the fire.

'What will you have?' the young man asks, smiling appreciatively at Dana.

'A vodka Martini please,' she says.

'Make mine a Scotch on the rocks, thanks,' Matthew says.

'I'm Bradley,' the young man says.

'I'm David,' says the man by himself.

'He's a criminal attorney,' the man across from him says. 'I'm Ian, and this is Lauren.' Lauren smiles at him.

'I'm Matthew, and this is my fiancée, Dana,' he says.

Ian leans over and indicates the women on the sofa. 'And these are Gwen and Riley.' Gwen nods and smiles demurely; Riley looks at them and gives the briefest of smiles before turning away to stare into the fire. 'We found them in a ditch not far from here,' he adds, smiling.

He seems friendly, Matthew thinks. Easy to talk to. Easy to like.

Gwen offers, 'We're lucky they came along or we'd probably still be out there, frozen to death by now.' The wind rattles the windows, as if to underline what she's said. 'I'll have to have a tow truck get my car out in the morning. They couldn't come tonight, obviously – the roads are too bad.'

'We're lucky we got here when we did,' Matthew says, 'or we might not have made it at all. I think the storm's worse than they expected.'

'I know,' Bradley says. 'Sometimes I wonder about the weather forecasters. My father says it's more useful to look out of the window. He's got the radio on in the kitchen. The main highway has been closed and they say the side roads are pretty much impassable. Some of our guests couldn't make it here, but frankly, that's a good thing. We're short-handed because of the storm.'

'Oh dear,' Gwen says.

'Don't worry, we can look after you all right,' Bradley says, with a brash confidence.

He's a good-looking young man, Matthew thinks, and very sure of himself – almost cocky.

'I hope the power doesn't go off,' Lauren says.

'If it does,' Bradley assures them, 'most of the rooms have fireplaces and the woodshed is well stocked with wood and kindling. And we have some oil lanterns if we need them.'

'That actually sounds kind of nice,' Ian says.

Matthew catches movement out of the corner of his eye and looks up. Another couple is coming down the staircase. They're older than he and Dana, maybe in their late forties. The man looks put out about something, and the woman beside him looks as if she's trying to make the best of it.

The man joins them and immediately says to Bradley, 'I could use a Scotch and soda.' He takes the drink from Bradley when it's offered and stands by the fireplace, leaving his wife alone by the bar trolley. Bradley asks her, 'What can I get you, ma'am?'

'I'll have a gin and tonic, please,' she says politely.

'Come and sit,' Gwen says, moving over a little and patting the empty spot on the sofa beside her. The woman looks at her gratefully and joins her, sinking down into the cushions.

Ian makes the introductions, and then looks pointedly at the man standing in front of the fireplace.

'I'm Henry,' he says, 'and that's my wife, Beverly.'

'Pleased to meet you,' Beverly murmurs to everyone.

'We were just talking about the storm,' Lauren says. 'Bradley was telling us that we are completely snowed in, and reassuring us that we have nothing to worry about if the power goes out.'

'There's no mobile reception up here,' Henry complains. 'And no wi-fi. It's like being buried alive.'

There's a startled silence at this.

'We've never had mobile reception,' Bradley says, flushing slightly at the rebuke. 'Or wi-fi. It's in our brochure. Many of our guests come up here to get away from all that.'

Matthew notices the sour look Henry shoots at his wife, as if it's her fault there's no wi-fi. Maybe that's what he's so annoyed about.

'The scenery is lovely, though,' Beverly says gamely. 'And I see there are lots of books here.'

It's true. Matthew has noticed bookcases around the hotel, filled with books of all sorts.

'I found an old Agatha Christie on my bedside table,' Lauren volunteers.

'That's me,' Bradley says. 'I put books in all the rooms. So much nicer than chocolates on the pillows, don't you think? Although we do the chocolates, too, of course.' He grins.

'I think it's refreshing,' Lauren says.

'We actually have a rather extensive library. I can find you something else if you like. I'm very familiar with what's in there – I've read most of them. Our guests like to read in the library, of course, but in the summer they read in the hammock, or by the pool, or in the gazebo.'

'We'll have to come back up here in the summer,' Matthew says, smiling at Dana, 'after we're married.'

'You should,' Bradley agrees. 'It's lovely here in the summer.

30

But it's just as lovely in winter. I can light a fire in the library after dinner if anyone wants to sit in there.'

'We'd like to see the icehouse,' Lauren says.

'What is the icehouse, exactly?' Beverly asks.

Bradley smiles. 'It's a little outbuilding made entirely from ice and snow. We had it made into a bar. Everything is carved from ice – the bar, the shelves, the stools, even. And there's some wicked sculpture. The only thing in there that isn't made out of ice is the bottles and the glasses and the bar equipment. It's pretty amazing. I haven't had a chance to clear the path out to it yet, but I'll get the snowblower out and it will be open tomorrow, I promise.'

'It sounds cold,' Gwen says.

'You'll need a jacket,' Bradley admits.

The atmosphere in the room has shifted slightly since the arrival of Dana and Matthew. Lauren couldn't help noticing how the men in the room reacted when Dana joined them. Bradley gawking at her as he served her drink. The older men are better able to hide their feelings; nonetheless it's impossible to ignore that Dana's remarkable beauty has affected everyone. It's as if they are all suddenly sitting up straighter. Even Ian. She gives him a little kick now, irritated, and he returns his attention to her.

Lauren knows that she herself is an attractive woman – and she has no doubts about Ian finding her so. But Dana is in another class altogether. It's not just her beauty, which is hard to ignore. It's her glamour. Her awareness of her own gorgeousness. She makes every other woman in the room feel second rate without even trying. There's something about exceptionally

31

beautiful women, Lauren has noticed, that makes them think they're entitled to anything they want.

Lauren finds herself staring at Dana. Suddenly, as if she can feel Lauren's eyes on her, Dana looks directly at her. The smile on her lovely face doesn't falter as her gaze lingers on Lauren.

Dana reminds Lauren of someone, she can't think who. Maybe she just reminds her of all those women who look out from movie screens and magazines, the ones who remind the rest of them of their own shortcomings. Lauren turns away first.

She catches Gwen and Riley watching Dana, too.

Friday, 6:45 PM

When James emerges from his kitchen and enters the lobby to check on the guests, he sees the cocktail hour is in full swing. The guests are chatting with each other, and everything seems quite convivial. They've been drinking for a while already, and there's something about being snowed in that has a way of bringing people together.

His son glances up at him as he enters the lobby. Bradley is holding an uncorked bottle of champagne – Veuve Clicquot – loosely by the neck. He's a rather striking young man, and now a lock of his hair is falling forward on his forehead, which lends him a certain rakish charm. He's tall and lean and athletic, and looks perfectly at ease in his slim black trousers and crisp white shirt. He wears clothes well. And Bradley is so good with the guests. So confident and outgoing, like his mother had been. James is more at ease behind the scenes, in his kitchen wearing his apron, or looking over his accounts. Still, he has his concerns about Bradley. He worries about him stepping over the line. He's still young and impulsive. He has to remember that he's a server, not a guest. There are boundaries to be observed. Bradley hasn't always been so good at observing boundaries.

All of the women are now drinking champagne out of old-fashioned coupe glasses. Occasionally a fussy guest will request a flute, but most enjoy the decadent, twenties feel of the coupes. James loves them, himself. They go so nicely with his hotel.

Bradley makes the introductions. Now James can put names to the faces.

'We've switched to champagne,' Lauren says, raising her glass.

'Excellent choice,' James agrees.

'Since we're snowed in here, we've decided we're going to make the most of it,' announces Dana, a strikingly pretty young woman with a large diamond engagement ring on her finger.

'The ladies are celebrating,' Henry says, standing in front of the fireplace and holding a drink aloft, 'but the men are just drinking.'

'Have we met everyone now, Bradley?' Ian asks. 'You don't have any other guests staying tonight in the hotel?'

'No, there's one more,' Bradley says. 'A woman arrived this morning. I don't think we'll see much of her. She says she's writing a book, and wants quiet.'

'A book?' Dana says. 'What kind of a book?'

33

'I have no idea. She didn't say.'

'What's her name?' asks Gwen.

'Candice White,' Bradley says. 'Do you know it?'

Everyone in the room shakes their head.

'Anyway, that's it,' Bradley says. 'And no more coming, not in this weather.'

Chapter Five

CANDICE WHITE SITS at the antique writing desk in front
of the window in her room and looks out at the wintry landscape, grateful that she arrived early, before the snow. She's
been able to put in a good day of work.

She'd driven up from New York City early in the morning,
desperate to escape. She's a bundle of resentment and raw nerves
these days. It's not that she has a family of her own that needs
her – a rumpled husband and adoring small children with sticky
hands. She revises – if she'd had children, they'd probably be
teenagers by now, and perhaps not so adoring. She does this
sometimes – imagines what her children would have been like,
at different ages, in different circumstances, if she'd had them. If
she'd been lucky in love. But no. She has not been lucky in love.
Not for her the happy ending. Instead, as the only unmarried
one of three daughters – and the only one who's gay – she has
been stuck with the lion's share of caring for their widowed and
declining mother, because her rather selfish sisters are too busy
with their own demanding families, who adore them.

Candice feels that she has been doubly cheated. Denied the happiness that her sisters seem to take for granted, and saddled with the thankless, grinding, demoralizing duty of elder care. It's not that she doesn't love her mother. But it's so . . . hard. And so sad – the dependency, the embarrassing bodily needs, the fact that her mother doesn't even know who she is half the time. It completely saps her creativity and makes it hard to work. That's why it's so important that she take this time away to finish her book.

Her sisters only step up when she's out of town on business, which has been infrequently of late. They have become complacent, depending on her all the time, visiting their mother less and less. Their own families are more important and *Candice doesn't have a family. Candice can do it.* She finds herself mouthing the words, silently and sarcastically, automatically, with a sour expression on her face.

Well. If this book is as good as she thinks it's going to be – as good as her agent says it is – then they will all have to adjust their thinking. The family dynamic will have to change. She drags her eyes from the swirling darkness outside the window back to the screen of her laptop.

She's let herself get off track. She ought to write another page before she goes down to dinner. She checks her watch and realizes she's missed cocktail hour. It's a sad thing for a writer to miss cocktail hour. She looks again at the screen of the laptop in front of her, regrets that last paragraph. It will have to go. She blocks it out and hits delete.

Candice takes off her reading glasses and rubs her eyes. Maybe she needs a break. She will carry on after dinner. There will be wine with dinner.

She tells herself again that she had to get away from her mother to finish this manuscript – she's trying not to feel guilty about it. She has to write the last ten thousand words, but she still has to eat.

Candice has a lot riding on this book. It's the first thing of her own that she's written in a long time. For almost two decades now she has eked out a living as an author of non-fiction, but more and more often lately she's been ghostwriting other people's books – everything from self-help to business books. Except most of these geniuses aren't particularly successful, so she's never thought their wisdom was worth the paper it was printed on. As long as they paid her, she didn't care. When she started out it was a good living. She got to keep her own hours and she met some interesting people. She got to travel – paid – and when she was younger, this was a valuable perk. Now she would like to travel a lot less and get paid a lot more.

She's hoping *this* book – her own book – is going to make her fortune.

Closing the laptop, Candice gets up, looks at herself critically in the full-length mirror, and decides she can't really go down in yoga pants. She puts on a decent skirt and tights and throws a silk scarf around her neck. She brushes her hair into a new, tidy ponytail, applies fresh lipstick, and heads downstairs.

Friday, 7:00 PM

At dinner they all move into the dining room. The meal has been set up as a buffet. There's a long table along one wall, laden with covered silver chafing dishes, platters of salads,

37

and baskets of various breads and rolls. A glittering chandelier provides soft lighting. There's a scattering of tables in the dining room – some for two, some for four – with white linen cloths. Soon there is the slight clatter of silver cutlery against good china as the guests collect plates and serve themselves.

David Paley slowly fills his plate, lingering over the roast beef, horseradish, and various hot side dishes – he chooses scalloped potatoes and asparagus – wondering where he should sit. He supposes he could sit down with anyone except the engaged couple, who look like they want to be alone, and have already nabbed a table for two in the corner. A woman he hasn't seen before, about his own age – she must be the writer – has taken a table for two. He supposes he could join her, but she seems rather forbidding, looking pointedly at a magazine on her table as she eats. She hadn't said hello to anyone when she entered the dining room. He would most like to join the dark-haired woman, Gwen, and her rather jumpy friend.

Gwen and Riley have already filled their plates and are sitting at a table set for four. He walks over and asks politely, 'May I join you?'

The two women look up at him, surprised; two pairs of nervous eyes size him up. Riley is glassy-eyed from too much drink too fast, he surmises. Gwen, he notices, is even prettier up close; her face is pale and fine, and she has lovely dark hair. Her features are subdued rather than flamboyant, the kind of face he imagines he could look at for a long time. He's surprised at himself for thinking this; he's only just met her. He suddenly wishes that she was here alone this weekend, like him, and that they could get to know one another. As it is, it's rather awkward, especially as her friend, Riley, looks as if she would prefer not to have company.

He sees Gwen glance at Riley, who shrugs her shoulders; neither yes nor no. Not quite rude, but not welcoming either. Gwen turns to him and says, 'Yes, of course. Please do.'

He sits beside Riley, across from Gwen, so that he can look at her.

'Are you here alone?' she asks, and then blushes slightly. He's charmed by the colour coming into her cheeks.

'Yes,' he says. 'I'm on my own. I came up here to get away, to think about things.' He's not sure why he's telling her this.

'I see,' she says politely.

He feels uncomfortable talking about himself, but he doesn't want to seem too nosy, either, by asking her about herself. It doesn't leave much to talk about, he realizes.

'You're a defence attorney,' Gwen says, when the silence verges on becoming awkward.

'Yes,' he says. Oddly, he can't think of anything else to say. He finds that he's tongue-tied. He's not usually, but he can feel her friend oozing barely veiled hostility, and it's disconcerting.

'That must be interesting,' Gwen says gamely. 'And challenging. Although probably exhausting, too.'

'Yes,' he agrees. For a moment there is only the chink of cutlery on fine china as they dine on their roast beef. David finds himself noticing the flickering candlelight reflected in the glass of the windows. 'What brings you here this weekend?' he asks finally. Perhaps her friend will go upstairs, and they can sit in front of the fire and talk. He would like that.

Gwen glances at Riley. 'We just wanted to get away, for a girls' weekend,' she says.

'Oh.' There's not much he can say to that. He can hardly crash a girls' weekend.

'Riley and I were at journalism school together. She's with the *New York Times*.'

He flicks a nervous glance at Riley, inwardly dismayed.

'But I never actually worked as a journalist,' Gwen confides.

'Is that right,' David says, his mind drifting from the conversation. 'What do you do instead?'

'I work in public relations for a small firm in New York City.'

'And do you enjoy it?' But he is already thinking of an exit strategy.

'For the most part,' she says. 'It can be exciting, but it can also be a grind. Like a lot of jobs, it sounds more glamorous than it is.'

They talk for a while, about nothing much. When they are about to start on coffee and dessert – English trifle and chocolate brownies have appeared on the long buffet table – Riley, slurring her words slightly, turns and looks directly at him and says, 'I've been trying to place you – what did you say your name was again?'

He looks back at her, refusing to shrink from her very direct gaze. 'David Paley,' he says, waiting for it. She's a journalist, after all. They have no compunction about anything. He knows his weekend is about to be ruined.

Beverly Sullivan struggles through her meal. She wonders how it can be possible that after twenty years of marriage there is nothing to talk about. Without the kids there, interrupting, distracting, it seems there is little for them to say to one another. They didn't use to be like this. They used to be good together. All those years of eating with the kids has made them lose the knack of conversation. They should have hired more babysitters, gone out by themselves to restaurants more, she thinks regretfully, like the experts always advise.

Unfortunately, she is positioned so that she is looking directly at the outrageously attractive engaged couple alone together in the corner. They do all the things couples in love do: they look into each other's eyes, they smile excessively, touch each other whenever they can. Every once in a while, they laugh.

They're so young, she thinks, they have no idea.

It's a good thing, she thinks, that the guests at the other tables are so engrossed in each other that no one seems to notice that she and her husband are hardly speaking to each other.

He still seems annoyed about there not being any wi-fi. Unless he's actually annoyed about something else. She can't think what it could be. The hotel is lovely. He agreed to come here. Perhaps he's feeling stressed and guilty about not staying at home and catching up on work. Finally, she says his name to get his attention, and when she has it, she asks quietly, 'Is something the matter?'

'What?' he says. 'No.' He takes another forkful of the excellent roast beef.

'You've hardly said a word to me since we got here,' she says gently, careful not to sound antagonistic.

In fact, she's a bit surprised. At home they have so little time for each other, but they are not deliberately neglectful of each other, merely too busy. Something's changed, and she doesn't know what it is.

'I have a lot on my mind,' he says a bit defensively.

41

'Do you want to tell me about it?' she asks. He looks at her, as if considering what to tell her. It makes her feel uneasy. Maybe there's a problem she's not aware of.

'It's just work,' he says, 'but I'd rather not talk about work this weekend.'

'Fine,' she agrees, taking another sip of wine and giving him a tentative smile. 'We came up here to relax and enjoy ourselves, after all.' She tries to set her uneasiness aside.

She has a nice surprise in store for him that will take his mind off whatever's bothering him.

Chapter Six

LAUREN WATCHES THE guests at the other tables with interest. She has always been curious about people, observing them, trying to figure out what makes them tick. Studying what they do. Why does that woman Riley, at the table with Gwen and David, seem so on edge, for instance? She keeps scanning the room as if expecting someone to steal her dinner.

Ian has slipped his foot out of his shoe and now he's touching her leg under the table with his socked toe.

'Are you flirting with me?' she asks coyly, her attention drawn back to the man sitting across from her. He's terribly appealing but she's never been able to focus on just one thing for long. Her quick mind darts all over the place. Fortunately, he doesn't seem to mind. He's almost as interested in their fellow guests as she is.

'What's up with that Riley?' Lauren asks him in a quiet voice.

'I don't know. She looks like she's escaped from detox or something,' Ian says, his voice a whisper.

Lauren shifts her attention now to the attorney, who's talking to Gwen. She's been observing his body language throughout the meal. Something has changed. He's sitting back now, stiffly, as if someone has said something he doesn't like. Just a little while ago, he was leaning in towards the pretty Gwen, smiling at her, tilting his head to one side, like a male bird looking for a mate. Perhaps Riley just told him to fuck off.

She lets her gaze travel to the corner, where the engaged couple is dining. She narrows her eyes. She'd taken a rather instant dislike to Dana while they were having cocktails in the lobby. Perhaps it was simply because of her rather intimidating beauty. Perhaps it was the way she ostentatiously waved that diamond ring around. She didn't exactly stick it under anyone's nose and say, *This is my engagement ring, isn't it gorgeous?* But she was constantly fluttering her perfectly manicured hands around, just begging people to notice it. The large diamond glittered when she smoothed her hair, when she picked up her champagne glass; her eyes sparkled when she looked at her fiancé. Everything about her was shiny and bright. She has a bright, shiny life, Lauren thinks. Then she directs her attention to the man to whom she's engaged.

What does she think of him? She thinks he is someone who collects bright, shiny things.

She moves on to the woman who must be Candice White, dining alone at a table for two, pretending to read a magazine. But really, she's staring at David, the attorney, who is positioned so that he is unaware of it. Lauren wonders why Candice is staring at David. Perhaps she finds him attractive. He certainly *is* attractive – anyone can see that. Well, good luck to her, Lauren thinks; he's obviously interested in the younger, more fetching Gwen.

Now Candice has turned her attention away from David and she's staring rather hard at Dana and Matthew. They are a good-looking couple, but something registers on her face – as if she recognizes Dana from somewhere. Or maybe it's Matthew she recognizes; Lauren can't be sure. But it seems now as if her interest is divided equally between the shiny young couple and the understated attorney.

The writer herself is rather austere looking. Dark hair pulled back from her face in a tight ponytail. Strong bones. No-nonsense skirt and sweater, equally no-nonsense glasses. She looks like she might make a competent nurse. The only flourish is a pretty scarf around her neck. Not unattractive but getting on. Maybe pushing forty. Lauren wonders idly about the book she's writing.

It's so pleasant here, Lauren thinks, in this enchanting dining room, with the lights low and the wind howling outside, slamming at the windows, like something wanting to get in.

Dana takes another sip of the excellent wine, tears her gaze away from Matthew for a moment, and looks around the dining room. How surprising life can be.

She's just thinking what a small world it is, when suddenly there is a loud, ominous crash.

Dana jumps a little in her seat. She notices everybody else raising their eyes from their meals, startled.

Bradley, replacing dishes over by the buffet table, smiles and says, 'Don't worry – that's just the sound of snow sliding off the roof.'

45

'Goodness,' Dana says, laughing a little, a little too loudly, 'it sounds like someone fell off the roof!'

'Doesn't it?' Bradley agrees.

Riley has the alcohol to thank for being able to keep herself together. She knows she made a bit of a spectacle of herself in the lounge, knocking back wine and champagne like a sailor. But she's a journalist; she can hold her drink. And she's been self-medicating more than she'd care to admit these last few years, since she started going to the ugly, dangerous parts of the world.

She hadn't enjoyed the meal. She hadn't liked the way the attorney insinuated himself into a place at their dining table. He was so obviously interested in Gwen. That bothered her. Riley always used to be the one men were interested in, not Gwen. Riley was the striking one, the one men noticed and pursued. Not tonight. Not any more. This, perhaps more than anything else, has brought home to her just how much she's changed.

But it's not jealousy that makes her wary of the attorney. There's something about him. Some memory floating around at the back of her brain, nudging at her thoughts. But she can't grasp it. His name is familiar; there's some whiff of scandal about it. She wishes that there were an internet connection here; she could have googled him.

Although Gwen was obviously flattered by his interest, Riley had thrown cold water on their little romance by asking him bluntly about who he was. Judging by the way he clammed up when he found out she was a journalist, she's pretty sure she's on to something. He'd skipped dessert and excused himself, saying that he was going to visit the library. Gwen has been quiet since he left.

She's sorry that Gwen has to be disappointed like this, but Riley has always been protective of her, from the time they were roommates. This weekend was supposed to be about Gwen helping Riley, but Riley has slipped again into her old role. It feels good, especially for someone who has trouble getting through the most basic aspects of her day.

Riley says, 'Shall we go up? I'm pretty tired.'

Gwen hesitates. 'I'm not that tired, actually,' she says. 'I think I might go stop by the library, get a book,' she adds, averting her eyes.

Riley is annoyed. 'I thought you brought a book?' she says coldly. They both know this is true. They both know this is about Gwen choosing to go up with Riley or to spend more time with the attractive lawyer. Riley wants Gwen to choose her. She wonders what kind of friend that makes her – a protective one, or a needy one?

'Are you okay going up on your own?' Gwen asks. 'I won't be too long.'

'Oh, don't worry about me,' Riley says curtly. 'I'll be fine.'

Friday, 8:25 PM

David finds himself alone in the library, a large room in a back corner of the hotel, to the left of the grand staircase, beyond a sitting room. It's like something out of a Victorian novel, a cross between a library and a men's smoking room. Like the bar at the front of the hotel, it's rather handsome. There's a

47

large fireplace against the west wall. Above it hangs an antique hunting rifle; above that, a buck's head with an impressive spread of antlers. It looks down at him with a glassy eye. There's a worn Persian carpet on the hardwood floor. An old sofa sits at a right angle to the fireplace, a pair of chairs facing it. French doors appear to open out to a veranda, but it's hard to tell with it being so dark outside. In the corner nearest the door is a large writing desk, which David briefly admires. But what he likes most are the beautifully made bookshelves. David touches them and admires the craftsmanship that went into them. The bookshelves are stuffed with every kind of book – from old, leather-bound sets to hardcovers and tattered paperbacks. It's all very orderly, with little brass plates reading 'FICTION', 'MYSTERY', 'NONFICTION', 'HISTORY', 'BIOG-RAPHY'. He thinks of Bradley – he suspects this is his handiwork. He pulls an interesting-looking book from a lower shelf – a coffee-table book really – full of photographs of the failed Shackleton expedition. It seems oddly suited to this room. There's a dim overhead light, but now David also switches on a lamp resting on a side table and sits down in the deep leather armchair. What could be nicer than to sit by a fire, in this lovely room, and read about the struggles of the ill-fated crew of the *Endurance* at the South Pole? But the fire hasn't been lit, and the room is a bit chilly.

He thinks regretfully of Gwen. How unfortunate that her friend is a damned journalist with the *Times*. He will stay away from both of them for the rest of the weekend. He doesn't need anyone dredging up his past.

He becomes absorbed in his book, until he is interrupted by the sound of a woman's voice.

'Is that you, David?'

It's Gwen, and, in spite of his earlier resolution, his heart leaps. 'Yes.' He turns to look at her, standing in the doorway, and sees that she's alone.

'I remembered you saying you were going to the library.'

How lovely she looks, he thinks, getting up out of his armchair.

'It's perfect,' she says, gazing around the room.

'Yes, isn't it,' he agrees. Somehow he knew she would appreciate it, too.

'I wonder where everyone is,' David muses. He feels awkward, adolescent.

'Riley is tired and has gone up to bed,' Gwen offers shyly. 'I think some of the others might still be in the dining room, having nightcaps.'

'I can ask Bradley to light the fire in here,' he says. She nods, but he can't tear himself away from her to find Bradley just yet.

Together they begin to peruse the shelves. He enjoys standing beside her, while the storm rages just outside. After a particularly loud gust of wind they both look towards the French doors.

'Do you think it's going to get worse?' she asks.

I don't care if it does, he thinks, but he doesn't say it aloud. He'd like nothing better than to be stranded here, with her. 'I don't know,' he says.

'What shall I pick?' she wonders out loud, as he stands close to her.

He points to the large book he'd chosen earlier, open on the coffee table where he left it. 'I'm reading about a tragic expedition to the South Pole.'

'Perfect for tonight!' She wanders along the shelves, dragging her index finger along the surface. Something seems to catch her eye, and she pulls a volume from its place. 'Oh – I've heard about this one,' she says. 'I've been meaning to read it.'

David reads the title – *The Suspicions of Mr Whicher, or The Murder at Road Hill House*.

'I love a good murder mystery, don't you?' she says.

Chapter Seven

Friday, 8:50 PM

AFTER DINNER, IAN escorts Lauren – they are both a little tipsy – up the grand staircase. He can't wait to get her into bed. Their room is located on the second floor, at the end of the hall. When they arrive there, Lauren fumbles with the key, and Ian idly notices another door near theirs. He suspects it opens onto another staircase that goes down the back of the building, presumably emptying out somewhere close to the kitchen. It would have been the servants' staircase; the maids would never have used the main staircase, which makes such a grand statement in the lobby.

He puts his hand on the door and pushes it open. He stares down the rather narrow, plain wooden staircase that winds below, dusty and dimly lit.

'What are you doing?' Lauren asks.

'Just looking,' he says.

'What's on your dirty mind, Ian?'

She is on his dirty mind. He grabs her hand and pulls her to him. 'Come with me, baby,' he says, nuzzling her neck. He slowly unbuttons her blouse. 'Come on, no one will see.'

She protests softly as he pulls her into the stairwell.

Henry and Beverly return to their room on the first floor after dinner. 'I think I'll read a bit before bed,' Henry says.

'I'm going to take a bath,' Beverly tells him.

She slips into the marble bathroom, taking with her the costly, sexy new nightgown that she'd bought in anticipation of this weekend. Henry doesn't even notice what she's up to, his nose already in a book.

It's been such a long time since they've made love. What with teenagers in nearby bedrooms, and the two of them both so tired and irritable at the end of the day, the physical part of their marriage has suffered. Time just slips away from you. But she's going to make an effort. She hangs the new nightgown – champagne silk with ivory lace – on the back of the door and admires it for a moment while the bathtub fills. Henry hasn't seen it yet. He'll be surprised. It's been a long time since she's worn proper lingerie – she's embarrassed to think of the tatty pyjamas she usually wears, day in, day out. This silky nightgown will make her feel attractive again. She adds bubbles to the bath, and as she gets into the tub and sinks below the bubbles, she decides that this weekend is going to be the beginning of a new start for her and Henry. Perhaps they will sleep late and have breakfast in bed, like they used to, a long time ago.

She emerges from the bathroom a short time later, feeling radiant in the champagne silk, smelling of roses, her skin soft, and approaches the bed. She looks at Henry sitting up in bed with his book, and when he lifts his head from the page she smiles at him coquettishly, though she suddenly feels shy. How ridiculous.

But he doesn't respond the way she expects. He looks more dismayed than anything. He certainly doesn't look at her as if he's pleased, as if he finds her attractive.

It's a shock.

He recovers quickly and says, 'I'm sorry, honey. I'm just . . . so tired.'

It's like a slap, even if she's only getting her own words thrown back at her. She feels her face go hot, and tears start to burn her eyes. She's so hurt that she can't think of anything to say. Perhaps she has misjudged things badly.

'I thought we came up here to be together,' she says, fighting tears. 'You don't seem that interested.'

He gives a big exhale and puts down his book. Then he says quietly, 'Maybe it's too late.'

Too late? He can't possibly mean that. He can't. Now she starts to cry, sloppily. She's hurt and scared and embarrassed, standing there in her filmy gown that hides nothing. That was the point, but now she wishes she'd never bought the damn thing, never popped into that fancy lingerie store a couple of weeks ago, blushing and hopeful. Suddenly she wishes they'd never come to this damn place, that she'd never had the idea. She doesn't want to see her marriage fall completely apart. She should have left well enough alone; perhaps they could have gone on amiably ignoring one another, being too busy to examine their lives, their relationship, focusing on the kids, who still very much need them. She's not sure she really wants to put the two of them – their relationship – under a microscope. Does she really want to open this can of worms? She's suddenly frightened of what he might say next. She's frightened of being alone, of being left. She has a career, but she doesn't feel that independent. Financially, a divorce would ruin both of them. They both know that. If he wants out, she thinks, terrified, he must be desperately unhappy.

Maybe it's too late. She feels like a fool for not seeing this coming, for not knowing what he was thinking. All this slips through her mind in a flash as she stands there exposed in her expensive negligee, goose bumps appearing on her chest and arms. Embarrassed in front of her own husband, she folds her arms in front of her breasts, which are billowing out of her nightgown in what now seems to be an unseemly fashion. Perhaps he is finished with her. Her thoughts are speeding away with her like a runaway train headed for catastrophe. She longs for her thick terry bathrobe to cover herself, but is too stunned to move. She sinks down onto the bed, takes a deep, ragged breath, and says, 'What do you mean?'

He sighs and says, sounding regretful, 'We haven't been happy, Beverly, for a long time.'

She doesn't know how to respond to that. Of course they haven't been happy. Her friends – with big mortgages, demanding jobs, problem teenagers, and ageing parents – aren't happy, either. It's impossible at this stage of their lives, with all the demands and stresses they face. He's simply being childish, she thinks, looking back at him in disbelief. He's probably having some kind of middle-age crisis, like some spoiled child who wants to be happy all the time, who doesn't understand that you can't always be happy. Life doesn't work that way. Henry can't be one of those men who realizes one day that he's miserable and decides to chuck it all and do what he wants. Surely not. *She* can't just throw everything aside and do what she wants so that she can be happy. Women don't get to make fools of themselves like that. Society won't let them. But men do it all the time. She feels bitterness rising in her heart, not only against him, but against the world. She feels so powerless, more powerless than he is. She has never had the selfishness, or even the time, to ask herself what would make her happy.

She sits looking at him, thinking how close she is to losing everything. But maybe it's *not* too late. If he would just say he spoke too hastily, that of course he loves her and wants to make it work, that they've had things stacked against them, he knows that, it's been hard for both of them, and they have to somehow help each other, try harder to be content together – then she's sure they could love each other again. She's not ready to give up. Not yet. But she waits, and he doesn't say it.

Finally she says, 'What do you mean you haven't been happy?' She sounds so controlled, but she wants to smack him as if he were a pouting child. That's what he is to her right now, a selfish child, and she wishes she could straighten him out the way she used to be able to straighten out the kids before they became wilful, unmanageable teenagers. When he still says nothing she adds, 'And what makes you think you have a greater right to happiness than anyone else – than me, for instance, or Teddy or Kate?'

*

Henry looks at his wife with veiled loathing. He hates it when she gets like this, all high and mighty. She's such a martyr; she has no idea how hard that's been to live with. How joyless must life be? She's a miserable woman, constantly complaining. At least, it seems that way to him. Maybe he's not being fair, he thinks now, rather guiltily. She is so exposed in that skimpy new nightgown that he feels a sudden pity for her. But he is still unable to reach out to comfort her.

He wonders how other people see his wife. What do Ted and Kate think of their mother? He doesn't really know. They complain that she nags them too much, but she clearly loves them. She's a good mother, he knows that. He doesn't know how the kids feel about either one of them. He doesn't know what teenagers feel at all. He loves his children, but he no longer loves their mother, which is what makes this so hard. He doesn't want to hurt them, or damage them in any way.

He's stuck between the proverbial rock and hard place. And now he's found himself here, snowed in with her for the weekend. What will they do with all this time they have together?

'I don't think I have a greater right to happiness than you or the kids,' he answers her stiffly. Surely that's not it. How typical of her to hear his *We haven't been happy* as *I haven't been happy*. He doesn't think he's more important than the kids are, or than she is. He doesn't think she's happy either. The difference between them is that he can see it, and she can't. Or maybe it's just that he can admit it. That he might be willing to do something about it.

Perhaps, by the end of the weekend, things will somehow be clearer.

Friday, 11:30 PM

Gwen knows she's being reckless but she doesn't care. Something has happened to her, and she's opening herself up to it. Perhaps it's the Veuve Clicquot that's gone to her head. Or maybe it's the way he smells – like expensive soap and imported suits. And he hasn't even touched her yet.

David has Bradley bring them more champagne. Bradley freshens up the fire, then discreetly pulls the library door closed behind him.

'I like that boy,' David says, and she giggles as he refills their glasses.

In the library, they talk. She loves the sound of his voice, especially now, when he's talking to her alone. It's lower, more intimate, but gruffer somehow, and it makes her feel desired. When he speaks low, he moves in close, so that she can hear, and she leans in more towards him, too.

They both know what's going to happen.

When they reach his room – he'd offered to walk her to hers, but she shook her head – he closes the door behind them with a soft click, and she shivers. She doesn't move; she waits in the dark.

He reaches behind her neck and unclasps her necklace and removes it and she feels as if he's undressed her. She breathes in, a little gasp, waiting.

He gently drops the necklace – costume jewellery, but pretty – on the bureau just inside the door. Then he kisses her.

The kiss releases something in her that's been pent up too long, and she kisses him back, but not frantically – slowly, as if she's still not sure. And he seems to get that. As if he's not entirely sure either.

Beverly has a difficult time falling asleep; she always does when she's away from the kids, and now her world is falling apart. It doesn't help that she can hear a muffled argument coming from the room next door – Dana and Matthew's room. Is no one happy?

It annoys her that Henry fell asleep so quickly, as if he didn't have a care in the world – and now he's snoring away. She doesn't know what's going to happen to them. She resents that she has to do the worrying for both of them. It always falls to her to do all the emotional work.

They'd agreed to stop talking about their marriage before either of them said something they might regret. They agreed to sleep on it and see how they felt in the morning.

Finally, deep into the night, she's falling asleep at last, when she hears a muffled scream. But sleep has her now, and the scream becomes part of a dream – a nightmare. Someone is trying to suffocate her. In that strange way of dreams, she is screaming loudly even while someone holds a pillow firmly to her face.

Saturday, 1:35 AM

Riley lies in her bed, staring at the ceiling. She wonders when Gwen will come to bed. According to her watch, it's after one thirty in the morning. She doesn't think for a minute that Gwen and David have been in the library all this time. She's gone to his room. She's gone to bed with him. Maybe she will spend the entire night with him and not come back to their room at all until morning.

It makes her terribly uneasy – the panic is rising inside her like a tide. Not because she's a prude – far from it. She's had a lot of lovers. And not because she's jealous, either. But because she's certain that there's some cloud hanging over this David Paley. She just can't remember what it is. Again she curses the lack of an internet connection.

She fights an irrational urge to get up and knock on David Paley's door. But she doesn't even know which room he's in.

She hates this constant, generalized anxiety she always feels now. She tells herself that nothing can possibly happen to Gwen here, among all these people. Riley knows that Gwen is with him.

Finally, she slips uneasily towards sleep. As she drifts off, she thinks she hears a scream, somewhere far away. She persuades herself it's not a scream, but a memory; she often hears screams as she's drifting off to sleep. She's used to it. They're a precursor to the nightmares.

Chapter Eight

MORNING COMES SLOWLY. Overnight, the falling snow, so peaceful, has turned to sleet, coating everything in brittle ice, making the landscape even more dangerous to navigate. It seems everything is about to snap. Inside the inn, there's a distinct chill in the air.

Lauren rises early, freezing, even with the warmth of Ian pressed up beside her. Her neck is stiff. She gets out of bed, shivering, and hurries to put warm clothes on, wondering why it's so damn cold. She slips on jeans, a T-shirt, a heavy sweater, warm socks. They hadn't closed the curtains before they went to bed, and now she glances out of the front window to the landscape below. Even though it's still quite dark, she can see that the branches of the huge tree in the front yard are bent, weighted down with ice. She sees where one of them has broken off; there's a large, pale gash where it has been ripped from the trunk. The heavy limb lies broken in three separate pieces on the ground below.

She walks quietly into the bathroom, leaving the door open. She doesn't want to turn on the light – she doesn't want to wake Ian. It's damn cold. She brushes her hair quickly. Her illuminated watch face says it's just before six. She wonders what time the staff get up and start their day.

She glances back at Ian snoring in their bed, only his head showing above the covers. He won't be up for a while. She opens the door quietly. It's dark in the corridor; the lights in the wall sconces are out. She slips out and walks down the second-floor hall to the main stairs in her thick socks. She doesn't want to wake anyone. She turns towards the staircase to the lobby, wondering how long it will be before she can get a cup of coffee.

Saturday, 6:03 AM

Riley wakes suddenly, sitting up abruptly in bed, eyes wide open. She thinks she's heard a scream – loud and piercing. Her heart is pounding, and she can feel the familiar adrenaline surging through her body. She glances quickly around the dim hotel room and remembers where she is. She turns to the other bed beside her, throwing aside the bedcovers, and is immediately accosted by the cold. Gwen is awake, too, and alert.

'What's going on?' Gwen says. 'I thought I heard something.'

'I don't know. I heard it, too.'

For a moment they remain perfectly still, listening. They hear a woman's voice, shouting.

Riley throws her legs over the bed and pulls on her robe against the chill, while Gwen scrambles to do the same, saying, 'Wait for me.'

Riley grabs the key as the two of them slip out of the door. The second-floor corridor is unexpectedly dark, and they stop suddenly, disoriented. Riley remembers that she needs to talk to Gwen about last night, but now is not the time. She's just grateful to have Gwen here with her. She doesn't know what she would do if anything happened to Gwen.

'The power must be out,' Gwen says.

Riley and Gwen make their way to the grand staircase, barefoot. Holding on to the polished rail, they race down the stairs as other footsteps can be heard running in the darkened hotel.

Then Riley stops abruptly. The faint light coming in through the front windows illuminates a ghastly sight below her. Dana lies sprawled at the bottom of the stairs, perfectly still, her limbs in an unnatural position beneath her navy satin robe. Her lovely, long dark hair spills all around her, but her face has an unmistakable pallor. She knows immediately that Dana is dead.

Lauren is kneeling on the floor beside her, leaning over her, her hand pressed against Dana's neck, feeling for a pulse. She looks up at them, stricken. 'I just found her.' Her voice is strained.

Riley continues slowly down the stairs until she is standing on the last step, right above the body. She can feel Gwen's presence behind her, hears her broken sob.

'Was that you who screamed?' Riley asks.

Lauren nods, tearful.

Riley notices Bradley and his father, James, standing nearby.

James is staring at the body of the dead woman at the bottom of his staircase, his face slack with shock. Bradley seems unable to look at Dana, staring at Lauren instead as she hovers over the body. Then James moves forward and reaches down hesitantly.

'She's dead,' Lauren tells him.

He pulls his hand back, almost gratefully.

David hears the scream and jumps out of bed. He throws on a bathrobe, grabs his key, and leaves his room. At the top of the landing he pauses and looks down at the ragged little gathering below. He sees Dana – clearly dead – lying at the foot of the stairs in her bathrobe, Lauren beside her. Riley and Gwen have their backs to him. James is pale and Bradley looks suddenly much younger than he did last night. David hears a noise above him, glances up quickly, and sees Henry and Beverly coming after him, also still in their pyjamas, drawing their robes closed and tying them shut.

'What happened?' David says, hurrying down the stairs.

'We don't know,' James says, his voice shaking. 'It looks like she fell down the stairs.'

David comes closer.

'I couldn't find a pulse,' Lauren says.

David squats down and studies the body without touching it, a grimness taking hold of him. Finally he says, 'She's been dead for a while. She must have fallen in the middle of the night.' He wonders aloud, 'Why would she have been out of her room?' He's noted the terrible gash on the side of her head, the blood on the edge of the bottom step. He takes it all in with a practised eye, and feels unaccountably weary.

63

'Dear God,' Beverly whispers. 'That poor girl.'

David looks up at the rest of them. Beverly has turned her face away, but Henry is staring solemnly at the body. David glances at Gwen – her face is tear-stained, and her lower lip is trembling. He longs to comfort her, but he doesn't. Riley's staring at the dead woman as if she can't tear her eyes away. He notices then that Matthew is missing.

'Someone has to tell Matthew,' he says, his heart sinking, knowing it will probably be him. He takes one more look at James and then at all the stricken faces now staring back at him as they remember Matthew. 'I'll do it.' Standing up, he adds, 'We'd better call the police.'

'We can't,' James says harshly. 'The power's out. And the phone. We can't contact the police.'

'Then someone has to go and get them,' David says.

'How?' Bradley asks. 'Look outside. Everything is a sheet of ice.'

James shakes his head slowly. 'The power lines must be down because of the ice storm. It's hazardous out there. Nobody's going anywhere.' He adds, his voice taking on an uncertain note, 'It's probably going to be a while before the police can get here.'

Candice's alarm on her mobile phone is set to go off promptly every morning at six thirty. She's nothing if not disciplined. She is a light sleeper, however, and this morning something wakes her before the alarm sounds. She's not sure what. She hears footsteps running along the hall below her, raised voices.

She decides she'd better get up. Plus it's goddamn cold. She flicks the light switch of the lamp on her bedside table, but it doesn't go on. It's very dark in the room. She crosses the floor, shivering in bare feet, to open the curtains. She's surprised by what she sees. Not the fluffy winter wonderland of last night – but the unleashed fury of an ice storm. Obviously the power is out. Fuck. Fuck, fuck, fuck. She wonders how much battery she's got left in her laptop. Maybe five hours, max. This is a disaster! She needs to find out when the power's going back on. She quickly pulls on some warm clothes and heads cautiously downstairs in the dark.

As she rounds the landing and sees down the stairs into the lobby, she stops abruptly. There's a cluster of people at the bottom of the stairs and they all glance up towards her. Every one of their faces is drawn and uneasy. And then she sees why. There's a woman lying at the bottom of the stairs, so still that she is clearly dead. It's Dana Hart. The attorney is standing over her, his face serious. There's no sign of Matthew.

David has volunteered to break the terrible news to Matthew, who as far as they know is still up in his room. Properly speaking, he supposes that it's the duty of the owner of the hotel to inform Matthew. But James doesn't look up to the task. This is what David tells himself as he treads back up. James accompanies him, obviously grateful that the attorney has offered. The others remain behind, standing in place, dumbly watching their quiet progress up the stairs.

'Which room is it?' David asks.

'Room 101,' James tells him in a distraught voice.

They stop outside the door. David pauses, preparing himself. He listens for any sounds within. But he hears nothing. He lifts his hand and knocks firmly.

There's no response. David glances at James, who appears even more anxious. David knocks again, harder this time. He's beginning to think about asking James to go and fetch the key when he hears movement within. Finally the door swings open and David is face to face with the man he met over cocktails the night before. David suddenly feels a terrible pity for him. Matthew still looks half asleep. He's clumsily pulling on a bathrobe.

'Yes?' he says, obviously surprised to find them at his door. Then he glances over his shoulder at the bed he's just got out of, as if he's missing something. He turns back and looks David in the eye and it registers all at once. Matthew's eyes sharpen. 'What is it?' He looks from David, to the visibly upset James, and back to the attorney. 'What's happened? Where's Dana?'

'I'm afraid there's been an accident,' David says, in his professional voice.

'What?' Matthew is clearly alarmed now.

'I'm so sorry,' David says quietly.

'Has something happened to Dana?' Matthew's voice is full of panic.

'She's fallen down the stairs,' David says.

'Is she okay?' But his face has gone white.

David shakes his head sombrely and says the dreaded words again. 'I'm so sorry.'

Matthew gasps, 'I don't believe it!' He looks ghastly. 'I want to see her!'

There's nothing to be done. He must see her. David leads him down to the landing, where he stops, respectfully. Dana lies below them like a broken doll, thrown across a room by a petulant child. Matthew sees her, cries out, and stumbles past him in his rush to get to his beloved.

'Don't touch her,' David advises.

Matthew collapses beside her and begins to sob as the others step back. He ignores David's warning and strokes her too-pale face, runs his thumb along her bloodless lips in disbelief. Then he buries his face in her neck, his shoulders heaving.

The others look away; it's unbearable.

Finally, Matthew looks up. 'How did this happen?' he cries, half crazed, at David, who has descended the stairs and has stopped above him on the second step. 'Why would she even be out of our room?'

'You didn't hear her go?' David asks.

Matthew shakes his head slowly in shock and misery. 'No. I was asleep. I didn't hear anything.' He covers his face with both hands and weeps wretchedly.

Bradley fetches a white sheet and they all stand by sombrely as he and David settle it gently over Dana's inert form.

Chapter Nine

Saturday, 6:33 AM

GWEN WALKS WITH Riley back to their room as if in a trance. She can't seem to take it all in. Dana is dead, just like that. She might have fallen down those stairs and died while Gwen was in David's room last night. It's possible she was already lying at the bottom of the stairs on the ground floor when she left his room on the first floor and climbed to the second floor to her own room. How fleeting and precious life is, she realizes. You never know when it may be snatched from you, just when you're least expecting it. Dana had everything to live for, Gwen thinks. It's too horrible. It makes her realize that she should try to enjoy every moment. Live life to the fullest. She hasn't been very good at that. Maybe it's time to try. Maybe it's time to let go of the baggage, the guilt, and try to live her life, she thinks. Maybe last night is a new beginning for her. She feels a surging warmth and happiness inside about David that she can't help, even though Dana is dead.

She'd wanted so much to go to him just now. But it would have been completely inappropriate. They'd managed a warm glance at one another, but that was it. There was time. They would be together again.

Riley won't like it that she was with David last night. Gwen knows that, but Riley is her friend, not her keeper. Riley should be happy for her that she's met someone. Gwen was always happy for Riley when *she* met someone, and Gwen usually didn't have anyone special herself. She's sorry it had to happen when they were supposed to be spending time together this weekend, but you must take good things when and where you find them. They are rare enough. Dana's dreadful accident has brought this home to her. Riley should understand that. It's not like she planned it this way.

They reach the room and Riley closes the door behind her. Gwen looks up at her warily, waiting for her to say something. When she doesn't, Gwen reaches for some clothes from her overnight bag. She would like a shower, but that seems out of the question. The water will be freezing.

'There's something I need to say,' Riley says at last, her voice serious, as she pulls a top on over her head and flips her long hair over her shoulders.

Here it comes, Gwen thinks.

'That attorney, David Paley.'

'What about him?' Gwen's voice comes out more sharply than she intended.

'Did you sleep with him?'

'Actually, yes, I did.' She turns and glares at Riley. 'Why, is that a problem? I'm a grown-up. I don't recall ever having a problem with any of your flings.' She zips up her jeans with an angry snap, and reaches for a thick sweater. She adds, 'God knows there were enough of them.'

'But you don't know anything about him.'

'Yes I do. He's David Paley, a defence attorney from New York City. And a very nice man.' She can't help adding, 'And we're *good* together.'

'Gwen, sit down for a minute,' Riley says, sitting down on her bed.

Gwen slumps down tiredly on the bed across from Riley and starts pulling on warm socks. She refuses to look at her, to show that she is listening. She doesn't want to listen. Riley should mind her own business. How quickly things have changed this weekend. She was supposed to be taking care of Riley, but somehow Riley is trying to re-establish herself in the role of her protector. Gwen doesn't like it.

'I don't know what it is, but something about him is bothering me,' Riley says, clearly tense.

Gwen looks up at her and says, in a voice that shows she means it, 'Riley – I don't want to hear it.'

Riley bites her tongue and finishes getting dressed in silence.

David returns to his room briefly to dress. His mind is racing. So much has happened in such a short time. Meeting Gwen. Now this awful accident. That looks like it might not be an accident.

He's learned to trust his instincts after all these years as a criminal lawyer. And he knows it's not actually that easy to die from a fall down a flight of stairs. Unless the neck is broken. And he's pretty sure Dana's neck was not broken. He thinks the cause of death was the blow to the head. And to die from a blow to the head from falling down the stairs, you have to fall in a particular way. You have to strike your head hard against the newel post, for instance. But it seems to him that she struck her head hard against the edge of the bottom step in a peculiar way.

It doesn't look like an accident at all. It looks to him like murder.

Matthew, simply as the dead woman's fiancé, is the most obvious suspect. David considers Matthew's reaction. Either it was completely genuine, or Matthew is a very good actor. David knows better than to underestimate anyone. He knows that people are complicated; life is complicated.

His own life is complicated. He'd intended to stay away from Gwen once he learned that her friend Riley had been a journalist with the *New York Times*. He didn't need the trouble. But then she'd sought him out in the library – and it was the most pleasant evening he's spent in years. It seemed so natural, so right, when she came upstairs with him. He unlocked the door and closed it behind them, and then it was inevitable. Somehow they'd found the bed. He'd felt himself come alive after years of being alone. He somehow sensed that she felt the same way.

He's been so lonely since his wife died.

Saturday, 6:55 AM

Beverly follows her husband to the staircase. They've hastily thrown on some warm clothes and are on their way to the dining room. Her heart races in time with her quick footsteps on the stairs. Despite her deep pity for the dead woman, she almost feels like they have been saved. This crisis has sidelined their own troubles. It's as if they've both been pulled back from the brink they'd faced last night. It's awful to think so, but she's hoping that it will prevent them from focusing again on their marriage in the cold, empty light of day. She does not want to go there, now that she knows just how precarious her position is.

And then, when they are home again, with all this drama and tragedy behind them, they will slip into old patterns, avoiding what's important, carrying on the way they should. The way they must. She's a little surprised at how, even in the face of something as calamitous as a young woman's unexpected death, she still considers her own interests first. But then, she didn't really know her. She suspects Henry is grateful to have something to distract them from themselves this weekend, too, rather than spending it arguing with his wife and blowing his comfortable existence apart.

They arrive at the landing and she recoils when she sees the body still lying at the bottom of the stairs, covered by the sheet. She hadn't expected it to be there. Why haven't they moved her, taken her away somewhere, where they don't have to see her? She shudders involuntarily. They make their appalled way down and step around the corpse, deliberately looking elsewhere, and hurry to the dining room.

When she and Henry enter the dining room, everyone turns towards them. Lauren is standing by the coffee, pouring herself a cup from a carafe. Beside her is her boyfriend, Ian, who for once isn't smiling. Gwen is standing by herself, but Riley is hovering nearby. Beverly doesn't see Matthew anywhere. The woman writer, Candice, is off in a corner by herself, drinking coffee and observing everyone with a sharp eye. She's not hiding behind a magazine this morning. The attorney stands quietly away from everyone else, looking troubled and sipping coffee.

Candice walks up to everyone near the coffee things and says, quietly, 'Are any of you aware of who Matthew Hutchinson *is*?' The rest of them look at her in surprise. 'No? He's from one of the most prominent and wealthy families in New England.'

Beverly had no idea, and looking around at the others, it seems that nobody else had any idea either. At that moment Bradley brings out plates of rolls, croissants, and muffins from the kitchen. He sets them down on the long side table where the buffet had been laid out the night before. 'Please, help yourselves,' he says.

Bradley seems quite different this morning, Beverly thinks. He has a distracted air, and he's missing his charming smile. Well, no wonder.

He glances around the room and says, 'I'm really sorry about the power. There's not much we can do about it but wait for them to fix the lines. I'm sure they're working on it. We'll try to make you as comfortable as possible in the meantime.'

Beverly is relieved that Matthew isn't there. He must have returned to his room. She imagines the others must feel as relieved as she does. No one would know how to act around him. A handsome young man in the prime of life, evidently the heir to a great fortune, engaged to such a lovely young woman – his happiness destroyed in an instant by this terrible, tragic accident. How sad and difficult the weekend will be, tiptoeing around his grief.

She wishes now, her own marriage hanging in tatters, that she'd never heard of this place. If only they could leave. She wants nothing more than to go home. She wants to go home with Henry and patch things up and carry on as normal.

The guests mill about awkwardly. Some step up and reach uneasily for croissants and muffins. Bradley soon returns carrying a big platter of eggs. 'Fortunately, we have a gas stove,' he says. He places the platter on the table and invites everyone to dig in. But many of them seem to have lost their appetite.

Finally James appears from the kitchen and says, with appropriate solemnity, 'This is such an awful thing to have happened. I am so sorry. And' – he hesitates – 'I apologize – but unfortunately, I have been advised that we must leave the body where it is for the time being.'

The guests shift uneasily where they stand.

'Advised by whom?' Henry asks.

'By me,' David answers.

'Are you sure you can't . . . move her?' Beverly asks, dismayed. It seems awful just to leave her there. Disrespectful, somehow.

'And no, we can't.'

'Why not? Surely it was an accident,' Lauren says.

'Better to wait for the coroner to determine that,' David says.

'You're not suggesting it wasn't an accident!' Gwen says.

'I'm saying it's for the coroner to decide.'

Suddenly Beverly wonders if the attorney suspects Matthew of pushing his fiancée down the stairs. She studies the others; she's pretty sure one or two of them just had the same thought. With a sick feeling in the pit of her stomach, she wonders if any of them heard what she heard, the argument between Matthew and Dana late last night. Should she say anything?

74

Surely it was just a lovers' quarrel. Matthew wouldn't harm Dana. They seemed so in love.

There's an awkward silence, and then Riley says abruptly, 'I thought I heard a scream last night.'

'When?' David asks.

'I don't know. I thought I'd imagined it.'

'Did anyone else hear anything?' David asks, looking around the room.

Beverly feels her whole body tighten. She doesn't want to get the young man into trouble if he hasn't done anything wrong. Perhaps someone else heard them arguing. She doesn't want to be the one to tell. But no one else offers anything. She looks down, uncertain, and lets the moment pass.

'What about the police?' Henry asks now.

James speaks up. 'As you know, the power's out and the phones are dead. We haven't been able to reach the police.'

'I know, but what about snowmobiles?' Henry asks.

James shakes his head. 'We don't have them here. They're noisy. We like to focus on nature – hiking, skiing, snowshoeing. We're old-fashioned.'

Henry rolls his eyes in disgust. 'I can't believe you don't have a generator,' he mutters.

'The police will get here eventually,' James says, ignoring him. 'Once the power's restored and we can use the phone. Or they clear and sand the roads and we can get out.'

'How long does it usually take,' Riley asks uneasily, 'to restore power up here when there's a storm?'

Bradley says, 'It all depends. But I imagine it's a pretty widespread outage. Ice is much worse than snow. It brings down the wires.'

'Until the police do get here,' the attorney says, 'we have to treat it as a possible crime scene.'

'But—' Beverly begins and stops, as all eyes turn her way and she flushes. She says, pointing out the obvious, 'We'll have to step past her body every time we go up or down the stairs. We'll see her lying there whenever we sit in the lobby.'

And then she thinks of that poor young man up in his room, waiting for the police. And whether she ought to say something about what she heard.

Chapter Ten

Saturday, 7:45 AM

CANDICE LINGERS IN the dining room with the others after breakfast. It seems like nobody knows what to do; they are all at loose ends now – with the exception of the lawyer, who leaves the dining room after breakfast with a subdued but purposeful air. Candice notices the dark-haired woman, whose name she's learned is Gwen, watching him go.

She can't have any idea who he is.

Candice would love to follow the notorious David Paley up the stairs. She'd bet dollars to donuts he's on his way to see Matthew Hutchinson, and she wishes more than anything that she could be there to hear what is said. Then she reminds herself not to be despicable, that the man has just lost the woman he was to marry.

This is something she has had to work on, not letting her curiosity trump her compassion. That's why she got out of journalism, after all, and started writing books instead. Long-form non-fiction had saved her from that at least. When she writes a book, she finds she can still feel for her subject, still find her sense of decency. Journalism can ruin you.

She glances at Riley, whom she recognized the night before as a war correspondent for the *New York Times*. She's got the look. Not the look of the hardened journalist who has necessarily grown a thick, protective skin. She's at the other end of the scale – she's broken wide open, raw. She wonders if Riley will ever be put back together again. She can recognize PTSD when she sees it; she's seen it before.

She's glad she's no longer a journalist. Still, there's a body lying at the foot of the stairs, and no one knows how it got there. She can read people pretty well, and she's not stupid – the attorney looks as if he suspects it was more than an accident. She's tempted to slip upstairs and listen outside Matthew's door. But she restrains herself.

'We can't go out in this,' Henry says gloomily, interrupting her thoughts. He's scowling outside at the ice.

The dining-room windows give on to the forest on the east side of the hotel. Everything is covered in sparkling ice. It's beautiful, as if the world is coated in diamonds. Long, pointy icicles hang from the eaves in front of the windows. They look rather deadly. If you were walking under one of those and it fell on you, it might kill you, Candice thinks.

The storm has made it too dangerous for walking, or skiing, or snowshoeing, or anything but taking your life in your hands. The best place to be during a major ice storm is safely inside where you can't get hit by falling branches or pierced through with icicles, or electrocuted by fallen power lines.

Not to mention the risk of slipping and cracking your head open on the ice.

No, thank you, Candice thinks. She's going to stay inside like everybody else.

David knocks on the door of Matthew's room. When there's no answer, he tries again, more loudly this time. Finally, with nervous hands he fumbles for the key he obtained from James and opens the door himself, afraid that Matthew might have done something drastic. He's seen it before. He pushes the door open quickly and spies Matthew sitting immobile in a chair in front of the fireplace. David's immediate relief shifts to uneasiness. Even though James had started a fire earlier, the room is chilly. David steps further into the room. No wonder; Matthew has let the fire almost go out.

David approaches and studies Matthew carefully. He's obviously been weeping. His eyes and face are puffy. He looks almost catatonic. 'Matthew,' David says. The other man does not respond. It's hard to tell if he's swamped with grief or guilt, or quite possibly, both at once.

Quietly, David moves over to the fireplace and sets the fire-guard aside. He chooses another log and carefully adds it to the fire, poking and prodding to make it catch. It's good to have something like this to do while he thinks about what to say. He wishes he could just keep poking and prodding the fire for ever, staring into the flames, and not have to do what he's about to do. But he's worried about this young man. He feels a responsibility. He would like to help if he can. Even though there is not much to be done; you can't go back in time and change things. He's just cleanup crew, really.

Finally, he sets the poker aside, replaces the fireguard, and takes the other chair beside Matthew. He pauses while he decides how to begin.

'The police will get here eventually,' he says at last in a low voice. 'If not today, then tomorrow. They will investigate. There will be an inquest into the cause of death.' He pauses. He knows to speak slowly; the mind in shock has trouble taking things in. 'It is my belief that they will not find the cause of death to be an accidental fall.' He waits. Matthew doesn't stir, doesn't even show surprise. Which is troubling. 'It appears to me that the injury to the head, which was most likely the cause of death, is not one that would naturally occur in a fall. It looks like it was caused by being pushed into the edge of the stair from the front and above.' He can't help himself; the cynicism takes over. 'If you're trying to make a murder look like an accident in a fall down the stairs, far better to push the head into the newel post in the direction of the fall.' That gets his attention.

'What did you say?' Matthew asks, lifting his head and looking at him for the first time.

David looks into his eyes. 'I said it doesn't look like an accident. It looks like your fiancée was murdered.'

'What?'

'I believe Dana was murdered.'

Matthew looks back at him as if it's finally dawning on him. 'Oh, God. No.'

'I believe so, yes.'

A long moment passes, and then Matthew says, 'You think I did it.'

'I don't know and I don't want to know. But I am a criminal

80

defence attorney and I am here to offer you some free advice until you can retain an attorney of your own.'

'I didn't kill her!'

'Okay.'

'I was asleep, I swear! I didn't even know she'd left the room! Why would she do that? She's never left our hotel room before. The bathroom is right here. She's not a sleepwalker.'

And that's just it. Why *would* she leave the room, David thinks – unless she'd argued with her fiancé? And then perhaps he followed her, in a rage. Lost control for a fatal moment. He doesn't want to ask – he doesn't want to get involved – but he does. 'Did you two have an argument last night?'

'What? No! Of course not. I love her! I could never hurt her!' His voice has risen and he lowers it again. 'There must be some reason she left. Maybe she heard something out in the hall. I don't know. All I know is that I slept through all of it.'

'You had no disagreements about anything, about . . . money? A pre-nup, perhaps?'

Matthew shakes his head dismissively. 'No. Neither of us wanted, or needed, a pre-nup. We were in love – that's the truth.' He asks desperately, 'Do you really think someone killed her?'

'It looks that way to me,' David says.

Matthew turns back to stare at the fire, fresh tears spilling from his eyes. 'Dear God.' He covers his face with his hands for a moment until he regains control. Then he removes them and turns to David. 'If someone deliberately killed her, then I want to know who, and I want to know why.' He looks back at David. 'It wasn't me, I swear.' He is clearly tormented.

David observes Matthew shrewdly. He's almost convinced the man is innocent. 'Okay. But here's my advice, anyway. Don't say anything to anybody about this. Just – say nothing. It may not be a bad idea to stay up here in your room until the police get here. And when they do get here, if they caution you, and arrest you – and even if they don't – say nothing. Get your-self a good attorney.'

Matthew has turned even paler. 'What about you?'

'I don't think so. But I can recommend someone, if you like.' David gets up to leave. He knows that with no phone service, there's no one that Matthew can call, no one he can talk to. He's isolated here. 'Are you going to be okay?'

'I don't know.'

'I'm here if you need me,' he says. He means it. 'I'll check in on you again in a bit.'

Matthew nods and turns back to the fire.

David lets himself out.

Matthew hears the door click closed and turns to look. He's alone again.

He stands up suddenly and begins to pace. He's overcome with grief for Dana, but he's also frightened and agitated by what David Paley has said. Dana is dead! And the attorney thinks he did it. If he thinks so, the police will think so, too.

He suppresses a sob as he paces the room. He told the attor-ney that he and Dana hadn't argued, and now he thinks he's made a mistake. He and Dana *had* argued, tension about the impending wedding erupting out of nowhere. They've both been under a lot of stress.

Dana had brought up his mother again – complaining that

his mother has never approved of her, never thought she was good enough. Dana got like that sometimes – more often, recently – emotionally overwrought, a little insecure. Looking at her, you would never be able to tell that sometimes she lacked confidence, but occasionally she revealed it to him. It didn't bother him. He was used to people – friends and girlfriends – being intimidated by his wealthy, powerful family.

He'd denied it, of course. Said that she was being oversensitive, that of course his mother approved of her. But he was tired of having to say the same thing over and over. Especially because it wasn't exactly true. His mother did think he could do better, and she'd had the audacity to tell him so, on more than one occasion. She'd tried to get him to wait, thinking he would tire of Dana, thinking that he was simply taken in by Dana's beauty and that his feelings for her would change. He'd made it clear to his strong-willed, wealthy matriarch of a mother that he loved Dana and that he was going to marry her. But it was wearying to be constantly caught between the two women, unable to entirely please – or appease – either one of them. Last night, his exasperation had got the better of him.

He wonders suddenly if anyone heard them arguing.

Chapter Eleven

Saturday, 8:00 AM

THE GUESTS FILTER slowly from the dining room into the lobby, subdued, avoiding the staircase, some of them still holding coffee cups.

Henry is cursing his luck. If only the snow had not turned to driving ice in the night this would have been a rather fabulous winter wonderland. He could have gone cross-country skiing all day, worked off some of this godawful tension. Now he stands close to the front windows of the lobby and looks gloomily out at the ice – coating everything like glass – and feels cheated. This hotel isn't exactly cheap and everything seems to be conspiring to make him have a miserable time. He makes the mistake of glancing at his wife, who is watching him.

He feels so restless. He leans forward and practically presses his nose against the cool glass of the window. He sees that a massive branch has broken off the enormous old tree on the front lawn and lies shattered in pieces, dark wood against sparkling white. He feels his wife come up behind him. Hears her say, 'You aren't thinking of going out in that.'

He hadn't been, but now she's decided it. 'Yes.'

'Don't be ridiculous,' she says, as if scolding one of the kids for some hare-brained idea.

He moves over to the coat stand near the door where most of them had left their coats the night before, their boots below them on the mat. He finds and pulls on his winter jacket, bends over and slips off his running shoes, and pulls on the winter boots that he arrived in.

'Are you sure that's a good idea?' Ian says, but without the overlay of hysteria and the need for control Henry detects so frequently in his wife's voice.

'I won't go far,' he tells Ian, pulling on his hat. 'I just want to get some fresh air.'

'Make sure you stay away from any power lines,' Ian advises him.

They're all standing watching him, as if he's some kind of canary, testing the conditions.

Henry turns around and opens the front door. He feels the cold air hit his face, and everyone's eyes on his back. He steps out onto the porch and pulls the door closed behind him. It's now that he notices the wind – how wild and loud it is. From inside the hotel it sounds like a constant, dull roar with the occasional shriek, something far away, but out here it's alive, it's a monster, and it's much closer. He looks towards the forest at the edge of the lawn and sees how the wind is whipping the tops of the trees back and forth. And the noise – it's like a keening. Worst of all is the creaking, sawing sound as the wind brings its force to bear on the ice-laden branches of the tree in front of him. He closes his eyes for a moment and listens; he imagines that this is what an old wooden sailing ship might have sounded like at sea, in a storm. Then he opens his eyes and lifts them up to the tree, wondering if any more branches are about to come down.

He's been still now for some moments and he knows they're all watching. He grabs the porch handrail and looks down. There's a thick coating of ice on the wooden stairs and he steps carefully, holding on firmly to the rail. It's very slippery, but he makes it to the bottom of the three steps without incident and stands there. He's beginning to wonder what he's doing out here. He starts walking – not walking, walking is impossible – but sliding his feet along the ice, trying to keep his centre of balance low. It's like walking after Teddy on the ice rink at hockey when he was little, just after the rink was flooded, only the rink was flat, and this ice slopes all over the place.

Without warning, Henry's feet go right out from under him in spectacular fashion and he lands heavily on his back, winded, not twenty feet from the front porch. He lies there trying to get his breath back, wheezing loudly, looking up at the clouds, feeling like a fool. He hears the front door open behind him. That will be his wife, telling him to come back in.

But before she can say anything there's a frightful cracking sound overhead. He turns his head towards the tree. His heart jumps in his chest as he realizes what's going to happen. He closes his eyes as part of a branch comes down and lands with a shudder no more than a few feet away. He slowly reopens his eyes.

That branch could have killed him.

Unable to get back up on his feet, Henry crawls and slides

on all fours back to the front porch and then hauls himself to standing at the front steps using the handrail.

The front door is wide open, and everyone is looking at him, alarmed. They practically pull him back inside the hotel.

Once he's regained his composure, his wife says, 'If you want something to do, you can go and help Bradley try to clear the walk out to the icehouse.' He looks back at her in annoyance and she adds, 'He told me there aren't any trees there. It should be relatively safe.'

Candice feels rather sorry for Henry, who is clearly frustrated at being trapped here. Most of them seem to feel that way. Either longing to get out, like Henry, or hanging listlessly about, like Ian and Lauren.

She's got plenty to do – as long as her battery holds up – and plenty here to interest her. She wanders over to Dana's body to have another look. She can feel the others' eyes on her, disapproving, as she lifts the sheet. This time she looks more carefully at the head injury, and then at the blood on the stair, and her heart beats a little faster at what she sees. Then she wanders back to the fireplace and stands in front of it for a moment, lost in thought, warming her hands. She really can't afford to let herself be distracted by this. But she suspects that someone murdered that poor girl.

Lauren startles her out of her thoughts by asking, 'What kind of book are you working on?'

Candice smiles a little evasively. 'Oh – I don't like to talk about it. I never talk about what I'm working on until it's finished,' she says apologetically. 'I find it just sucks all the energy out of the project.'

'Oh,' Lauren says. 'I thought writers always liked to talk about what they were working on.'

'Not me,' Candice replies.

Gradually the guests begin to leave the lobby, scattering in different directions, subdued by the tragedy that has occurred in their midst. Bradley had brought a couple of oil lamps and some matches and left them on the coffee table, but most of them opt to use the torch app on their iPhones to help them find their way up the dark staircase and around the unlit corridors upstairs. It's unnervingly dark once you leave the ground floor, where the windows across the front of the hotel let in daylight.

It's time to get to work. Candice skirts the corpse and trudges up the staircase to her room on the second floor. The corridor is lit only by the rather small windows at each end, and it is dark and gloomy, made even more so by the dark carpet and dull wallpaper. Candice supposes that all the bedrooms have windows – hers certainly does – and that if the curtains are pulled back, there will be enough light for most purposes, but probably not enough to read easily.

Upstairs, it's colder. The large fire in the lobby makes it undoubtedly the most hospitable place to be, if you are able to ignore the presence of the dead body. But most of the guests seem to have gone back up to their rooms, badly spooked.

Candice finds her room too cold, too gloomy, and too dark for her liking. She returns downstairs carrying her laptop and discovers the library. She searches out Bradley, finds him in the dining room clearing things away, and asks him to build a fire in the library for her. Bradley looks a bit harried and harassed. It must be difficult, Candice thinks, to keep a hotel going while short-staffed during a power failure.

'I thought I heard you were shovelling the path to the ice-house,' she says as they walk to the library.

He smiles at her briefly. 'Yes, but I've got Henry helping with that now. It's tough going but he's having some luck with the snowblower.'

She follows Bradley into the library. She longs to complain about the awful position the power failure has put her in, but she doesn't want to burden him any further. And she is aware of how petty it would be, when there's a young woman dead, and there may be people out there in real jeopardy from this storm.

Still. There is no question the power outage is causing her great inconvenience. She came up here to work, and she can't work without a functioning laptop. She has only a few hours of battery left at most. She may be reduced to writing with a ballpoint pen, wrapped in a blanket. It's not what she imagined. She thinks of her mother trapped in her bed, and wonders if her sisters are taking care of her the way they should.

She settles herself into a comfortable armchair by the crackling, spitting fire, thanks Bradley profusely, and asks him to bring her a hot cup of tea when he gets a chance. Then she opens her computer. But it's a while before she can stop thinking about Dana, and get down to work.

Saturday, 9:15 AM

Gwen had found breakfast in the dining room – which she couldn't help comparing unfavourably to the delightful breakfast experience promised to her in the Mitchell's Inn brochure – excruciating. She only managed to eat half a muffin, without tasting it.

David hadn't approached her, but Riley had been standing beside her oozing a fierce protectiveness. Or maybe it was because he was distracted by what had happened to Dana. Gwen knew he was concerned about Matthew. She didn't really give a shit what Riley thought, but she hadn't liked the idea of Riley grabbing her arm if she tried to walk over to David, and creating a scene. Riley was unpredictable. When David left the dining room, Gwen decided she would find him later, when she had the possibility of a little privacy.

She couldn't help thinking about him. Just a few hours earlier he'd been touching her, loving her.

They'd wandered out to the lobby and watched Henry make a fool of himself on the icy lawn. Then Riley had suggested the two of them explore the hotel together. Gwen showed her the library, then they went into the sitting room next to the library. It was quite charming, with an array of plump chintz sofas and chairs and low tables and an oil portrait of a woman over the fireplace.

'Shall we stay here?' Gwen suggested, rubbing her hands along her arms for warmth. But Riley was restless and wanted to keep looking around. They explored the little corridor off the lobby and came to the bar.

'This is nice,' Riley says now, glancing around the bar approvingly. 'I'll make a fire for us here.'

Of course she can start her own fire, Gwen thinks, watching her. She's lived in Iraq, and Afghanistan, in the roughest of conditions. She wonders what else Riley can do that Gwen can't. Drive a car with a manual gearbox. Treat a wound. Protect a source. Negotiate with terrorists. She realizes that Riley has never really shared any of these kinds of details with her; she probably thinks Gwen wouldn't be able to handle it. Riley is the strangest collection of impressive skills, fierce bravery, and now, a terrible, unpredictable fragility.

Gwen is acutely aware of the bottles behind the bar and worries that Riley will want to get into them, even though it's just past breakfast. She turns her back on the bar and wanders around the room, perusing the titles of the books shelved along the walls, studying the paintings.

Suddenly Gwen finds herself thinking about the last year of journalism school, when everything changed for her. Riley knows what happened; she was there. She knows why Gwen thinks she doesn't deserve to be happy. But Gwen knows that if she wants a chance with David, she must confront the past. She must face it and come to terms with it somehow.

They were out one night at a party. There was a lot of drinking – it was the end of the year and everybody was partying hard because they would soon be graduating. Gwen witnessed a terrible crime. She watched three men rape a young woman. And she did nothing. Nothing at all.

She remembers how she'd been up all the night before, finishing some assignment. She'd had a lot to drink, and needed to lie down. She found a bedroom – it was a house party – with a bed and a spare mattress on the floor. She crawled under some blankets on the mattress. Then a girl came crashing into the room, waking her up. It was dark, with only the light from the streetlight outside penetrating the room. Gwen recognized the girl – she was in some of her classes. She was trying to shrug some guy off, but he wasn't having it. He started pulling off her clothes. Gwen was about to get up – she thought the two of them could make him stop – but then two more men came in and closed the door behind them. One of them propped a chair up under the doorknob so no one could open the door. Gwen was paralysed with fear.

The other girl screamed, but the music was so loud no one could have heard her. They held her down on the bed while they raped her. They were laughing. It all happened so fast. She hadn't wanted them to know she was there. She was afraid they would do the same to her.

They left the girl there, sobbing, on the bed. As soon as they were gone, Gwen threw up. She went over to see how the other girl was, but she'd passed out. Gwen turned her on her side so that she wouldn't choke on her own vomit, and then she went to find Riley. And Riley told her she should have fought back.

Riley has told her since then that she doesn't think that any more. When Gwen found Riley at the party and told her what had happened, they went up to see the girl together. Gwen told her she'd been in the room; the girl didn't say anything, but Gwen could see the reproach in her eyes. She asked Gwen if she would be able to identify the men who raped her, and to corroborate her story. She'd told Riley that she thought she'd be able to recognize them, but the minute the girl put her on the spot, Gwen panicked. She didn't want the responsibility. She told her that it was too dark, and that she couldn't bear to watch, that she'd hid under the covers. That she wouldn't be able to identify them. That she couldn't help her.

The girl wanted to press charges, but she didn't want to do it without Gwen's help. But Gwen didn't help her, even though Riley urged her to. She told her that she couldn't be a witness. She did nothing. She graduated and moved away and tried to forget about it. But she's always been haunted by the thought that those college boys – whoever they were – are now grown men. And if they could behave that way once, they could do it again. She heard that the girl killed herself not long after. And Gwen's been living with the guilt ever since.

It has defined her, shaped her life. She's a coward, someone who failed to do the right thing. She knows she no longer deserves any of the good things life has to offer.

Riley has always judged her for it. Even now, years later, Riley's generally holier-than-thou attitude infuriates her. She sometimes wonders if Riley did everything she should have done in all those war zones, whether she'd always done every-thing absolutely fucking morally perfectly. She wonders if Riley ever made a mistake, if she'd ever been afraid, all that time in Iraq and Afghanistan.

Lost in her thoughts, she suddenly hears Riley suck in her breath with a loud gasp. She turns, startled, and sees Riley in the chair in front of the fire, her face drained of colour.

'Oh, no,' Riley says.

'What?' Gwen's alarmed at the visible change in Riley. 'Are you all right?'

'I knew I'd heard his name before.'

Gwen turns away uneasily.

'Come over here. Listen to me.'

Gwen looks at her warily, and reluctantly goes and sits across from her.

'I've just remembered who he is.' She leans forward and looks at Gwen intensely, genuine concern on her face.

Now Gwen is starting to worry. Surely there's nothing wrong with David. There can't be.

Riley says, 'He's the attorney who was arrested on suspicion of murdering his wife.'

Chapter Twelve

Saturday, 10:00 AM

JAMES SCRUBS THE frying pan in the big kitchen sink and ponders how to rejig things so that he can feed his guests adequately without any electricity. The refrigerator isn't working. At least he can cook with the gas oven. But he's without a dishwasher. Breakfast was easy enough – eggs and pastries, and nobody much felt like eating anyway, from what he could see, after that poor girl fell down the stairs.

He's lost his appetite, too. He feels terrible for that man's loss. And the whole thing makes him sick with anxiety. It's the kind of situation every hotel owner loses sleep over – an accident in his hotel, a fatal accident at that. He has insurance, but Christ. What a thing to happen. He knows he's not to blame. His carpets aren't loose – he'd gone up to the landing and checked over that carpet himself the first chance he got. It was fine. She must have stumbled for no reason. There's absolutely no way anyone can blame him or his hotel.

He thinks again about how much she might have had to drink the night before. He'd asked Bradley, in the kitchen earlier when they were preparing breakfast.

'Do you think she was drunk?' he asked him in a low voice. 'Do you think that's why she fell?'

Bradley shook his head. 'Don't worry, Dad. She wasn't drunk. I was serving, remember?'

'But I had you put that bottle of champagne in their room, remember? Do you know if they drank it?'

Bradley shook his head again. 'I don't know. I haven't been in there this morning, David didn't want me in there.'

James chewed his lip, something he does when he's worried, a habit he's been trying to break. He hadn't looked for the champagne bottle when he was in the room, hadn't thought of it.

'Dad, don't worry,' Bradley repeated firmly. 'You have nothing to worry about. She didn't fall because she'd been drinking.'

But James couldn't help noticing that Bradley also seemed shaken by what had happened. He looked tired; there were rings under his eyes, as if he hadn't slept.

'Were you up late last night?' James asked.

'No,' Bradley said, picking up the trays. 'I need to take these out.' Then he'd taken the muffins and croissants out to the dining room.

James finishes with his frying pan and puts it on the drying rack. He wishes the power would come back on. He misses his bloody dishwasher. He wishes the police would get here and take the body away. He can't believe he's got to take care of almost a dozen people without electricity and that there's a dead body at the foot of the grand staircase in his beloved hotel and he can't do anything about it.

Saturday, noon

Lauren descends the staircase into the lobby, stepping with distaste around Dana's body, Ian right behind her. It's a rather horrible choice they all have to make – whether to use the creepy back staircase or the main one with the body at the bottom. When she looks up, the lobby is empty except for Candice, who hurriedly puts a book down on a side table and turns to face her. It's Lauren's book.

'That's mine,' Lauren says. 'I *thought* I'd left that book down here.'

Candice asks, 'Do you know where Bradley is? I came out to ask him to bring me some hot tea.'

'I can tell him if I see him, if you like,' Lauren says.

'Oh, would you? And tell him to bring my lunch to the library. Thanks. I didn't really want to bother his father in the kitchen.' Candice hurries away.

Lauren watches her go.

She sits down on the hearth of the lobby's big stone fireplace and pulls Ian down beside her, trying to warm up while they wait for the others to appear and for lunch to be served. Lauren stares across the room at the front windows. She can't stop thinking about it. Dana is dead, at the foot of the stairs. She avoids looking in that direction as best she can. 'This is so terrible,' she whispers to Ian.

'I know,' he agrees, beside her. He takes her hand, clasps it in his own. 'I don't know what I'd do if something happened to you.'

She lightly kisses his cheek. Then she whispers, 'I don't see why she can't be moved. Why do we have to wait for the coroner?'

97

'It's awful to leave her lying there,' Ian agrees.

'Do you think someone might have pushed her?' Lauren whispers.

'No, of course not. It must have been an accident. David's an attorney – he's just following procedure.' He adds, pushing a strand of her hair behind her ear, 'Lawyers always think they know everything.' He glances over his shoulder at the body and says, 'But if the police don't get here soon, surely we can't just leave her there. It's too creepy.'

One by one, the guests reappear in the lobby, as if summoned by an invisible bell. Hungry, no doubt, David thinks, wondering what there is to eat.

After speaking to Matthew, David had spent the morning in his room. Thinking about Dana at the bottom of the stairs. About how it might have happened. Thinking about the bereft young man holed up in his room, waiting for the inevitable visit by the police.

Thinking about Gwen. Thinking a lot about Gwen.

Now, in the lobby, David looks at her. She seems even more distressed than she had earlier that morning, at breakfast. And she hasn't turned his way once since he entered the lobby. She's sitting by the fire, holding her hands out to it for warmth, not looking his way. He would like to go to her, but he senses she doesn't want him to. He tries to understand it. She can't be one of those women who enjoy one-night stands but want nothing more. He doesn't think she's the type. He's certain of it. Of course, they're all distressed by the death of Dana.

And he doesn't know what her friend Riley might have said to her, once they were alone together. Warned her off him, no doubt.

He knew it was better not to get involved, with any of it. Not with her, and not with Matthew. He's had enough trouble. What he wants now is peace. But he fears that peace might have to wait.

Gwen catches David looking at her and averts her eyes. What Riley told her about David – *it can't possibly be true*. Maybe she's just saying this to restore the balance of power between them to what it was before. Maybe Riley is deliberately sabotaging her. That is what Gwen doesn't know. How easy it would be to do – to warn her to stay away from David all weekend, and then when they get back to civilization and google David Paley, he probably won't be who she's thinking of at all. The only thing he will have in common with the man who was arrested for murdering his wife is that they are both attorneys. And Riley will just laugh it off, *Oh, I was so sure. Sorry.* But it will be too late. Her opportunity with David will be gone. She's already thirty and she might never meet anyone else. She studies Riley resentfully and then turns away.

Or maybe it's not deliberate at all; maybe Riley's paranoia is simply spilling over into everything.

Henry is sitting beside his wife, not looking at her. His muscles are pleasantly tired from clearing the path out to the icehouse, and he's built up an appetite. Surely lunch will be soon.

He can feel Beverly looking sidelong at him. He wonders what they would be doing right now, if this hadn't happened. Dismantling their life together bit by bit, he thinks, over cold cups of coffee in some corner of the hotel. He realizes that he is almost glad of the diversion the accident has brought.

He thinks about what the attorney said. *It's for the coroner to decide.* He dips his head down now to his wife and whispers, 'Do you think she was pushed?' She looks back at him, worried.

Beverly answers him anxiously, 'I don't know.' Should she bring up the argument she overheard between Dana and Matthew? She tells herself it's none of her business.

She's decided to say nothing, at least for the time being. No one ever really knows what goes on in other people's relationships, or what another person's relationship is like. Perhaps they quarrelled all the time, and it means nothing.

She looks now at Henry and realizes that she doesn't actually know what goes through his mind most of the time. She makes assumptions, that's all. And believes they are the truth. All these years she thought she knew him so well, but did she really? How utterly shocked she'd been last night when he said it was too late for them to fix their marriage. The truth is, she doesn't know what he's thinking at all.

Perhaps he has a mistress. It's the first time the thought has occurred to her. Maybe it isn't so hard to believe. She hasn't been that interested in sex for a long time. Perhaps he's found someone else, and that's why he wants to leave her. Otherwise, she doesn't think he'd bother. That's it, she thinks, that must be the reason for this bombshell he's dropped so callously. He can't want to tear their family apart just so that he can be away from her – they're not that bad together. He can't be looking forward to being financially ruined and living alone in some sad apartment, missing his children, just to be away from her. No. There must be someone else. Someone who makes him think that leaving her and the kids is going to be some fun, giddy, sex-soaked adventure. She wonders who it is, whether it's someone she knows.

She remembers how annoyed he'd been when he realized there was no wi-fi here at the inn. Perhaps he was hoping to be able to stay in touch with his girlfriend; perhaps she had expected him to stay in touch with her – the girlfriend that Beverly is now afraid actually exists.

How quickly and how absolutely trust – built over many years – can collapse. She needs to be sure. She realizes she needs to look at her husband's mobile phone, but he always keeps it on him, or at least near him. And she has no idea what his password is; she can't even guess. But she is suddenly certain that if she could get into his mobile phone, she would find the truth.

And then she would know what she's dealing with.

Chapter Thirteen

LAUREN WATCHES HENRY and his wife, Beverly, seated side by side. They are barely speaking to one another.

Riley and Gwen are sitting far apart; Lauren senses a rift. She has been watching Riley especially. The edge of hysteria that Lauren first noticed when they'd rescued her out of the ditch the night before is still there. Amplified, even. Riley fidgets endlessly, twirling the silver ring on her index finger, her eyes constantly scanning the room as if looking for something, some threat. Lauren notices that Gwen is ignoring Riley, which is odd. Last night, Gwen had seemed overly solicitous, trying her best to manage Riley's mood, but now she doesn't seem to care. Something must have happened. Lauren remembers last night, noticing the little flirtation between David and Gwen in the dining room coming to an abrupt halt. She wonders if Riley had anything to do with that. And if she did, what her reason might have been. Jealousy, probably.

*

Riley knows Gwen is angry at her. But it had to be done. Riley studies David, watching him, trying to remember what she knows about the case. She's almost certain he's the New York attorney who was arrested – and released – for the violent murder of his wife, three or four years ago. She tries to recall the details. It was a bludgeoning death, a particularly brutal one. The woman had been so badly beaten that her back was broken. She'd been struck repeatedly in the head with something heavy, in the kitchen of their home, in one of New York's expensive suburbs. The murder weapon had never been recovered. The husband claimed that he'd returned home late from work and found her. He'd called 911. But there was some discrepancy about the details that didn't work in his favour. There was some lost time. A neighbour had insisted that he'd noticed the husband's car drive in considerably earlier than the 911 call. The attorney had then explained it by saying that he hadn't gone into the kitchen when he first got home. It hadn't sounded likely.

She stares at David's hands, hanging down by his sides as he stands near the fireplace, calmly waiting for lunch. Strong, masculine hands. She wonders what he is capable of. She lifts her eyes and catches him staring at her. She looks away.

There were other suspicious circumstances, Riley recalls. The marriage had been in trouble. There had been talk of divorce. That might describe half the marriages out there, but there had been an insurance policy – a large one. And there had been no sign of forced entry.

As far as she can remember, the charges had been dropped. They could find no bloody clothes, no murder weapon. With no physical evidence tying the husband to the crime, and no witnesses – other than the neighbour who said he'd been home

103

earlier than he at first claimed – there wasn't enough. They let him go. And as far as she remembered, the case was still unsolved.

Riley studies David's face as he stands near the fire, and asks herself if it is the face of a killer. She thinks of him in bed with Gwen, his hands on her – imagines him pummelling his fists into Gwen's face, over and over . . .

She is breathing too quickly. She must stop thinking like this. She must control her thoughts. If only they could get the hell out of here.

Finally, James and Bradley appear and invite everyone into the dining room. They've put together a huge plate of sand-wiches and supplied more coffee.

Gwen finds herself wishing for a stiff drink, even though it's only lunchtime. She hears Lauren say to Bradley, 'Candice wanted me to mention that she'd like you to bring her lunch to her in the library, if that's all right. Oh, and hot tea.'

'Yes, I figured as much,' Bradley answers, and bends over the platter and selects a few sandwiches with a pair of silver tongs and arranges them on a smaller plate. He heads off towards the library.

Even with the corpse lying at the foot of the stairs in the next room, only yards away, the sandwiches quickly vanish from the platter.

Gwen watches the others eat with distaste. She wants to leave. She doesn't want to spend another night here, in this hotel, in what will be almost total, claustrophobic darkness, with no heat.

She steals a glance at David. She can't believe what Riley said about him this morning is true. It can't be. He can't have killed his wife. He can't be a murderer. The idea is absurd. Riley must have it wrong.

When they've all finished eating, they drift together out towards the lobby, and the warmth of the fire.

Gwen says, 'I don't know about anyone else, but I could use a drink.'

Ian is delighted that someone else has mentioned drinks, so that he doesn't have to. He's surprised that it's the pretty, pale Gwen who has suggested it, rather than her hard-drinking friend who looks like she's escaped from rehab.

'Yes, why don't I fetch the bar trolley,' Ian offers now, glancing at Lauren, as if for permission. Bradley isn't there, and James has returned to the kitchen. 'I think we could all use a little something, considering.'

Ian gets up and wheels the trolley closer, then starts serving drinks. For a time, there is only the tinkling sound of ice against glass and the wind howling around the building.

There's an awkward silence, as if no one knows what to say.

Saturday, 1:30 PM

Riley is sitting on her own, away from those arranged around the coffee table near the fire, looking out occasionally across the lobby to the windows. But she is listening to their conversation as they hover over the game board on the coffee table. Ian had found some games on a bookshelf and suggested they play Scrabble.

She sees Bradley return to the lobby and tend to the fire.

It's Ian who starts it, bluntly asking the attorney why he seems to be suggesting that Dana's death might not have been an accident.

'Oh, please, let's not talk about it!' Gwen says, obviously preferring to focus on the game. She has always excelled at Scrabble, Riley knows. And she's also good at avoiding things she doesn't want to face.

'Why not?' Ian replies. 'It's all any of us are thinking about. He's a criminal attorney – I want to know what he thinks.'

'I'd like to hear what he thinks, too,' Henry chimes in.

Riley turns and stares now at David, who has just been put on the spot.

'I don't know any more than the rest of you,' the attorney says evasively. 'I simply said that I think we ought to wait for the coroner to decide what happened.'

'I'm not asking you what you *know*, I'm asking you what you *think*,' Ian presses.

'Very well,' David says, looking around at the rest of them, as if considering what to say. He takes a deep breath and exhales. 'I don't think that Dana's death was an accident.' He pauses and adds, 'In fact, I think she was pushed. And then I think her head was deliberately and forcefully smashed against the bottom stair.'

Riley almost spills her drink. She sees Ian's eyebrows go up in surprise.

'Seriously?' Ian says. 'You think someone *murdered her?*' He shifts in his seat, looks uneasy. 'I thought . . .' But he lets his sentence trail away.

Riley is trying her best to appear completely calm, completely normal. She's had two glasses of wine already, which helps. She sees David look at Gwen; Gwen averts her eyes. *Frightened little Gwen*, Riley thinks. *If she could bury her head in the sand, she would.*

'I think it's a distinct possibility,' the attorney says crisply.

Riley grips the arms of her chair tightly. She feels the tension build in the silent room; it's palpable. Then Riley blurts out what they're all thinking: 'Did Matthew do it?'

She hears several gasps from the guests around her. She has been impolite. She doesn't care. They all seem to think she's a train wreck anyway.

David turns to her and says, 'I have no idea.'

Ian asks, 'Are you acting as his attorney?'

'No, I am not. I have enough cases on my plate as it is,' he answers rather irritably. 'I've merely suggested he remain in his room.' He takes a last drink from his glass, finishes it. 'The police will sort it all out when they get here – which I hope will be soon.' He adds, 'But for now, nobody is moving the body.'

Chapter Fourteen

'IT SEEMS TO me,' Henry says, in his slightly pompous way, 'that if this *is* a murder, it would be almost impossible to solve. It seems to have happened in the middle of the night. We were all asleep in our beds. There are no witnesses. Unless someone wants to confess, or share some helpful information about seeing someone creeping about in the night, I don't see that there's much to go on.'

Beverly listens to him, licks her lips nervously, and waits. No one else volunteers anything.

Finally, she blurts out, 'There's something I should probably say.'

All eyes turn her way. She almost loses courage. She doesn't know if the argument between Dana and Matthew is relevant or not, but it will certainly sound damning.

'What is it?' David says calmly, as she hesitates.

'I heard them arguing, last night.'

'Dana and Matthew?' David says, as if in surprise.

'Yes.'

'What was the argument about, do you know?'

She shakes her head. 'I heard them shouting, but I couldn't make out any words. Their room is next to ours, on the same side of the hall.' She looks at her husband. 'Henry slept through it all.'

'What time was this?'

'I don't know, but late.'

'Did it sound . . . violent?' David asks.

'I don't know. It was just raised voices. No crying or anything. Nothing slamming, if that's what you mean.'

There, she's said it. If Matthew's done something wrong, then it's good that she's told them.

David can sense the heightened distress of the others. They don't like what Beverly has said; it makes them uneasy. They don't like to think the unthinkable. He can see from their faces that they are all imagining it – the argument, the push down the stairs.

He's sorry for their distress, but he's only telling it how he sees it. It doesn't seem possible that Dana could have been injured like that from her fall, and he doesn't want them messing about with the body. And now this new information – Matthew had told him that he and Dana had not argued. If Beverly is to be believed, Matthew lied to him.

It depresses him. Matthew seemed so shattered, so genuinely grief-stricken. But David reminds himself that many a murderer – especially one who kills in passion – is genuinely regretful at what he's done, and he's still guilty.

Perhaps it's more personal than that. Maybe David is giving Matthew the benefit of the doubt because he has himself been accused of killing his wife, and he knows how it feels. Perhaps that is all.

Perhaps he's wrong, and Matthew did force Dana off the landing and then finish her off. He just doesn't want to believe it.

But he definitely thinks it's murder. And if Matthew didn't do it, who did?

Gwen gets up suddenly and walks away from the little circle by the fireplace. She can't bear to sit there any longer. She goes to the front of the room and paces back and forth before the windows. She glances out occasionally at the icy drive, as if hoping for rescue.

She flicks a look over her shoulder at the rest of them, still sitting by the fireplace. No one is pretending to carry on with the game of Scrabble without her. What David said – and now what Beverly has said – has unsettled them all far too much.

She couldn't bear to be near David any longer. That delicious tension that had existed between them last night has been corrupted. Now she's not sure what she feels when she looks at him – it's a confusing mix of attraction and fear.

She digs her nails into the palms of her hands. How can he be so detached about a man – even if he is a complete stranger – killing a woman he purports to love?

After a while, Riley joins her by the windows. Gwen turns to her briefly. Riley's eyes are large and alert. For a moment the two of them stand together looking out at the frozen landscape that holds them trapped here.

Finally, Gwen leans in close to Riley and speaks quietly. 'Do you think David is right? That Dana may have been murdered?'

Riley looks back at her, her eyes huge. 'I don't know what to think.'

Gwen studies Riley closely. She's very pale and there is perspiration on her face, as if she's running a fever. Maybe she shouldn't even be talking to her about this. Riley's brought her wineglass with her; her hands are visibly trembling.

'Are you all right?' Gwen asks her.

'No, I'm not fucking all right,' Riley says. 'Are you?'

'No. I'm not all right either,' Gwen says, her voice low. 'But you have to pull yourself together, Riley. Ease up on the booze.'

Riley narrows her eyes at her. 'Mind your own business.'

'Oh, because you mind yours?' Gwen snaps back bitterly. She doesn't know, suddenly, whether she will remain Riley's friend after they get out of here. And she's not even sure she cares.

Riley softens a little. 'I'm sorry. I did what I thought was best. But I think David Paley is exactly who I say he is.'

'Well, I don't.'

'Why don't you ask him?'

'I'm not going to ask him.'

'Then I will,' Riley says, and turns away.

'Stop!' Gwen hisses, and reaches out and grabs Riley by the arm. 'Wait.'

Riley turns and looks back at her. 'Why? I think we should clear this up, don't you?'

'Just – wait,' Gwen pleads.

Riley hesitates.

'Don't say anything about David. You could be wrong.' Gwen watches Riley anxiously as she considers.

'Fine,' Riley says. 'I won't say anything – for now.' She lifts her wineglass to her lips and takes a long, needy swallow.

Chapter Fifteen

BEVERLY HAS CHANGED her seat so that she is no longer sitting beside her husband and so that she doesn't have to see Dana's shape beneath the sheet.

So this is what has become of their weekend away, for which she'd had such hopes. Her marriage facing imminent ruin. Stuck in an isolated hotel in the thrall of a deadly ice storm, without power, sharing the lobby with the corpse of a woman who may have been pushed down the stairs by her wealthy fiancé. If so, what a shock that must have been to her.

She watches Gwen and Riley return. Gwen sits back down in the chair across from David that she'd abandoned earlier, without looking at him. David glances at her guardedly. Something has happened between the two of them, Beverly is sure of it. She'd noticed the chemistry between them last night; that chemistry is gone, replaced by something else she can't quite put her finger on. Some kind of awkwardness or wariness.

Riley says suddenly to David, fidgeting nervously with her ring, 'I don't think you should be jumping to conclusions.'

'I'm sorry?' David says, turning to her politely.

'Saying that Dana's fall wasn't an accident.'

'She's right,' Henry says accusingly, glaring at David. 'You don't know what happened – unless you killed her yourself, which I highly doubt.'

Beverly watches her husband, cringing at his supercilious tone. She knows Henry can be a bit of an ass. He's probably feeling too hemmed in, and it's making him a little aggressive. He's like a Border collie; he needs a job to do.

The cornered attorney says mildly, 'I never intended to imply that I *knew* what happened. I was asked what I thought, and I gave my opinion. I don't pretend to be an expert.'

But he *is* an expert, Beverly thinks nervously, and the rest of them aren't.

Lauren examines a broken fingernail, trying to recall whether she brought a nail file with her. She glances at all the gloomy faces around her. No one appears to be enjoying themselves – even if they wanted to, it would be in bad taste. Candice going off to the library to work, as if nothing has happened, seems a bit callous. God, she'd love to get out of here! And it's barely past lunchtime. She wonders how much longer they will be trapped in this hotel.

David thinks it's not an accident, but murder. She tries not to let it get to her.

Lauren thinks of Matthew upstairs. He's keeping to his room, on the attorney's advice. Beverly says she heard them arguing. She wonders if that's true, and if it is, whether that makes Matthew look guilty. She would like to know what the attorney thinks.

Bradley, always observant – it's one of the things that makes him a good waiter – notes the various undercurrents in the lobby of his father's hotel. All the guests are behaving very differently from the way they had the night before.

David seems thoughtful and preoccupied, and Gwen seems distressed. Ian no longer has the relaxed, pleasure-seeking demeanour he had the night before, and his girlfriend, Lauren, seems quiet, observant. And whatever had been bothering Henry and Beverly the night before only seems worse today. Only Riley seems unchanged – she was a nervous wreck when she arrived, and she's a nervous wreck now.

When David said he thought Dana had been murdered, every one of the guests looked startled, but Bradley also sensed fear.

Bradley goes about his work, turning things over restlessly in his mind.

Saturday, 2:00 PM

They are all still huddled in the lobby. Beverly has been brooding about her situation. She has become fixated on the idea of Henry being involved with someone else. She tells herself that the idea is absurd. Henry is not a particularly exciting man, not the type to have an affair. The idea's never even crossed her mind until this morning. She tries to push the unwelcome thought away.

114

She catches David observing Bradley as he scurries about his tasks. David suggests casually, 'Why don't we pitch in and ease the load on Bradley? Henry, do you mind making a trip to the woodshed with me to bring in more wood for the fireplace? And maybe for the stove in the kitchen.'

'You don't have to do that,' Bradley says, flushing.

'No problem at all,' David assures him. 'You must have your hands full.'

Beverly watches Henry drop his good sweater in his chair by the fire and follow David to grab his jacket from the coat stand. Bradley provides them with a single torch, whose rechargeable batteries, he advises them, probably won't last long. David takes it with them to the woodshed.

Beverly looks at the others – they all seem lost in their own worlds. She finds herself staring at her husband's sweater on the chair close to the fire. She's pretty sure his mobile phone is in the pocket. She needs to get his phone out of his pocket without these other people noticing what she's up to.

She gets up and walks over and sits down by the fire. The sweater is beneath her. No one is showing any interest in her. She can hear, faintly, James and Bradley rattling around in the kitchen.

Beverly feels quietly around in the sweater until she finds Henry's mobile phone and closes her hand around it. She slips it into her own pocket. She doesn't want to look at it here, in front of everyone. And she doesn't want her husband to come back in from the woodshed and find her in his seat.

She gets up and moves around restlessly, as if looking for a new magazine among the ones in the lobby. Maybe Henry won't notice that his mobile is missing for a while.

They've got the torch, and he wouldn't be looking at his phone otherwise, since there's no coverage. She only wants to see his old messages. If he misses it, he won't have any particular reason to believe she has it. She has her own phone with the torch app.

She clutches it inside her pocket. She tells herself not to hope for too much; she has no idea what his password is.

Henry and David come in with their first armfuls of wood and drop them by the hearth. David tosses another log onto the fire. Sparks fly up in a shower and then he prods at it with the iron poker to get the fire going again. Then they leave for more wood. Her husband hadn't even looked at her.

'I'm going to go back up to my room for a bit,' Beverly says.

Lauren suggests to Ian, 'Maybe we should go up, too.' She picks up her book from the little table at the end of the sofa.

It seems as if no one really wants to stay in the lobby any longer, Beverly thinks. They are already tiring of one another. She walks towards the staircase, eager to slip into the privacy of her room to see if she can access her husband's phone. As she turns on the landing, she looks down and sees Gwen nudging Riley up, too.

It doesn't take Beverly long to get to her room on the first floor, lighting her way with her own mobile phone. She opens the door with her key and closes it behind her.

She sits down on the bed in the gloomy room and pulls her husband's mobile out of her pocket and looks at it. She's seen him use his phone countless times. And he always does the same thing with his index finger – two quick swipes down, one across. Inspired, she tries the obvious, a capital H, for Henry. But it doesn't work. She thinks hard about the last time she saw

116

him using his phone and realizes he must have changed the password. He wouldn't do that unless he has something to hide. She stares at the phone, frustrated. She tries different combinations of numbers but gets nowhere. Then she moves her finger in a capital T pattern, for Teddy, her husband's favourite child, and the phone opens. For a moment, she's exhilarated. She thinks what a fool her husband can be, and how frequently he underestimates her.

She quickly goes through his emails but there's nothing but work emails, long and boring; if he's hidden a mistress in there, she'll never find her. Then she looks at the texts. She starts from the top of the list, ignoring names of people she knows, but then she sees a woman's name she doesn't recognize. She clicks on it and opens the text; there is a picture of her. Beverly's heart almost stops. She starts at the bottom, with the most recent text, and works her way backwards.

Idk. I have to go away this weekend with the nag.
When will I see you again?

The nag. That is what he calls her to his girlfriend. A wave of hurt swells inside her. She knows she nags him and the kids. She nags them because they don't listen. If they did what was expected of them the first time she wouldn't have to nag. But the word *nag* also makes her think of an old, broken-down mare – whiskered, swaybacked, and ugly. She fights tears and continues reading.

I miss you terribly!
Do you miss me?

117

Attached to the text is a picture of her, topless, with a shameless grin. Beverly stares at the photo, shocked to her core. She's young, and gorgeous. A home-wrecker. She knows nothing about life at all.

She can't imagine what this girl sees in her husband. If she's after money she's going to be disappointed. He's not going to have any left when she's done with him, Beverly thinks furiously. And then she stops herself, takes a deep breath.

She's not going to divorce him. Surely this is just a temporary infatuation, a midlife fling. He's made a mistake. A mistake that they can recover from. She doesn't want to lose him. She needs him.

She tabs up quickly through the rest of the texts to the beginning of the thread, anxious to see how long this has been going on. Only about a month. He met her at a bar.

She's married to a cliché.

Well, now she knows.

Her finger itches to send a text of her own to this bitch. But she hesitates. And then she remembers there's no coverage here anyway. Just as well. Finally she drops the mobile back in her pocket. She's going to hurry back downstairs and slip it back into her husband's sweater until she decides what to do. She must handle this the right way. She opens the door to the hall.

Chapter Sixteen

Saturday, 2:20 PM

MATTHEW SITS ALONE in his first-floor room, the lunch tray that Bradley brought on the side table untouched. He desperately needs to talk to his father, but he has no way to reach him. His father would know what to do. He's always good in a crisis.

Matthew rises from his chair and goes restlessly to the window. He looks out at the icy landscape below. He can't drive in that. He couldn't possibly get back to New York City. And even if he could, how would it look – if he fled before the police arrived?

No, he's stuck here. Waiting for the police.

Henry, drowsing by the fire, starts at a sound and opens his sleepy eyes. His wife is coming down the stairs, holding the rail until about halfway down, when she starts to make a wide detour to avoid Dana's body at the bottom of the stairs. There's a look on her face that makes him uneasy.

He knows his mobile phone isn't in his sweater pocket. He doesn't think he's dropped it, and besides, he's retraced his steps. It's nowhere to be found. But when he sees the expression on his wife's face, the realization hits him. She has it.

That can only mean that she suspects the truth about him and Jilly. He wonders if she was able to get past his password.

Christ, he thinks wearily, watching his wife approach. Maybe it will be better to have it out in the open. Now she'll understand that she has to let him go. She'll be bitter, at first, but he's in love with someone else. Beverly has a good job. She'll manage. It will be difficult for both of them – harder for her, of course – but he will get back on his feet, and life will be good again.

His kids might hate him for a while, but they'll get over it. Both Ted and Kate have friends whose parents are divorced. It's totally normal these days. Kids don't even blame their parents for it any more – they practically expect it. They even work it, playing the guilt card, to get more stuff they want. He prepares himself as she sits down across from him, her serious face on.

Beverly's heart sinks when she sees Henry sitting there, as if he's expecting her. There's no way she'll be able to put his phone back. Very well. They have to talk about it sometime – it might as well be now. There's no avoiding it. Maybe it's for the best.

'There's something I need to say,' Beverly begins, taking the chair across from him and pulling it a little closer.

Her husband gives her a particularly hard stare. 'Did you take my phone?'

She looks down for a minute at her lap, gathering her courage, and then looks up again. 'Yes.'

'I knew it,' he says coldly.

'I wanted to find out if you've been unfaithful to me.' She waits a beat and then continues. 'I managed to figure out your password.' She looks at Henry, who seems surprised. 'I bet you didn't think I'd be able to do that, did you?' She tries a smile but stumbles, unnerved by the expression on his face. But she has to keep going; she has to do this. Maybe Henry will see how ridiculous his affair is. She also wants to hurt him just a little – if only to show him how terribly hurt she is. Maybe she wants to shame him into dropping this girl. 'I found the texts between you and your . . . girlfriend.' When he doesn't respond, she can't help it, her annoyance shows. 'It was very illuminating! I saw pictures of her. I even know what she looks like naked.' She says this quietly, her eyes on her husband, while he sits frozen. 'She's considerably younger than you, isn't she?' She tries to keep a lid on her disgust. 'I can't believe what you call me, you two lovebirds.' The outrage has crept into her voice, even though she has done her best to keep it under control. 'The nag. You call me the nag.' She tries to look into his eyes, but he shifts his gaze away. The coward. 'How do you think it makes me feel to know that the two of you are having sex behind my back, and calling me the nag? *I have to go away for the weekend with the nag.*' He still won't look at her.

'Do we have to do this here?' Henry asks her now, his voice tight. 'Can't it wait till we get home?'

'Actually, yes. We do. Why wait? Why pretend? It feels good

to get this off my chest.' She's getting carried away now. 'Do you know what I call you? I call you the man-child. Because you're a grown man, facing the sad fact of ageing and mortality and disappointment just like the rest of us, but you're having the childish, selfish reaction that so many men in midlife get – and it's . . . sad. Sad and unnecessary.' She pauses for a moment, gathering her thoughts. 'You don't love her, Henry – it's just a phase.' She lets that sink in. At least she hopes it sinks in. 'You think you can run off with this young woman and it's going to be fabulous. You'll move into her apartment, maybe buy yourself a convertible. No more people carrier for you, ferrying the kids to soccer three nights a week! You'll see the kids at weekends – when you feel like it – and renege on your support payments, like most men do. It'll be all sex and dinners out and vacations and no obligations. Well, think again, because that's not how it's going to be.' She waits a moment to let that sink in, too, and then pauses for a long moment and says in a more conciliatory tone, 'It won't last. You'll get tired of her. She'll get tired of you. You'll miss me and the kids. There won't be enough money. You'll regret it – I'm sure of it.' Her husband lifts his eyes and looks at her at last. 'Henry, don't destroy what we have. Forget her.'

This is his chance to choose her, Beverly thinks. She waits, holding her breath. But he doesn't say anything at all. Her heart plummets, a body going over the falls in a barrel.

Suddenly she remembers how she felt the evening before, when they arrived here at the inn – it seems so long ago now. How foolish, how wrong she'd been to think that they'd merely drifted apart and needed only to spend time together to recall what they liked about each other. She remembers how he didn't even come up to the room with her with the luggage, how he'd stayed down here, in the lobby, looking at excursions to keep them busy so they wouldn't have time to think, to talk.

She remembers how he looked at her in her new negligee.

He'd known all along that he was in love with someone else.

Well, she won't accept it. Infatuation isn't love. He just needs time to come to his senses. This is a kind of middle-aged madness. He will come back to her. It will be fine. She must be patient, that's all.

'Think it through, Henry,' she says. She slowly rises and makes her way back to her room, leaving Henry alone by the fire.

Saturday, 3:30 PM

Candice's laptop battery is dying. She curses out loud to the empty library. She saves her work again and then decides to shut down while she still can. She needs to save some battery – in case she needs to refer back to something in her draft. She should have printed it out and brought it with her. *Fuck*. She won't ever make that mistake again. From now on, she promises herself, she will always print the manuscript and bring it with her whenever she goes anywhere. She gets so little undisturbed time to work.

She looks down at the closed laptop and thinks about what to do next. She will have to write longhand, she supposes. It's too bad her handwriting is so illegible – even she has trouble reading it. And of course she didn't bring any paper with her. The paperless society. Ha! She looks up and scans the room around her. She gets out of her comfortable chair by the fire and approaches the desk in the corner of the room next to the door. It must be original to the hotel – the age is about right. Its surface is almost pristine – just an old-fashioned leather blotter with an elegant letter opener on its surface. She tries the top drawer. It opens easily. There is nothing inside but a single, lonely paper clip. With her frustration rising and her hopes falling in equal measure, she tries the side drawers next. *My kingdom for a pen and paper* she mutters under her breath. Nothing. *Shit.*

Then she recalls the writing desk in her room. Surely there was a folder with full-sized notepaper printed with the hotel letterhead sitting on the side of the desk. Of course! Most hotels provide notepaper, and a pen. And if she runs out of paper, she can borrow more from the other guests. No one else will be using it. She hopes she doesn't have to rely on quill and ink in this quaint hotel.

She hastens out of the library with her laptop hugged to her chest. It's still warm, which she appreciates. She turns to her right and starts to walk back to the lobby and the main stair-case, but then she remembers that there's a servants' staircase near the kitchen. Curious, she turns back and finds the hall that runs along the back of the hotel. At the end of the hall, outside the closed kitchen door, is the door to the servants' staircase. She pushes it open.

She's shocked at how dark it is inside the stairwell. It's like falling to the bottom of a well. She thinks about retreating, but then takes her mobile phone out of her pocket and turns on the torch, noticing with resignation that her phone, too, is almost out of battery. She climbs up the narrow, plain wooden staircase, slowly making her way to the top, feeling tense. Perhaps she would have been better off going back to the lobby and taking the main staircase, after all, sheeted corpse or not. At last she makes it to the top and opens the door onto the second floor. With relief, she finds herself in the dim corridor, lit only by the narrow window at the end. Her room, number 206, is across the hall. She hurriedly inserts the key and enters the room, not bothering to close the door – she's planning on getting what she needs and going right back down to the fire in the library. The chill up here makes her bones ache.

Her eyes fall on the writing desk across the room nestled under the windows. She spies the folder of notepaper. She crosses the thick rug – so thick it muffles all sound – and opens the folder eagerly. It contains several sheets of creamy, good-quality A4 writing paper, and a pen. She smiles with relief.

Chapter Seventeen

Saturday, 4:00 PM

THE GUESTS START to drift down to the lobby again around four o'clock, eager for their tea. They continue to do their best to ignore the corpse at the bottom of the stairs, filing past it quickly on their way to the dining room. Matthew still does not appear. James has made scones to go with the tea and coffee, and they all agree that they are delicious.

Gwen sips the scalding tea, grateful for the warmth of the cup in her hands, and wonders if she will ever speak to David.

Henry says, 'I suggest we all check out the ice bar. The path's all clear, and I had a sneak peek. It's really something.'

'Thanks to your hard work with the snowblower,' Bradley says.

Gwen goes with the rest of them to grab their jackets and boots at the front of the hotel and then they all follow Bradley down the back hall and into the woodshed – smelling wonderfully of freshly chopped wood – where they don their outdoor gear. Bradley opens the door and a bitter wind gusts into the woodshed. Bradley and Henry go out first, then Ian and Lauren. David goes next, and Beverly steps in front of Gwen and follows David.

Gwen goes last, behind Riley, and pulls the woodshed door shut behind her. The sky is sullen and the wind violent. Gwen can't see much directly in front of her – just Riley's back – as they trudge single file down the cleared path, banks of snow on either side. But she looks up to the forest beyond, where the wind is giving the trees a thrashing. Riley says something to her over her shoulder, but Gwen can't catch the words before the wind tears them away and they are lost. The tip of her nose is already freezing. At least there are no large trees to come crashing down between the woodshed and the icehouse. Finally they stop and the path widens out into a cleared area in front of the icehouse and she can see.

It looks like an igloo, or a Nissen hut made of snow. The front, however, is made of large blocks of ice cut and fitted together. A pair of wooden doors is affixed to the ice somehow. Gwen studies it with interest.

'The doors are the only part not made of ice or snow,' Bradley says, his breath puffing out clouds. 'It has to be rebuilt every winter – and then it melts.'

'That's a lot of work for something that just melts,' Beverly says, her face pinched with cold.

'But the beauty of it is, it looks different every year,' Bradley says. 'They do different designs, different sculptures. Wait till you see inside.'

'So you don't make this yourself,' Ian says.

'Hell, no.'

Bradley opens the door and they all step inside.

Gwen gasps. It's like stepping into a sparkling, twinkling fairyland. Beneath a vaulted ceiling, the curved bar is sculpted out of translucent ice. In front of it are several barstools, also carved from ice. Behind the bar, bottles rest on ice shelves, shimmering in the unusual light.

Bradley steps behind the bar, a bright spot of colour with his red wool hat, and says, 'I highly recommend the vodka Martinis.'

Gwen waits for her drink and looks around. Apart from the bar itself, there are small round tables with curved seats, also made of ice. But it's the sculpture over the bar that really takes her breath away. It's a bird of prey with its wings spread out and its feet extended – even the claws – as if it's about to land on its quarry. It's huge – the full length of the bar – and it seems to hover over Bradley as he mixes the Martinis.

David appears beside her and hands her a large Martini glass with gloved hands. Now that she's facing him, she finds she's nervous. 'I wouldn't want to be in here without my winter coat,' she says.

She can feel Riley's eyes on her, watching her, but she doesn't care.

'Quite beautiful,' David says.

'It is, isn't it?' Gwen agrees.

'I wasn't talking about the icehouse,' he whispers.

She feels herself melting, even in all this cold. Riley is wrong. David cannot be the man she's thinking of. Riley is confused. Riley's confused about a lot of things.

David takes a gulp of his Martini, watching her. Gwen flushes and says, more loudly, 'Candice really should see this.'

'She's in the library,' Bradley says, from behind the bar. 'She asked not to be disturbed.'

'I think she'd be sorry to miss the ice bar,' Gwen says. 'It's pretty fabulous.'

Bradley smiles. 'I think you're right. I'll run in and see if I can coax her to come out,' he says, stepping out from behind the bar.

'Relax,' David says, chiding her gently. She smiles nervously at him and sips her vodka. He lowers his voice and says, 'I think we should find a time and a place to talk. Just the two of us.'

She nods. They obviously can't talk now, in this confined space, with so many people around. With Riley looking on. But they must talk soon. She is both looking forward to it and dreading it.

Bradley steps back outside into the blustery wind and heads for the woodshed, his head down and collar up. The pleasant smile falls away. There's always so much to do, owning a hotel, he thinks tiredly. It's endless. Running around, being nice to people. This bunch is pleasant enough. But he doesn't want to work in this hotel for ever. Serving drinks and meals, picking up after people, being at their beck and call. His father wants him to take over the hotel some day, but Bradley doesn't want to be stuck out here in the country, far from everything. As much as Bradley loves the place – and loves his dad – he's itching to leave. He doesn't want to be trapped here, catering to people with more money than him, with the freedom to go wherever they want. And unlike his father, he doesn't love to cook.

But whenever he thinks about leaving, the guilt kicks in.

He can't leave his father here alone. He knows his father's worried; he's always worried. If his father would sell the hotel and retire, then Bradley would be free.

When he looks in the library, Candice isn't there. He takes a quick look around the ground floor, but doesn't find her. She must be having a nap in her room, but he doesn't feel like running up two flights of stairs to find out. For a moment he forgets about Candice. He has big plans. He's going to get some money together and—

He hears his father call him from the kitchen. 'Bradley, is that you?'

Bradley pops into the kitchen. 'Yeah.'

'I need you to help me with the food prep. Can you start chopping?'

'No, I can't,' Bradley snaps. His father looks up at him in surprise. 'I'm supposed to be serving drinks in the icehouse.'

'What's the matter with you?' his father asks, looking at him more closely. He says cautiously, 'I hope I don't have to remind you about not crossing the line with our guests.'

And that's another thing Bradley can't stand – being reminded of his place. He feels his temper flare. He doesn't answer, just slams the door on his way out.

David is thinking how appealing Gwen looks in her bright red ski jacket and pink-and-red-striped hat, when Bradley returns.

'She wasn't in the library,' Bradley says. 'I'm not sure where she is.'

By now everyone has finished their drinks and they're getting cold. They decide to go back inside. When they leave the icehouse it's starting to get dark. David sticks close to Gwen as they file back up the path to the woodshed in the deepening dusk, accompanied by the shrieking wind.

'This is what the wind is like on Mount Everest,' Riley says, once they're inside the woodshed.

'Have you been?' Henry asks.

'No, but I saw the documentary.'

They return gratefully to the fire in the lobby. Some of them keep their hats and gloves on for warmth. Gwen stands in front of the flames, rubbing her hands together. David considers asking her to come with him somewhere else, where they can talk. Maybe they could go to the bar. He could make them a fire, and they could be alone. Bradley has gone to the library again to see if Candice is there. Lauren is in front of the reception desk, leaning over it, looking for a pen for a crossword.

Bradley returns to the lobby shaking his head. 'She's still not there. I've looked around down here. She must be in her room. I'll check.'

David feels a twinge of unease. He wonders why Candice isn't where she said she'd be. 'I'll come up with you,' he offers.

'I'll come, too,' Gwen says.

No one else shows any interest in going up those dark stairs. Bradley grabs one of the flickering oil lamps off the coffee table and uses it to light their way. It's getting properly dark out now, hardly any light at all filtering in through the windows.

Bradley holds the lamp high, and David and Gwen follow. The oil lamp throws shadows on the dark-papered walls as they ascend. David has his mobile phone's torch on to provide more light for their footing. There's not much charge left.

As they trudge up the stairs, Bradley says, 'I saw her after lunch when I went to take the tray away. I told her we'd be having tea at four o'clock. She said she would come out if she wanted any tea, but otherwise she was not to be disturbed.' He adds, 'It's really a shame she missed the ice bar. But we can always go back out again.'

They reach the second floor, which if anything, David thinks, seems darker and gloomier than the floors below. It's bloody cold. Candice's room is to the left of the stairs, across from the housekeeping closet. Bradley knocks on the door. There is no response from within. He knocks again. David's uneasiness has grown to a mild alarm, but he tries not to show it.

Bradley turns to him, looking worried. 'Do you think we should open it?'

David hesitates. 'Is there anywhere else she might be?'

'I've looked everywhere else.'

David nods. Bradley hands him the lamp and fishes the appropriate key out of the bunch. He feeds it into the lock and slowly opens the door. David holds the lamp high.

He sees Candice lying on the floor, her scarf pulled tightly around her neck.

Saturday, 5:35 PM

In the lurid light of the oil lamp, Gwen sees the body slumped on the floor, a flash of pale face, the pretty scarf around Candice's throat, and screams. She feels David grab her with one strong arm and quickly pull her head into his chest so she can't see Candice, but it's too late. She feels the acid corroding her stomach, feels the bile slip up her throat.

Gwen trembles against David's chest, trying not to be sick, her mind reeling. Dana had at least *looked* like an accident. Gwen hadn't allowed herself to even think that it might be deliberate murder, despite what David said. She didn't want to believe it. But there's no mistaking this. Candice has been strangled with her own scarf.

Filled with dread, she hears the sound of running footsteps stumbling up the darkened stairs.

Chapter Eighteen

RILEY HEARS GWEN'S scream, and despite her own immediate fear, tears up the stairs. The others are close on her heels. She arrives at the open doorway to Candice's room. The first thing she sees is Gwen with her face buried in David's chest, to her right, and then, beyond them, the body on the floor. She gives a strangled cry, feels as if all the breath has left her body.

The others crowd around her, trying to see. Candice is clearly dead. They spill from the open doorway into the room. Riley steps to one side, allowing the others in. She feels her anxiety spiking as her mind desperately tries to make sense of what this means. She sees Gwen pull away from David, and David places the oil lamp on the desk. It creates a pool of light around Candice, as if she's an actress on the stage, under a spotlight. She doesn't look real.

Riley can't bear to look at the body any more; she turns her attention to the others instead.

Bradley is staring at Candice as if he's seen a ghost, grabbing the edge of the desk to steady himself.

David's mouth is set in a grim line.

Gwen, beside him, has her hand pressed hard against her mouth, trying not to throw up.

Ian mutters, 'Dear God,' and stands flat-footed, as Lauren pushes past him to the body. She moves to pull the scarf loose, touching Candice's neck.

'Get back, everyone,' David commands harshly. 'There's nothing we can do for her.'

Lauren sits back on her heels and looks up, pale and shaken.

Riley hears a sob and turns to see Henry and Beverly standing inside the open doorway, looking at Candice. Beverly is obviously trying to control herself. And now Matthew, tall and dishevelled, appears in the darkness of the doorway, James, out of breath, behind him.

Riley turns her attention back to the body and forces herself to look. Candice is lying on her stomach, her head turned to the left. Her face is bloodless against the dark carpet. Her eyes are open wide in surprise. She is . . . ghastly. Terrifying.

There's no coming back from death.

She begins to feel the familiar sensation of panic, and she closes her eyes briefly and breathes deeply, trying not to give in to it. She opens her eyes again. Everyone is in the room now, ignoring David's command to stay back. She wonders, fleetingly, who is going to keep order now. She knows how quickly things can fall apart; she's seen it.

Riley looks now at Gwen – Gwen is still standing close to David, and is looking at the dead woman, too. Her face is crumpling like she's about to cry. She's too squeamish for this, Riley thinks.

135

'We must leave her as she is,' David says quietly. 'The police will deal with it when they get here.'

'When is that going to be?' Lauren says, her voice tense.

'I don't know,' David says.

'How can you be so calm?' Lauren asks, her voice shrill. 'She's been murdered! We need to get the police!'

'How the hell are we going to do that?' Henry shouts.

'I don't know!' Lauren snaps. 'But we'd better think of something.'

Henry finds the sight of the body deeply disturbing. He can't bear to look at it any longer, so instead he studies Matthew, whom he hasn't seen since Dana's body was first discovered early that morning. Gwen's scream has pulled him from the seclusion of his room. Some of them, he thinks, suspect that Matthew pushed his fiancée down the stairs. This changes things. He glances at David. The attorney's usually calm exterior is definitely ruffled.

The fact that Candice has been murdered – it means that there is definitely a killer here, in the hotel. And the police aren't coming.

Henry looks around at the rest of the little gathering and can see they are of one mind. The fear is palpable.

He can hear Beverly breathing heavily through her nose beside him. Henry wonders just how much danger they're in. And suddenly he has a terrible thought. He realizes that if only it had been Beverly who had been strangled, instead of Candice, all his problems would be solved. It's the first time he's recognized that he would be free if only his wife were dead. It makes him feel strange, agitated. He has a fleeting fantasy of finding her strangled in their room, but it's interrupted by David.

'It might be one of us,' David says.

There's an awful silence.

Then Beverly shakes her head in disbelief. 'Surely not,' she says. When David doesn't answer, she begins to protest. 'You think that one of *us* is a murderer?'

'It's possible,' David says.

'But that's absurd,' Beverly insists, looking around wildly at the rest of them. 'You seem to think that almost anybody is capable of murder. Murderers are not normal people.' She looks desperately around the room at the others.

Henry silently agrees with his wife – the idea that it's one of them is ludicrous, like something out of a novel. He was willing to credit that Matthew may have, in a fit of anger, killed his fiancée. But he doesn't think that Matthew also killed Candice, in cold blood.

David has spent too much time with criminals, Henry tells himself now. He can't picture any of his companions pushing that young woman down the stairs, then smashing her skull against the step. Nor can he imagine any of them strangling Candice. There must be someone else here. He looks around anxiously in the flickering dark.

Saturday, 5:45 PM

'We should search the hotel,' David suggests, as they stand above Candice's corpse.

The others turn his way, startled.

David knows they are all in shock, and probably not think-ing clearly. 'Two people are dead. Murdered. We may not be the only ones here,' he says bluntly.

Frightened faces look back at him from the shadows.

'Whoever did this must be insane,' Lauren whispers.

'There's no one else staying at the hotel,' James stammers.

'No other staff we don't know about?'

James shakes his head. 'No. Just me and Bradley. Because of the storm. The others couldn't make it in.'

'Someone might be here without our knowing it,' David says.

'No,' Bradley says, shaking his head. 'The rooms are kept locked.'

'This room was locked,' David says, 'and there's a dead body inside. How did that happen?' They all fall silent for a moment.

'Maybe she answered the door,' Matthew suggests, no doubt thinking of his own Dana, inexplicably found dead outside her own room.

'Possibly,' David says, thinking aloud. 'But judging from the position of the body, she was standing at the desk with her back to the door when she was strangled. She either answered the door to someone she knows, and trusts, or at least recognizes – one of us perhaps – and was comfortable enough to let them in and then turn her back on them, or someone unlocked the door without her being aware of it.'

'But that's not possible,' James says. 'The keys are kept behind the reception desk.' Then he colours, as if realizing the inadequacy of his argument.

'But there isn't always someone there,' David points out. 'Not this weekend.'

Henry says, 'Someone could have taken the key – if there was no one in the lobby to see them.'

'But wouldn't she have heard the door open?' Ian asks.

David raises a hand calling for quiet. The sound of the wind howling violently outside answers Ian's question.

'Jesus,' Lauren says, in deep dismay.

Riley blurts out, with barely concealed hysteria, 'You're suggesting that there's someone else in this hotel? A killer? Who can get into our rooms?' Her eyes are wild.

Gwen looks anxiously at Riley and says quickly, 'Maybe the door was already open. Maybe she left it open. Maybe she just came up to get something.'

'Maybe,' David says.

There's a long silence as everyone ponders the position they are all in.

David says again, 'I suggest we search the entire hotel, including our own rooms – unless there is anyone here who objects?' He surveys them all carefully. He wants to know if anyone has anything to hide. And he wants to find out if there is someone else here. Someone they don't know about.

The guests look at each other uneasily, but no one objects.

'Shall we cover her?' Bradley asks, his voice uneven.

'No, leave her as she is,' David says. He adds, 'It would probably be better if only some of us search and the rest of you go back downstairs and stay by the fire. I'll need James and Bradley with me.'

'I'll go back downstairs,' Riley offers quickly.

'I'll come with you,' Lauren says. 'I don't want to go around this place in the dark.'

139

'I'm staying with you,' Ian says protectively. 'I'm not letting you out of my sight.'

Henry says, 'I want to help search.' He turns to his wife and says, 'Why don't you go back downstairs and stay warm, with the others.'

'No, I want to be with you,' Beverly says, as if being with her husband is the only way she will feel safe. Her husband is the only one she knows here.

David turns to Matthew. 'What about you?'

'I'll join the search party,' Matthew says decisively.

David says to Gwen, 'Why don't you go with Riley and the rest of them?' He's worried about her. She looks so frightened and vulnerable.

She nods and slips away from him. David watches Ian usher Lauren, Gwen, and Riley out of the door on their way back to the lobby.

Riley follows Ian, Lauren, and Gwen out of Candice's room. She sticks so close to Gwen that she almost steps on her heels. Out in the hall, the darkness seems absolute, even though there's a pinprick of light ahead from Ian's mobile phone. But she is at the back of the little group. As they make their way silently down the stairs from the second floor, Riley tries to extinguish the image of Candice's lifeless body from her mind. But she can't discipline her thoughts. Her imagination takes control – she imagines what Candice's final moments must have been like. Someone came to find her in that cold, dark room and snuffed the life out of her. Riley imagines how it must have felt to have that scarf pulled so tightly around her neck that she couldn't breathe. She must have struggled . . .

Riley can feel her own breath quicken and become shallower. She glances uneasily over her shoulder, into the dark. The darkness is like a curtain of rich black velvet – you can't see past it. She realizes she is falling behind, her feet not as steady on the stairs as the others. She grips the banister tightly. She ran so quickly up these stairs, just a short while ago, but now – since seeing Candice dead – she feels like she's walking through molasses, one slow, thick step after another. She's not herself. She tries to hurry, to catch up before the others make the turn on the landing and the small beam of light disappears.

She can't shake the sense that there is someone else in the hotel, someone watching their every move. He must have been watching Candice, and now she's dead. Maybe he's watching Riley now, maybe he's behind her on the stairs, waiting to pick her off, the straggler left behind . . . Suddenly she can feel him watching, knows that he is behind her, behind that black curtain, a grim reaper reaching out for her.

She senses movement above and behind her on the stairs, hears someone, something. Panicking, she rushes towards the others, stumbling, leaning heavily on the banister. 'Wait!' she cries. She tumbles into Gwen in front of her; Gwen is not so far away, after all. Gwen takes her in her arms.

'I'm right here, Riley,' she says.

'I think there might be someone up there!' Riley gasps.

The light from the mobile phone flashes in her face, almost blinding her, then moves off, playing against the stairs and walls behind her. They all look up. They can't see far.

'I don't think there's anyone there, Riley,' Ian says firmly.

'Come on,' Gwen says, taking her by the arm. 'We're almost there.'

David turns to the others. 'Let's start with the empty rooms on this floor.'

David notices that this time, Bradley seems more distraught than his father. He watches as James quietly takes the keys from Bradley – whose hands are visibly shaking – and sorts through them. They start with the room next to Candice's, which is across the hall from Lauren and Ian's. James inserts the key into the lock, as David holds the oil lamp up so James can see what he's doing. David glances over his shoulder at the rest of them, hovering in the darkened corridor. The door swings open, and David enters the room first, carrying the lamp. The others follow, some with iPhones giving off beams of light.

There's nothing there. The room is pristine, as if waiting for the next guest. They check the bathroom, the wardrobes, look under the neatly made bed. There's nothing.

They exit the room and move on to the next unoccupied room, the one next to Candice's on the other side. It's empty as well.

It's when they move to the last unoccupied room on that side, across the hall from the room currently occupied by Gwen and Riley, that they find something disturbing. James inserts the key and opens the door, David beside him with the light. James's face registers surprise, and David turns his attention away from the owner to the room itself. The first thing he notices is that the bed has been slept in.

'Nobody move,' David says tersely. He stands still, listening keenly for any sound. His eyes fly to the bathroom door, which is open. Someone has been in this room. Maybe he's still here, in the bathroom. He feels a chill of fear. But something, perhaps his sense of hearing, or smell, something running below his conscious radar, tells him that there is no one else here. He steps quickly to the bathroom and looks inside. It's empty.

'What's going on?' Beverly asks from the corridor, her voice shrill.

'Nothing, it's fine,' David says.

The others spill into the empty hotel room and David hears their gasps of dismay at the sight of the unmade bed.

'Christ,' Henry says, his voice tense.

David walks up more closely to the bed, its covers thrown back in disarray. The oil lamp casts a small pool of flickering light as he moves observantly about the dark room. There's no luggage, no clothing, no sign of anyone's effects. It's as if the person had checked out and the room had not been made up. But there is no customary tip for the housemaid lying on the pillow, or resting on the desk or the bureau, as you would certainly expect. David opens the wardrobe doors, but finds only empty hangers. He looks again into the bathroom, more closely this time. There is water splashed around the sink, a towel left on the counter, but no personal items. The others are milling around the room now, clearly distressed.

'I don't understand this,' James says, visibly unnerved.

David asks, 'Is it possible that housekeeping simply missed this room? That the previous guest checked out and the room was missed somehow and not made up again?'

'That would never happen,' James says emphatically. 'This is a small hotel. It's not hard to keep track of the rooms.'

'Bradley?'

'I don't know,' Bradley says, sounding shaken. 'I think it's very unlikely. It's never happened before.'

'Well, it's either that, or someone we don't know about has been using this room, and possibly moving about the hotel without us knowing,' David says. The room is directly across the hall from the room Gwen and Riley are staying in. He feels a sudden fear for Gwen clutching at his heart. He looks around at the others, huddled together, their faces drawn.

'Let's move on,' David says.

Chapter Nineteen

HENRY DOESN'T KNOW which is worse – the possibility that one of the people in their little group might be a murderer, or the possibility that there is someone they're not aware of, moving about the hotel, who has already killed two people.

As they search Gwen and Riley's room, Henry wonders what it is they're even looking for. He's not sure why David suggested they search the guests' rooms, too, not just the empty ones, or why they all agreed to it. He doesn't know what David expects to find. It feels like they're playing at something, some sort of parlour game, or murder mystery evening, with the lights out. Only no one's having fun.

Beverly finds some medication in Riley's bag and holds it up to the light.

'What is it?' Henry asks, for all of them.

David looks at it. 'For anxiety,' he says, and Beverly puts it back in Riley's overnight bag.

Continuing with the second floor, they search the sitting room by the stairs and then the housekeeping closet. In Lauren's

room, they discover that she uses strong sleeping pills –
Ambien. But they don't find anything else of interest.

At last they are finished with the second floor. They move
down to the first floor, where the rest of the guests have their
rooms. David's room is in the northwest corner, directly
below Gwen and Riley's, next to the sitting room. Across the
hall from the sitting room is Dana and Matthew's room,
diagonally opposite David's. Next to it, across from David's,
is another unoccupied room.

They start with the empty room across from David's. It
looks the way a properly made up hotel room should look.

Next, David leads them to his own room, across the hall.
Henry's certain they're not going to find anything there. They
move about in the dark with their fading iPhones, pulling open
the drawers of the bedside table, the dresser, the bathroom vanity
unit. Matthew stirs the cold remains of the fire in the grate with
a poker. The room – the entire hotel – is chilly, and Henry wishes
he had a thicker sweater, or his jacket. Henry looks under the
bed. Beverly looks through David's luggage while David watches,
picking through the contents of his overnight bag – boxer shorts
and socks, clothes, books – and opening zippered pouches.
Meanwhile Henry lifts the mattress and looks beneath it. He
remembers hiding porn mags under his mattress as a teenager.

Finally, they are finished, and as they all leave the room,
Henry casts an anxious look out of the window. The sky is black
outside. The wind howls around the hotel. He can hear the
creaking of the ice-coated branches sawing in the wind outside
the windows. He feels a sinking sensation in his core – more
than that – it's a sensation of dread.

*

They step out of the room, and David closes his door behind them. The others are already entering Matthew's room, where David leaves it to them to feel through luggage, open drawers, lift carpets, stir ashes. He watches Matthew's reaction as his and Dana's room and private belongings are searched. He is uncomfortable at having his things examined, but nothing more than that.

David is startled when Henry finds a gun. It's in Matthew's luggage, properly locked and stowed, along with ammunition.

'I have a permit,' Matthew says a little defensively. 'I don't normally take it anywhere,' he tells them. 'I keep it in my bedside table at home, in case of intruders. But I thought it might be handy if we did some skiing or hiking up here. There are bears. Better to be prepared.' He turns to James. 'You can scare them off easily with the sound of a shot. Isn't that right?'

James nods nervously. 'Yes.'

David nods, and Henry returns the gun carefully to the overnight bag and puts the bag back down on the floor.

Matthew leans over and grabs the overnight bag and pulls it towards him and puts it on the bed. He takes the gun out of the bag and methodically loads it. David freezes. Everyone has stopped what they're doing to watch Matthew. He grabs extra ammunition and shoves it into his pockets. He's not looking at anyone. He holds the gun in his hand; David wonders if he should say something, do something.

Time seems to stop. David's heart is racing. Everyone is transfixed by the sight of Matthew handling his gun. As if they are afraid that Matthew is the murderer, and he is going to kill them all. But then Matthew looks up, and it's just Matthew.

'We could use this, for protection,' he says. And the moment passes.

Henry and Beverly's room is beside Matthew's, across from the empty housekeeping closet. They find nothing there. Now even David doesn't know what they're looking for. He's starting to think he's on a fool's errand, searching the guests' rooms. The two rooms across from each other at the end of the hall, near the back staircase, are unoccupied, and cleaned, prepared for the next guests.

Saturday, 6:30 PM

'We'd better search the rest of the hotel,' James says. 'The entire ground floor, and then the cellars.' James is very disturbed by the appearance of room 202. Nothing like this has ever happened before. He asks himself if it is possible that there is someone here that they're not aware of – some interloper. But he has no enemies. Not that he can think of. No mad relatives hidden away. No disgruntled employees. He wishes now that he'd installed security cameras, but he hadn't wanted them in his quaint, old-fashioned hotel. He hadn't thought they would ever be necessary. But now, if only he'd had cameras installed in the corridors, they might have shown what happened to Dana – if it happened before the power went out. But then he realizes they wouldn't have been able to review the video anyway, without electricity.

James glances at Bradley. Bradley is standing in the hall with the rest of them, staring down at the floor, unaware that he's being observed. There's naked fear on his face. And something else that James can't quite read. It's a look he's seen before . . .

James feels his stomach drop with a sickening lurch. He doesn't really know everything about his son. No parent does. Bradley has had some brushes with the law. James thought those days were behind them. Dear God, he hopes Bradley hasn't become involved with something bigger than he can handle. But then he assures himself that anything Bradley might be involved in couldn't have anything to do with this. Bradley is a good boy, who once got involved with some bad people. But he'll talk to him when he gets a chance.

He comes up beside his son and whispers, 'Are you okay?'

Bradley looks up at him, startled. 'Yeah, I'm fine.' And that look on his face is gone and he looks like he always does, and James tells himself he's worrying for nothing. This has nothing to do with Bradley. He's just frightened like everybody else.

'Bradley,' James says, 'you've got the lamp, why don't you lead?'

This time, they take the back staircase down to the ground floor. It's the first time Beverly's seen it. It's narrow and un-carpeted. They go down single file, their steps echoing.

'This was the servants' staircase,' Bradley says.

'Is there an attic we should be checking out?' David asks.

'No,' James says.

They arrive at the bottom of the stairs where a door opens onto a hall that runs along the back of the hotel. Immediately to the left is the kitchen.

'Let's leave the kitchen and cellars for last,' James says. 'Let's try the woodshed.'

Down the hall from the kitchen is the door to the woodshed. They follow Bradley. Beverly hadn't really looked closely at the woodshed when she was here before, being in a hurry to follow the others to the icehouse. But she looks at it now. It's really cold in here. The walls are simple barn board. It's not insulated. There's a large wooden stump with an axe plunged into it in the centre of the earthen floor. Logs are neatly stacked all around. Kindling, too. There are some gardening tools, and a musty smell, but there is nowhere to hide in here.

They move further along the hall at the back of the hotel and turn left, towards the lobby. On the right-hand side is the library. James opens the glass-paned door and they all follow him. There's nowhere to hide in here, either.

They move on next to the sitting room, but again, there's nothing to find.

When they get back to the lobby, they turn down the corridor towards the bar. It yields nothing. Further down the corridor is the door to James and Bradley's apartment. James unlocks the door and invites them in. The apartment is small but tidy and nicely appointed. There's no one there, either. As they return to the lobby, Beverly is both relieved and disheartened. She doesn't know what they are going to do, how they will find the killer.

'There's nothing left but the kitchen and the cellar,' Bradley says.

Beverly feels uneasy at the thought of going down to the cellar, but she follows along as they go back to the kitchen.

'Come in,' Bradley says. With Bradley holding the oil lamp aloft, they enter the enormous kitchen. It's half country kitchen, half industrial. Beverly notices the enormous refrigerator that must be eight feet wide, and which is now full of food that must be thawing and spoiling. There's an oversized island in the middle of the kitchen – obviously a busy workspace on most days. Cupboards line the walls, and there's a large double sink and an industrial dishwasher.

Beverly watches James open the large refrigerator and look inside. Nothing. Then he opens the larder and they all look inside with the aid of the sputtering oil lamp. It's empty, too.

James turns to them and says, 'Only the cellar left.' He opens an old wooden door and automatically reaches for the light switch before remembering. 'Give me that,' he says to Bradley, and reaches for the lamp.

'No, let me go first,' Bradley insists, and pushes past his father with the light.

They creak down the rough wooden stairs. There are no backs on the stairs, and there's no handrail, either. Beverly keeps her hand against the rough stone wall for balance. When she arrives at the bottom, it's like stepping into another century. Thick, heavy ceiling beams support the building overhead. The foundation walls are made of stone.

'Two feet thick,' Bradley says, pointing casually.

Beverly looks, impressed, at the whitewashed stone. The paint is flaking off.

'Are there rats down here?' she asks. There are probably rats. Beverly is terrified of rats. This is the country, and the cellar is directly below the kitchen.

'We take care of them,' Bradley says. 'Don't worry.'

'How?' Henry asks.

'Warfarin,' James says curtly, and Beverly's uneasiness increases.

James seems uncomfortable about his guests seeing this rather primitive cellar, and possibly rats; it's nothing like the fancy hotel upstairs. He must feel like he's stripping down to his underwear in front of them, Beverly thinks.

She sees a rude wooden shelf built into the stone wall that must be original to the building. It's empty. Bradley sees her looking at it.

'We don't use the basement much,' Bradley explains. 'We keep everything in the pantry upstairs.'

Beverly gazes around the very large open space. The cement floor is uneven. There are some small windows set into the stone high up in the wall. A modern electrical panel stands out for being clean and new. The furnace is relatively new as well.

'There's no one here,' David says, peering around behind the furnace.

'We're not done yet,' Bradley says. He moves towards the back of the cellar and slips through another opening to the right. 'The cisterns are in here,' he says, his voice sounding far away.

Not wanting to be left behind, Beverly reluctantly follows the others and glances through the rough doorway. There are two large square concrete cisterns to the right.

'Empty now,' Bradley says.

Beverly shudders. She doesn't go inside the room with the cisterns. She stands at the opening, watching as Bradley looks down inside each one, holding the light aloft. David comes up beside him and looks down with him.

Bradley shakes his head. 'All clear,' he says.

'Look,' David says, his voice sharp.

Beverly follows where David is looking. There's a window on the far wall, near the ceiling.

'Shit,' says Bradley.

Beverly watches, tense, as Bradley approaches and examines the window. She can see that the glass is broken; there are fragments on the floor below.

'The window is still latched,' David says, standing beside Bradley, studying the window.

'So it might just be a broken window,' Bradley says.

'Or it could have been deliberately broken, unlatched from outside, and someone could have slipped in this way and latched the window again.'

Beverly feels herself go a little faint.

David says, 'We'd better go outside and take a look around. See if there are any footprints. Bradley and I will go. Everybody doesn't have to come.'

Matthew says, 'I'll come.'

Saturday, 7:10 PM

Matthew pulls on his winter jacket and boots and follows David and Bradley outside onto the porch. The wind is a force to be reckoned with, angry and noisy; the trees seem to cower before it. They've checked all the ground-floor windows and doors from the inside, and they are all secure. There's just the one broken basement window they have to go and look at now. Matthew wonders how they're going to make it around the east side of the hotel to check the window, given how slippery it looks out there.

They've had to leave the oil lamp inside because no one wants to scramble over the ice holding an oil lamp. Instead they've got Matthew's iPhone torch – David has hardly

153

any charge left in his and wants to conserve it. But Matthew isn't going to lead the way – he's given his phone to Bradley.

'Follow me,' Bradley says.

They slide slowly across the front of the hotel, and then round the corner and make their way along the side of the hotel, their hands against the wall for balance. As they near the basement window, they can see there's a broken branch lying in front of it, fallen from a nearby tree crippled by the storm. They bend down and peer at the window, Bradley shining the light.

But they can't tell if the branch fell and broke the window, or someone used the branch to break the window. With the ice, they can't see any footprints.

'What do you think?' Matthew asks, studying the window, the branches strewn about in front of it.

'I don't know,' David says, looking worried.

Chapter Twenty

DAVID, BRADLEY, AND Matthew return to the lobby, to the anxious faces of the others waiting inside.

David sags into a chair by the fire and explains their findings to the others. He finishes wearily, 'So, we have a room that looks like it's been used, and a mysteriously broken window. Other than that, we haven't seen any sign of someone else in this hotel. Or of anyone going in or out.'

They all glance at one another in silence, as if they can't possibly make sense of this information. They're visibly on edge.

'So is there someone else here or not?' Riley asks, her voice strident.

'I don't know,' David says. 'Maybe. Maybe not.'

Ian says, 'Are you really suggesting that it might be one of *us* that killed Dana and Candice?' Ian's voice rises with incredulity. 'Why on earth would one of us kill either of them? We don't even know them.'

'We don't know that. We don't know that no one here knew Dana or Candice,' David says evenly. 'I don't know anything about anyone here.' He looks around them as if daring someone to speak. 'As far as I know – as far as we've led each other to believe – we are all strangers. But maybe that's not the case.' He looks around slowly at the assembled group. 'In any event, when the police get here there will be an investigation. They will look very carefully into Dana's background and Candice's background – and into all of us, as well.'

And he knows what that's going to be like. He watches the others as they look uneasily at each other. 'Just for a moment, let's assume it *is* one of us. We need to know where everybody was this afternoon. Bradley saw Candice alive when he picked up her lunch tray from the library – when was that, Bradley?'

'It was about one thirty,' Bradley says.

David continues. 'All of us were here in the lobby together, with the exception of James and Bradley, until around two, when Henry and I went to get wood and everyone seemed to go their own way. We all met down here for tea at four o'clock. All of us then went out to the icehouse together and came back together. With the exception of James.' He pauses, and adds, 'Of course, Bradley, you came back in to look for her, when the rest of us were in the icehouse.' He gives everyone a frank glance. 'But let's focus on where everyone was between about two o'clock and four. I was in my room, alone.'

Gwen says, 'Riley and I were in our room.'

Lauren says, 'Ian and I were in our room, too.'

Matthew says, 'I was in my room – you told me to stay there. I only came out when I heard that scream when you found Candice dead.'

156

Henry says, 'I was down here, in the lobby. I fell asleep in my chair for a bit. Then I went upstairs to freshen up just before four.'

Beverly nods. 'I was in our room – I came down briefly to chat with Henry in the lobby, but went back up to our room after. He came up just before four.'

James says, 'I was in the kitchen, and Bradley was helping me.'

David says wearily, 'So, that doesn't help much, does it?'

'If you think it's one of us,' Henry says into the ensuing silence, 'if I had to guess, my money would be on Matthew.'

Matthew turns to him in shock.

Henry's been thinking about this during the long, cold search of the hotel. If it's even possible that the murderer is one of them, maybe it's time to shake things up a bit. He's decided to play devil's advocate. 'You're the most likely culprit,' he says mildly, turning on Matthew. 'Maybe you killed Dana after your argument and Candice figured it out and you had to shut her up.'

The others watch in alarm, but no one tries to defend Matthew.

Lauren says, 'How could she have figured it out?'

'I don't know. She seemed kind of snoopy to me. Or maybe' – he's thinking out loud here – 'maybe Candice was writing a book about Matthew – the famous, wealthy businessman. Or about Dana, who was about to marry him. And Dana argued with her about it at the top of the stairs and Candice pushed her down. And Matthew knew it must have been her who killed Dana, so he strangled her.'

'That sounds pretty far-fetched,' Ian says.

'*Murder* is far-fetched,' Henry says. 'We're not dealing with

157

normal here. Somebody around here is a killer. Somebody had good enough reasons to kill Dana and Candice. I'm just trying to figure out what they are.'

Lauren turns to Matthew and says haltingly, 'Candice *was* staring at you and Dana at dinner last night.'

Matthew looks back at her, frowning. He shifts uneasily in his seat. 'Was she? I'm well known in the business world. Our engagement was announced in all the society pages. So yes, it's possible she recognized me and knew who I was.'

Lauren says, 'She knew who you were – she told us all at breakfast this morning.'

'But I didn't know *her*,' Matthew snaps, 'and Dana didn't either. If she was writing a book about us, we didn't know about it. And neither of us have anything to hide, so we wouldn't give a shit.'

Then Riley says, 'But maybe Dana *did* have something to hide, something you didn't know about. Maybe Candice knew about it, and was writing about it, and she and Dana fought on the stairs and Candice pushed her down.'

'But if I didn't know about it, why would I conclude that Candice pushed her down the stairs and then kill Candice?' Matthew says sarcastically.

'Maybe you *did* know about it,' Henry says. 'We only have your word for it.'

Matthew leans forward and says, deliberately, 'I didn't kill anybody.'

Riley says, her voice intense, 'You brought a gun. Maybe you knew Candice was going to be here. Maybe you planned to kill her all along but the thing with Dana happened first.'

'I don't have to listen to this,' Matthew says.

Beverly breaks in. 'Hold on. Maybe the fact that Candice is dead too means that Matthew didn't kill Dana, and that he has nothing to do with this – did you ever think of that?' She turns to Henry and says, 'Doesn't it make him *less* likely to be guilty?'

'Possibly,' Henry says.

'That's kind of what I was thinking,' Gwen admits. 'If it was just Dana, then yes, I'm sorry, Matthew, but you would seem like the obvious suspect. Especially since Beverly heard you arguing late last night.' She turns to the others. 'But once there's another death, doesn't that make it seem less likely that Matthew did it?'

'She kind of has a point,' Ian says.

Henry watches everyone carefully. He doesn't know anything for certain, but he's going to keep his eyes open.

'If we could all just stop pointing the finger at me for a minute, there's something I'd like to bring up,' Matthew says. He knows he sounds a bit aggressive; he doesn't care. They've practically accused him of murder, for God's sake.

'What's that?' David says.

'I think James and Bradley are hiding something.'

James looks completely taken aback. Bradley flushes to the roots of his hair. 'What do you mean?' James stammers.

Matthew leans towards James and Bradley, who are seated together. 'This is your hotel. Maybe you know something the rest of us don't.'

'Like what?' James says, on the defensive.

'I don't know. But I've seen you two whispering together. What have you been whispering about?'

'We haven't been whispering,' James says, colouring.

'Yes, you have, I've seen you.'

'Oh, for Christ's sake,' Ian interjects, 'they've got a hotel to run.'

David turns to James, his face serious. 'Is it at all possible that there is someone who might wish you – or your hotel – harm?'

Matthew watches James closely. Out of the corner of his eye, he sees Bradley shaking his head.

James shakes his head stiffly. 'No. If I thought that was possible I would have said so.'

Matthew sinks back in his chair, dissatisfied, unconvinced. 'I don't believe you.' He looks from James to Bradley and back again. 'I still think there's something you're not telling us.'

David watches as Gwen rises restlessly from her chair and wanders over to the windows. It's darker by the windows but he can see her in the gloom. She looks out, pointlessly. No one is coming. David leaves his seat and goes to her. He can feel the others watching, but he doesn't care.

She turns towards him as he approaches. Her eyes are troubled.

'There's something I have to ask you,' she says without pre-amble, her voice a whisper.

Here it comes, David thinks. She's going to ask him about his wife. She's been listening to Riley, he's sure of it. He should have told Gwen about his past first. He should have told her last night. But it wasn't the right time. You don't tell a woman you're terribly attracted to that you were once arrested for murder.

'Anything,' he says, his voice low, his expression open. He will tell her the truth. It's up to her whether to believe him or not. He can't hide it; it's all over the internet.

Gwen glances back at the others around the fire. 'Not now,' she whispers. 'But we need to talk, privately, at some point.'

He nods. It will give him time to prepare what he's going to say to her. How to put it. He doesn't want to frighten her away.

All Beverly wants is to go home. She wants to see her children. This hotel no longer seems lovely and luxurious to her – it's dark and cold and awful. She shudders when she remembers the cellar. It looked like it could be the setting for some horror film. She feels like she's *living* in a horror film. This can't really be happening, not to her. She's a very normal woman, with a very normal, even dull, life. Nothing exceptional ever happens to her. And deep down, she likes it that way.

It's horrible to have Dana's body still lying at the foot of the stairs. Really, it's too much. She feels a bout of tears coming on, and forces them back.

She wants that body moved. She thinks it's beginning to smell. It has been lying there since sometime last night. It must be decomposing by now. That must be what that smell is. Can't anyone else smell it? She's always had a very acute sense of smell. She's sensitive; she's always been sensitive. Teddy's like that, too. Doesn't like tags in his clothes, very fussy about his socks. She lifts her wrist to her nose and tries to breathe in her own fading perfume.

As the time ticks by, she finds herself staring at Dana's body, draped in the ghostly sheet. She couldn't even look at it before, but she's glowering at it now. Because she's afraid of it. She doesn't want to turn her back on it. It's irrational, but that's how she feels. She's unravelling.

She thinks she sees something moving in the dark, over by the body. A dark shape, a rustling. And now it looks as if Dana is moving slightly under the sheet. She's heard about that, about bodies moving after death, shifting, because they're full of gas. She stares more intently.

What is that? Is that a rat? She screams.

Henry bolts out of his chair.

'There's a rat, over there, by the body!' Beverly cries, getting up and pointing. Everyone turns to squint into the dark where she's pointing.

'That's impossible,' James says defensively, jumping out of his chair.

'You already admitted you have rats,' Lauren points out uneasily, tucking her feet up underneath her on the sofa.

'Not up here!' James says.

'But there's a dead body up here,' Lauren says, 'and maybe it's . . . attracting them.' She shudders visibly. 'Oh, God, I can't stand this!'

Beverly agrees with Lauren; she can't stand it either. She starts to sob and shake; out of years of habit she turns and buries her face in Henry's chest. He puts his arms around her, and even though she's still furious with him, it's comforting.

'We need to get that body out of here!' Henry says crossly.

'We really shouldn't move it,' David begins.

'To hell with what we should and shouldn't do,' Henry cries. 'There's a dead body there, it's festering, and attracting rats, and it's frightening my wife!'

Beverly lifts her head from Henry's chest and looks at Matthew. He's gone white. She's suddenly sorry for her outburst.

'I'm sorry—'

But Matthew ignores her and picks the oil lamp up from the coffee table and goes over to Dana's body. He holds the light over her, looking down, looking for a rat. It's a macabre sight, but Beverly finds she cannot look away.

'I don't see any rats,' Matthew says sullenly. 'There aren't any. You must have imagined it.'

Ian gets up and stands beside him. 'Still, maybe we should move her,' he says gently. He turns and looks back at David.

David looks around the room, as if gauging the mood. Finally, he nods, as if he knows he's outnumbered. He takes his mobile phone out of his pocket, pulls back the sheet and snaps some pictures. Then he makes a sound of frustration and says, 'Now my phone's completely dead.' He looks up at the others. 'Okay. Where can we put her?'

'The woodshed?' Bradley suggests tentatively.

'No!' Matthew says. 'There may be . . . rats might get her there.'

It makes Beverly feel sick, the thought of rats gnawing on Dana.

'How about the icehouse?' James suggests. 'It's cold. It's completely sealed. Nothing can . . . disturb her there.'

Finally Matthew swallows and nods. Beverly feels the most awful pity for him. She watches as David lays the sheet down on the floor beside the body. Then he takes Dana's feet and Matthew takes her shoulders and they clumsily lift her onto the sheet. Her head falls suddenly to the side. They wrap her up tightly in the sheet to make it easier to carry her.

163

Bradley, Matthew, and David put on their coats and boots and begin the sad, awkward journey with the body out to the icehouse.

Once they're out of sight, Beverly bursts into tears.

Chapter Twenty-one

Saturday, 8:30 PM

ON THEIR RETURN from the icehouse, David puts two more logs on the fire and gets a good flame going. Then he turns reluctantly to the others, seated around the fire, their faces glowing in the firelight. Matthew sits apart, alienated from the others by his grief and by the suspicion that has been cast on him.

The room is quite dark, with just the light thrown by the fire and the single, sputtering oil lamp. The other has run out of oil, and Bradley has explained, embarrassed, that there is no more. No one was expecting to have to use oil lamps.

Riley fidgets nervously with the ring on her index finger, her version of wringing her hands, David thinks.

She says, 'What are we going to do?'

David thinks that someone should give Riley another drink. Or one of those pills of hers they found upstairs. He says, 'We're going to stick together. We're going to make it through the night.' The storm shrieks around them, slamming against the windows, as if mocking him. 'And in the morning, when it's light, I think we should try to make it out to the main road.'

He detects some nods in the shadows.

'We'll stay here, in the lobby. If anybody has to go to the bathroom, we'll go together, in groups,' David instructs. 'And then, at daybreak, we'll go. Maybe the road crews will be out by then. We'll get help. But we have to stick together. Nothing can happen to anyone if we all stick together, understand?'

Everyone stares back at him. Now, one by one, they nod. Even Riley, who licks her lips nervously.

'It's still cold in here,' David continues. 'We need to stay warm. We have to keep the fire going.' He stops to think for a minute. 'We should get some more blankets from the rooms.'

'I'm not going back upstairs,' Gwen says with feeling.

David is distracted for a moment by how anxious she looks. But they're all frightened. Other than keeping them warm and fed and all together in one place, he has no idea how to keep them alive.

'Our phones must be very low on battery; mine's out,' David says. There are nods all around.

'Mine's still working, for now,' Matthew says. 'But it won't last much longer.'

David turns to Ian and Bradley. 'Why don't we go upstairs now and grab some blankets.'

Bradley and Ian nod, and the three of them head for the central staircase, into the dark, Bradley holding up the oil lamp to light their way, leaving the others by the light of the fire.

*

Gwen stares into the dark after them. She's reminded some-how of the story of Hansel and Gretel, lost in the dark forest, trying to make their way home, where they aren't even wanted. The fairy tale had terrified her as a child, and now she feels as if she's inside the story, in the dark forest, aban-doned by those who love her. She shivers. She's letting her imagination run away with her.

Riley watches and waits, her heart beating fast, like an over-revved engine that might burn itself out. She listens to every little sound – the wind against the windows, the crackling of the fire, the startling sound of the logs shifting suddenly in the fireplace. But she's listening for something else, something unexpected. She's listening for something that shouldn't be there.

She pulls the blanket more tightly around her body. She tells herself that they have to make it to the morning, then they can try to get the hell out of here. She tries to think. Maybe there's a connection here that they don't know about, as David suggested. If anyone here knew Dana or Candice previously, they aren't admitting it. It's possible that Mat-thew's right, and James and Bradley are hiding something. She had seen James and Bradley whispering, too. Or Mat-thew might simply be trying to shift attention away from himself.

She knows she's become a little fixated on David Paley. Yet as much as she thinks he might have murdered his own wife, she's not particularly afraid of him now.

But she wishes Gwen would stay the hell away from him.

Saturday, 9:05 PM

They settle into their sofas and chairs around the fireplace. They've eaten a meal hastily thrown together by James and Bradley, with David keeping them company in the kitchen. James has brewed another big pot of coffee.

No one wants to sleep tonight. No one wants to even close their eyes. They sit together in a charged silence. No one is talking about the elephant in the room.

Gwen squirms in an attempt to find a more comfortable position on the sofa. She doesn't know who or where the killer is. She can't bear to think about it any more. Her neck is stiff with tension. She just wants to survive. They will try to make their way out of here first thing in the morning. She's holding on to that.

They sit wrapped in blankets with their fingers around their mugs of coffee for warmth. There's a bottle of Kahlua taken from the bar trolley sitting on the coffee table. They take turns topping up their coffees with it.

Maybe it's not such a good idea to get drunk, Gwen thinks, but the Kahlua tastes good, and it's soothing. She notices gratefully that David isn't putting anything in his coffee. He's going to keep his wits about him. Their protector. She has more faith in him than in Matthew, with his gun, which seldom leaves his hand. He plays with it restlessly. She wishes he would put it down. She wishes David would tell him to put it down, or take it away from him. It's making her nervous.

The rest of them are now trying to talk about other things – other hotels they've stayed at, in other countries – anything to keep their minds off the long dark night stretching out in front of them. She finds her eyes drifting more and more to David as the night wears on. She keeps thinking about the two of them together the night before. Occasionally – in fact, more and more frequently – he glances her way.

He looks dark and solid by the meagre light of the fire and the oil lamp. He's unshaven, but he wears it well, and a lock of his hair falls forward over his forehead in a way that she finds appealing. She wants to brush it back. She wishes that the two of them were sitting close together, sharing a sofa, but she's sharing a sofa with Riley.

She wonders what David would think of her, if he knew the truth about her. She's not going to tell him. Not yet. There's only one person who knows the truth about her, about what she did – and she's sitting right beside her. But Riley isn't going to say anything.

Chapter Twenty-two

RILEY'S BEEN SLIPPING Kahlua into her coffee at a faster rate than the rest of them. They already think she's got a problem with alcohol. Maybe she does. But that pales in comparison to the problems they've all got tonight. She just wants to take the edge off.

She notices the way Gwen and David are looking at each other, and decides she's not having it. She can be a bit mean when she's had a couple of drinks.

'So,' she says, venturing into a conversational lull, 'maybe we should get to know each other a little better.' She's looking right at David. She's pretty sure, from the way he was last night at the dinner table, that he knows she's on to him. She knows who he is.

She can feel Gwen tightening up beside her. Bristling.

But then Lauren says, 'Sure, why not?' She stares at Riley across the coffee table, challenge in her eyes. 'Why don't you tell us a bit about yourself, Riley? Like, what exactly is bothering you so much?'

Riley looks back at her, surprised and thrown off course. She doesn't like Lauren. She's seen her rolling her eyes. And now she's giving her a hard time. *How dare she?*

Riley hesitates, angry at Lauren. Then she says, 'You don't want to know.' There's a warning in her voice.

'Sure I do,' Lauren says.

Pushy bitch, Riley thinks. She pauses and then says, her voice icy, 'I've seen things that would make your guts turn inside out. So don't you dare judge me.'

'I'm not judging you,' Lauren says. 'I just want to understand you. I remember when we first got here thinking that maybe you were ... disturbed in some way. Because you seemed freaked out *before* any of this started happening.' Lauren leans forward in the dark. 'So do you know something about what's going on? Because *I don't trust you*.'

Riley freezes in her seat, speechless. She can't believe what she's being accused of.

'What are you saying?' Gwen protests from beside her, clearly indignant. 'She doesn't have anything to do with this!'

'Really? She may not be the one killing people, but I wouldn't be surprised if she knows something! Look at her!'

Now everyone is staring at Riley. She can feel herself becoming agitated. She tries to stay in control.

'She has a point,' Matthew says, glaring at her. 'You've been really nervous since we all got here. Everybody can see it. I thought there was something wrong with you. So did – so did Dana.'

'Maybe we should all take a step back,' Ian says calmly.

'I don't know anything about what's happening here!' Riley protests.

'Tell them,' Gwen says beside her, her voice bold and furious. 'Tell them what you've been through. Tell them, or I will!'

Riley flashes Gwen a grateful look. She sighs heavily and says, enunciating carefully, 'I'm a journalist.' She hesitates a bit too long. Takes another gulp of her drink – more straight Kahlua than coffee by this point.

'Yeah? So what?' Henry says provocatively.

Riley, feeling cornered, turns her eyes on him. She hasn't really given Henry any thought, but suddenly she despises him. She looks around the room. She despises all of them, except for Gwen. Gwen is the only friend she has here.

'I was stationed in Afghanistan – mostly in Kabul. I spent almost three years there. I saw terrible things.' Her voice begins to shake. 'I saw so many civilians killed – children, babies. Limbs torn off by bombs, just lying in the street. So much brutality—' She stops. She can't say any more. Her voice has fallen to a whisper now, and she feels Gwen put her arm around her shoulder. She focuses on the pressure of Gwen's arm around her, grounding her. 'Then I was taken hostage.'

'What?' Gwen says beside her, obviously shocked. 'You never told me that.'

Riley stares down into her lap. 'It was kept quiet. I was held prisoner for six days, until they negotiated my release. Every day they would hold a gun to my head and pretend they were going to fire. They would pick someone at random and shoot them on the spot.' Her entire body is shaking now, and it makes her feel ashamed, even though she knows she shouldn't be ashamed. 'I thought I could do it. These were important stories, they had to be told. So I stuck with it for as long as I could. You try to cope. Until you crack.' She waits a beat. 'But after that,' she falters, her voice a whisper, 'I couldn't do it any more.'

Gwen is rubbing her back now, in large, slow circles, comforting her. The others are deadly quiet.

Riley focuses on the feeling of Gwen rubbing her back in firm circles. It feels good, actually, to get this out. She's tired of pretending she's fine, when everybody's looking at her like they obviously think she's got a screw loose. At least now they'll know why. She reminds herself it's nothing to be ashamed of. Her illness is a sign of her humanity. When she speaks again, she tries to make her voice sound more matter of fact.

'I had to come home. I'm trying to get well. I've got PTSD. I take medication for it,' she says. 'These horrible images keep coming back to me, and I never know when they're going to come. I hear a sound – it's like something trips in my head, and I'm back there, in the chaos, waiting for the killing to start.' She raises her eyes then and looks at each one of them, their pale faces looming above their dark blankets, as if their heads are disembodied and floating in the air.

Gwen whispers, her face close to hers, 'Oh, Riley – I'm sorry, I didn't realize – I had no idea what happened to you.'

Riley's hands are trembling, and she clasps them together. 'Last night, when I was falling asleep, I thought I heard a scream, but I ignored it, because I didn't think it was real. I hear screams in my head every night when I try to go to sleep.' She lowers her voice again to a whisper. 'And I hear them every night when I dream.'

When she stops speaking, the silence is complete, except for the crackling of the fire. Even the wind has died down for the moment.

Then Lauren says, 'I'm so sorry.'

Henry says nothing.

Matthew plays nervously with his gun.

Beverly shrinks into her blanket, chilled to the bone. She's sickened by what Riley has said. She watches Gwen rubbing Riley's back. Riley's obvious terror is contagious.

Beverly's frightened of what's out there, lurking in the shadows. She doesn't think the killer is one of these people sitting around the fire. She thinks he's out there, waiting. She feels like a cornered mouse, eyes bright, chest heaving rapidly with each breath.

Henry is sitting near the fireplace in the dark. She thinks about their children, Teddy and Kate. How will they cope if their mother and father don't come home? She just wants to go home with Henry, she tells herself. She wants things to be the way they used to be.

David drinks his coffee down to the dregs, even though it's cold now. He must stay awake. He got very little sleep last night, and now his eyes burn and feel gritty. He surveys his little flock of sheep. For that's how he thinks of them. They seem like sheep because they are all frightened, and they don't know what to do.

Matthew is making him uneasy. He seems a bit agitated. David would like to get the gun away from him, but doesn't want a confrontation. He can't predict what Matthew might do.

He can't predict what any of them might do. The revelations about Riley make sense. Her history, her experience – they explain her volatile personality, her startled eyes, constantly scanning, her tension, her drinking. He knew she was a journalist, but if she's been in Afghanistan for the last three or four years, maybe she doesn't know about him at all. Maybe she was just jealous that he was interested in Gwen rather than her. Maybe Gwen has no idea about his past.

But Gwen told him there was something she wanted to talk to him about. No doubt it's his murdered wife. Or – it just occurs to him now – maybe it's something about her. Maybe she's involved with someone, and neglected to tell him last night.

He will have no possibility of any kind of future with Gwen if they don't make it through the night. He needs to think about the problem right in front of him. To hell with Riley and what she might think she knows.

David tries to look at the situation analytically, the way he would look at a case. The most likely scenario is that Dana's fiancé, Matthew, killed her. They'd argued. Perhaps he'd pushed her down the stairs. Perhaps he hadn't meant to, but once he'd done it, he realized he had to finish her off. Maybe.

But Candice ... Maybe she did have something on Matthew or Dana. Or maybe she knew something about Dana's death – perhaps she'd seen something, heard something. Had she been snooping on Dana and Matt? She knew who they were. She might have been listening outside the door, overheard their argument, and then scuttled out of sight when the door opened and seen – or perhaps heard – Matthew push Dana down the stairs. If so, why didn't she say anything?

Maybe she was too afraid to say anything until the police arrived, and was biding her time. Maybe that's what got her killed.

If he had to give an opinion, he's with Henry on this one: he thinks it was probably Matthew. He lied about the argument; he's the most likely one to have murdered Dana. Candice might have known something, or have had some connection to them in some way. And Matthew may be trying to throw suspicion on James and Bradley, while bolstering the view that there's someone else out there.

Or maybe there is someone out there, killing them for sport.

And if he's killing them for sport, because he can, because he wants to – none of them is safe.

Chapter Twenty-three

Saturday, 10:20 PM

GWEN TRIES TO relax into the sofa. She feels relatively safe here, surrounded by the others. She watches Matthew out of one eye. He's hypervigilant, his eyes constantly scanning the dark void beyond them, as if alert to any threat. But the effect of his attentiveness is not calming at all, but the opposite. She has more confidence in David. His presence makes her feel safe. She pulls the blanket more tightly around her neck and withdraws into herself. She's relieved that the truth is out about Riley. She hadn't known about the PTSD, about her being held hostage, but it all makes sense. She thinks it will help Riley for people to understand her, to be supportive. And she will try to be more supportive, too.

Trauma changes people. She should know.

She broods into the dark.

If they survive this – of course they will, she tells herself, they are all together now, and nothing is going to split them up – then she has to tell David the truth about herself. But first, she wants to ask him about who *he* is. She hopes – it's frightening just how *much* she hopes – that he's not the person Riley believes he is. She hopes he's someone else altogether, that Riley's confusing him with someone else. But Riley is usually right about things.

First, they have to get out of here. She closes her eyes briefly and says a little prayer, begging for the police to come.

Sunday, 12:05 AM

It's after midnight when things start to unravel. The lobby is quiet, but no one is sleeping.

Riley finds the silence unbearable. She needs conversation to keep the terrifying images at bay. She keeps glancing into the dark at the spot where Dana's body used to be, remembering her awful, lifeless face. Candice, with her scarf wound tightly around her neck. She doesn't want to think about the killings, or about what might happen to the rest of them. So she thinks about David Paley instead. She becomes fixated on him until it's like an itch she has to scratch. She can't stop herself. She leans towards David, who is also wide awake, across from her on the other side of the coffee table, and whispers, 'I know who you are.'

For a moment, she thinks he's going to ignore her, pretend he didn't hear. She's about to repeat herself, more loudly, but then he leans towards her. She can see his face, resolute, in the glow of the oil lamp.

'What is it that you think you know?' he says back in a low voice. But he's not whispering.

178

Riley feels Gwen tense beside her. Gwen places a restraining hand on her leg, under the blanket, but she disregards it. 'I knew I recognized your name, last night, but I couldn't place it. But I kept thinking about it and then I remembered, this morning.' She's not whispering any more. She's aware of the others – now alert – listening. He stares back at her, waiting for her to say it. So she does. 'You're that attorney who was arrested for murdering his wife.'

The silence around the fireplace suddenly takes on a different quality; it's fraught with the shock of the others, hearing this for the first time.

'Arrested and *cleared*,' he says crisply.

'So it *is* you,' Riley hisses with satisfaction. It feels good to be right. She turns to look at Gwen, wanting to gloat. But Gwen looks back at her with something almost like hatred in her eyes, which throws her for a minute. 'I told you!' Riley says to her.

'The charges were dropped,' David says, more firmly. 'I didn't do it.' He's looking now at Gwen, to gauge her reaction.

'Just because the charges were dropped,' Riley says, 'doesn't mean you didn't do it. It just means they didn't think they could prove it.' She smirks and adds dismissively, 'It's always the husband.'

Gwen says, 'Shut up.'

Riley looks at her in surprise. 'I'm doing you a favour. I told you this guy is bad news.'

Gwen says, 'He says he didn't do it.'

'Oh, and you believe him?' Riley says sarcastically.

Lauren says, looking at David in shock, 'Your wife was murdered?'

'Yes,' David admits. 'But not by me.'

179

There's a lengthy, stunned pause as everyone takes this in. Then Ian asks, 'Did they get the person who did it?'

'No.'

'Hang on,' Henry says, his voice accusing. 'Why should we believe you?' He's raised his voice. 'We're sitting around here waiting for someone else to get killed and we find out that your wife was murdered?'

'Let's all calm down,' Ian says. 'Why don't we let him tell his story?'

'I can tell you the story,' Riley says, without taking her eyes off David. 'It was in all the papers. Some of you must have heard about it. Respected New York City defence attorney comes home late one night and finds his wife lying in a pool of blood in the kitchen of their upmarket home in an expensive suburb. She'd been beaten to death.' She leans aggressively towards David. 'Her head was bashed in and her back was broken, I believe. Have I got it right so far?' she asks him. He doesn't answer, but stares woodenly back at her.

Riley continues. 'He claimed he came home and found her dead. The trouble was he didn't call 911 for almost an hour. They didn't get along. And she was insured for a million dollars. He was arrested almost immediately, but *he got a very good lawyer*. Because, you see, he knows people.'

She sits back in satisfaction and looks at everyone else in the room, one by one, except for Gwen – she doesn't dare look at her. They've all been listening attentively to her – and now they all turn and stare at David.

Hearing Riley tell it, in her accusing, sneering way, David knows how terrible it sounds. He's aware of them all staring at him and feels angry that he has to defend himself – again. He is always having to defend himself. At this moment, he hates Riley. Hates her not because she has outed him – he's used to people recognizing him, after all, whispering about him; his was a very public disgrace – but because of her ugly motives. She wants to prevent Gwen and him from getting closer. He was going to tell Gwen himself. But now she's heard it the worst possible way.

What happened to him will never go away. He will always be defending himself. And there will always be people who don't believe him. He's learned that people will believe what they want to believe. And it's truly frightening how easily they'll believe it.

He'd come home late from work, like most nights when he was in the middle of a trial. He can hardly remember the details of that trial now – he didn't finish it in any case; someone else from the firm took it over. His wife's violent murder had resulted in an investigation, and his arrest; he hadn't worked for months afterwards.

He remembers coming home that night. The house was mostly dark; there was one light left on over the porch, but inside, the only light was coming from the kitchen, the stove light. They usually left it on all night, as a sort of night-light for the ground floor.

He came in the door quietly, like he always did those days. He didn't call out, 'Barbara, I'm home,' like he used to. The way he did back when she was still happy to see him. He took off his coat and hung it in the hall cupboard. His first thought was that she'd already gone to bed without him. It was perfectly true that they hadn't been doing too well together at the

181

time. He couldn't deny that they'd been having marital problems.

Just like he couldn't deny that her life was insured. It didn't seem to matter that he was financially well off already; they seemed to think that even the financially secure could never be too greedy. It had been a strike against him. He'd been astonished. He was insured for the same amount, but that hadn't mattered either. They thought a million-dollar life insurance policy was excessive.

He'd sat down in the living room, exhausted. Trials wore him out. He'd sat there for some time, thinking about how things had gone in court that day, how they might go tomorrow, and then about his life, how hard things were with Barbara. He was too depleted even to get up and go into the kitchen to pour himself a drink. Which, as things turned out, was very bad for him. But eventually he got up and made his way through the dark living room and dining room to the kitchen. It was only when he was almost there that the little hairs on the back of his neck began to stir. He still doesn't know why. He suspects that he could smell the blood – on some level, even though he was not consciously aware of it. Then he made it to the kitchen door and saw her—

She was crumpled on the kitchen floor in her nightgown. It looked as if she'd been struck down while making herself a cup of herbal tea. There was a cup on the counter, an opened packet of tea beside it. But she was on the floor, soaked in her own blood. She'd been bludgeoned to death. Her head smashed in, her face beaten to a pulp. One arm was splayed beneath her, obviously broken.

Through his paralysing horror, one of his first thoughts

was to wonder if she'd suffered. Whether the first blow had caught her by surprise, and whether it had killed her. But he knew Barbara, and he suspected she fought back tooth and nail. There was blood everywhere. Of course she'd fought back. Barbara had never been meek. Her arm had indeed been broken. And it turns out – they told him later – that her back had been broken as well. She had been kicked viciously after death. That's another thing that made them suspect him – it looked like a crime of passion. But perhaps it was just made to look that way. That's what David thought at the time. Someone had tried to set him up.

He finally speaks. 'Most of what you say is true. I was working late that night. When I got home, the house was dark. I assumed Barbara, my wife, had already gone to bed.' He takes a deep breath, exhales. 'We hadn't been getting along; we'd talked about separating. It wasn't a secret. She'd told some of her friends, I'd told a friend or two at work. It's also true,' he says, looking directly at Riley, 'that she had a life insurance policy for a million dollars. As did I. We'd both had those policies for many years, from early in our marriage.'

He looks around the group, his eyes resting finally on Gwen. He tries to read her expression, but he can't; it's too dark. She is leaning back against the sofa across from him, in shadow. 'I didn't kill her. She was already dead when I got there. I found her lying on the kitchen floor, covered in blood.' He hesitates. 'I switched on the overhead light. It was the most horrible moment of my life.' He pauses for a moment, to recover himself. 'I thought she'd been stabbed repeatedly, there was so much blood. But there was no knife there. She was so badly beaten . . .' He covers his face with his hands.

Slowly, he brings his hands down again and continues speaking. 'I called 911 immediately. I said that I'd come home from work and found her. My mistake was that in that 911 call, I didn't mention that I'd been sitting alone in the living room for almost an hour before I found her. I didn't think to mention it. I was very distressed – I wasn't thinking clearly. And then my next-door neighbour told the police that he had noted the time that I drove in the driveway and parked the car. He'd seen the lights, and knew the exact time. Then, when they asked me about the discrepancy between the time I got home and the time of the 911 call, I immediately told them the truth, but they were suspicious. They arrested me. After all,' – he gives Riley a bitter look – 'I was the husband. People knew our marriage was in trouble. Then somebody made a big deal about the insurance policy.'

He takes a deep breath and exhales. 'It was a living hell. An unbelievable nightmare. My wife had been murdered and I was arrested for it – put in jail, denied bail – and I hadn't done it.'

There's a long silence while everyone tries to digest what they've just heard.

'But they dropped the charges,' Gwen says, her voice low.

He looks back at her. She's leaned forward a bit. 'Yes. They didn't have any evidence against me. They assumed I had a motive, but there wasn't one scrap of physical evidence to pin the crime on me. If I'd done it, I would have had blood on me, on my clothes. They tried to figure out how I could have killed her and cleaned myself up and destroyed any evidence in that hour. But they didn't have anything. They didn't even have the murder weapon.

'The most damning thing was that I didn't have an alibi. I was sitting alone for that hour, in my own living room. They determined that the time of death must have been very close to around the time I arrived home. I must have missed whoever did it by a few minutes. The investigating officers asked the neighbour if he'd seen anything, but he'd been out at his bridge game up until just before he saw me arrive, so he was no help. And the neighbour on the other side of us was out of town, and the ones across the street go to bed early. No one saw anything.' He looks intently at the small group seated around him, listening with wide eyes. 'Anyone could have parked on the street and walked up to the front door – or sneaked in the back. Nothing was stolen. There was no sign of forced entry, but Barbara might have let someone in if she knew him. She wasn't afraid of anyone. Maybe she was having an affair. I don't know. I never suspected such a thing. They didn't find anything like that.'

David shakes his head slowly. 'Someone obviously wanted her dead – or was setting me up,' he says. 'I'd like nothing more than to find out who.' He frowns deeply. 'They had to drop the charges. But this – stigma – has become part of my life. I wish I could say I've got used to it, but I haven't. I don't think I ever will.'

He looks at each of them in turn. 'I can't make any of you believe me. I've told the truth, but I've found that people believe what they want to believe. I can't help that.'

185

Chapter Twenty-four

GWEN HAS LISTENED to both sides of David's story with a feeling of horror. She is much colder inside her blanket now than she was before.

It sounds worse than she expected. She thought at first that maybe they'd arrested him simply because he was the husband, and had quickly realized their mistake. But this sounds so inconclusive. Unsatisfactory. There hadn't been enough evidence to send him to trial – *but does she believe him?* Riley is right about one thing – he would have had the best possible defence lawyer.

It's very disturbing, the admission of the missing hour between his arriving home and calling 911. And he's a criminal defence attorney. He would know what to do – how to destroy evidence, or get rid of it. She doesn't know what to believe.

Henry squirms uncomfortably in his seat. His breathing is shallow. This entire situation is becoming more and more surreal. All these revelations are bizarre – Riley with her stories of being held hostage, of having a gun held to her head, of severed limbs in the streets – no wonder she's so peculiar. And this thing about David has given him a nasty jolt – *my God, did he murder his wife?*

Henry suspects he is looking at it from a slightly different perspective than the others. He looks at his wife, seated a short distance away, and allows his gaze to rest on her. He doesn't doubt that David killed his wife. Because he can understand it. He can understand the impulse to want to kill your wife. To just want to end things, and to be able to move on, without all the carping. He would like to reach over to the hearth and grab the iron poker – it's an arm's length away – and strike his unsuspecting wife over the head with it. He knows just how it would feel, how the poker would feel in his hand, because he's been tending the fire occasionally. He imagines leaning down as if to poke the flames, then changing course and turning suddenly, raising his arm and bringing the poker down as fast and as hard as he can and spilling her brains. Would she look up in time to realize what he was doing? What would her face look like? He would have to make the first blow count. He wonders if a poker would do it, if it would be heavy enough. Would he have enough force in his arm? How many times would he have to hit her, to be sure? Perhaps something heavier . . .

Henry realizes he's clenching his hands into fists underneath the blanket. He blinks his eyes rapidly, as if to dispel the fantasy, which has run away with him. Of course he wouldn't do that. Even if there was no one here watching, he still wouldn't do it. Thoughts are not actions. They aren't the same thing at all. But he can understand the impulse. So he has no difficulty believing that David might have murdered his wife.

187

He catches his own wife staring back at him in the dark. For a moment, he wonders nervously if she can read his thoughts.

But then he has a thought, and before he fully considers it he voices it out loud. 'Maybe Candice knew *David*. Maybe she was writing a book about *him*.' He leans towards David. 'You say the case was in all the papers.'

'That's ridiculous,' David says dismissively.

'Is it? Maybe she knew something about the case and was going to put it in a book, and you found out she was going to be here and you came up here to put a stop to it.'

'That's nonsense!' Gwen says indignantly. 'Then how do you explain Dana's death? Why on earth would he kill her? That's ridiculous.'

'No, it isn't. Because here's my theory: Matthew argued with Dana and pushed her down the stairs. David killed Candice because she was writing an exposé about him. The two are unconnected – pure coincidence.'

'Who do you think you are?' Beverly snipes. 'Hercule Poirot?'

Henry gives his wife a dirty glance.

Lauren says slowly, 'I did notice Candice staring at David at dinner last night. She was paying attention to Matthew and Dana, and David – nobody else. You had your back to her, David, but she was definitely staring at you.'

'Maybe it's time for another drink?' Ian says into the charged silence that follows.

When Bradley doesn't move from his seat, Ian gets up and pulls the bar trolley closer himself. It's hard to see in the dim light. He picks up the oil lamp from the coffee table and holds it aloft over the trolley. 'There's still plenty here,' he says.

Ian pours and hands out the drinks, sits down again in his place nestled next to Lauren, and says thoughtfully, 'I have a story to tell, too. It's not much, really. No dark secrets. I haven't been accused of murdering anyone. I've never been arrested. I've never been to a war zone and seen people slaughtered. I had a pretty normal childhood growing up in Iowa with two parents and my brothers.' He goes quiet for a moment. 'Except – when I was thirteen, my younger brother died. He was ten. That was tough.'

Gwen asks, 'What happened?'

'He drowned. In a local pond.'

'I'm so sorry,' Gwen says.

He nods, and looks down at the drink in his hand. 'My mother was beside herself. He'd gone to the pond by himself. He wasn't allowed to go on his own, but the rest of us were all off doing something else, and he went anyway. He was like that. Wilful, hard to manage. Didn't do what he was told – always did what he wanted, to hell with the consequences. When he didn't turn up for supper, we went looking for him. It wasn't that unusual, we were always coming home late for supper.' He hesitates a moment, takes a gulp of his drink, then says, 'I was the one who found him.'

Lauren reaches out and takes his hand, pulls it into her lap. He'd already told her this.

'My parents never really got over it. It pretty much shattered them. So I guess that's a blip in my otherwise normal childhood.'

'That's tragic,' Riley says, with genuine sympathy.

'It was a long time ago,' Ian says, and reaches for his drink.

*

David is observing Ian carefully. He's been observing all of them, while trying to appear as if he isn't. There was something about the way Ian told the story about his brother that bothers him.

David's used to interviewing clients who are pretty damned good at lying. Usually he can tell. The way the eyes drift up and to the left. The hesitations. The fleeting facial expressions. There's just enough light from the oil lamp to see Ian's face. And if he'd been asked to give an opinion on whether Ian was telling the truth about his brother, he would have said no.

He knows it's not always possible to tell if someone's lying. He's been proven wrong before. And he's tired, stressed, and the circumstances are highly unusual – for all of them. But something about Ian just now – a man he has so far found to be warm, open, and uncomplicated – has put him on notice.

Chapter Twenty-five

THERE'S A STRANGE, compelling sort of intimacy in this room, with the oil lamp flickering and the fire crackling, all of them sitting around together wrapped in blankets because they're afraid to go to their rooms. It's seductive.

But Lauren says quietly, 'I'm afraid I don't have any dark secrets either.'

That's not exactly true. She has survived a dysfunctional family and an awful, short-lived stint in a foster home, but she has survived. She has made something of herself. She doesn't have to share that with anyone if she doesn't want to. 'Of course there have been some things in my life that have been difficult, which I won't share with you. Family problems, the usual. I don't think anybody comes out of a family unscathed.' She smiles wanly. 'But I certainly haven't got anything to hide.'

'Nothing?' Riley prods.

Lauren studies Riley, who is looking at her as if she doesn't believe her. Riley seems to have something against her. Fair enough. Lauren was a bit hard on her a little while ago. She pretty much told her she thought there was something seriously wrong with her. At least now they know what it is, and why. Still, she's not going to take any shit from Riley.

'Why is that so hard to believe?' Lauren asks her point-blank.

Riley shrugs, looks away.

Lauren decides to let it go.

But Henry asks, 'Then what's with the sleeping pills?'

Lauren is taken aback. 'I have trouble sleeping. I always have. So I take sleeping pills.'

'It's true,' Ian says, nodding beside her.

Then, surprisingly, Riley turns to Gwen and says, 'If it's true confession time, why don't you tell everyone *your* deep dark secret?'

Startled, Lauren watches Gwen give Riley a hard look. But Riley has drunk down her glass of wine very quickly and seems to be shedding her inhibitions and possibly her good sense. She's a sloppy drunk, Lauren's noticed. She's suddenly very curious about what's going to happen next. She wonders what Riley has on Gwen. She'd like to know.

'Piss off, Riley,' Gwen says.

Her heart is fluttering anxiously. She doesn't want to be put on the spot. Gwen doesn't want to share her past with anyone. She doesn't want to spill it all in front of this group of strangers. Not in front of David. Definitely not like this.

But she wonders how it would feel to unburden herself, to confess to someone other than Riley. Perhaps it would be liberating, perhaps she would be able to forgive herself then. Riley would no longer have this hold over her. Maybe they would no longer be friends.

192

She looks across at David, his handsome face inscrutable. She wants to tell him; she wants to see how he'll react. She looks at him and doesn't even know what kind of man she's looking at. He could be a man who killed his wife – with sufficient presence of mind to successfully cover his tracks. Henry suggested that he might have killed Candice. She doesn't know. She wishes they had never come here to this horrible, god-forsaken place, wishes she had never met David, who has her in turmoil, or any of these other people, either.

'Are you okay?' David asks her.

His concern is so tempting, but she must guard against it. She feels herself go suddenly cold, emotionless. 'I'm fine.'

She knows her voice sounds harsh, as if she's pushing him away. She wants to push all of these horrible people away – especially Matthew, playing incessantly with his gun. But, she tells herself, it must be very disorienting to suddenly, violently, lose someone who knows you better than anyone else, someone you've counted on to anchor your world.

Sunday, 1:10 AM

David slumps back against his seat, exhausted, stinging from Gwen's rebuke. Matthew's fidgeting is putting everyone on edge.

David says abruptly, 'Matthew, put the gun down, it's making everybody nervous.'

Matthew's hands go still, but he doesn't put the gun down. Instead he says, 'You can all sit here and wait. I'm going to go after this sonofabitch.' He gets up suddenly from his chair. 'Where's that torch?'

193

'You can't,' David tells him sternly. 'You can't go anywhere on your own, even with the gun. It's too dangerous.'

'What do I care?' Matthew looks with contempt at the rest of them. 'Are you going to give me the torch or not?'

'It's almost dead,' David reminds him, as Matthew snatches it up.

'Don't do this,' David says. This is what he feared, the group splitting up. He thinks they should stick together. He doesn't want Matthew going off on his own – nobody wants a jumpy, overwrought man running around with a gun in his hand. His little flock is coming apart. There might be someone out there, waiting for one of them to break ranks and run into the dark to be his next victim. *Or the killer might be right here within arm's reach.*

Should he just let Matthew go?

Maybe he will be killed out there, and then they will know it isn't one of them. He's tempted to use Matthew as bait, David realizes with a sickening feeling.

'Does anyone want to come with me?' Matthew asks.

David wrestles with himself – should he go, too, leaving the rest? He glances at the others, watching Matthew nervously. No one else answers, either.

'Fine, I'll go myself.'

'But,' Gwen says, 'how do you think you'll find him? We've been all over this hotel. Stay here, with us. In the morning, we'll all go together out to the road.' She pauses and adds, 'Please.'

He gives her a last, dismissive look, turns away towards the staircase, and is slowly swallowed up by the darkness.

*

Beverly watches anxiously as the group remaining falls into a fraught silence. There are nine of them left sitting around the fireplace: Gwen and David sitting across from one another; Lauren and Ian on one of the sofas; she and Henry sitting in armchairs across from each other; Riley, who has left the sofa where she'd been sitting with Gwen and moved to the hearth; and James and Bradley sitting together close by.

Beverly wonders if Matthew has just gone to his death.

Suddenly David gets up, mutters an expletive, and follows Matthew into the inky blackness.

Riley says, 'What an idiot.'

Beverly wishes fervently that David would come back. She wants to get out of here alive. She wants to survive the night. She can't bear that he has deserted them.

For Matthew, the loss of Dana has been completely destabilizing.

He walks quickly up the dark staircase and arrives on the second floor of the old hotel, holding the fading torch, which casts a faint light on the floral carpet.

He pauses in the corridor. How cold and dark it is up here, he thinks. It's as cold as a morgue. He hears a sound below him. He looks back over his shoulder towards the staircase behind him, fading to black. He switches off the feeble torch and immediately can't see a thing. He stands perfectly still and listens carefully, tilting his head. Then he hears David, calling his name. It sounds like he's on the first floor, below him.

Matthew doesn't answer. David will only want him to go back to the others. But Matthew doesn't feel like part of this little group. He doesn't have to follow their rules. And he has a gun. His heart pounding, Matthew makes his way quietly

195

along the hallway to his right, silently trying all the door-knobs as he goes. His hands are sweaty. All the doors are locked, of course. Coming back down the hall towards the stairs, he peers into the dark sitting room. He stands still for a moment. There is the faintest light coming in from the windows; it's slightly less dark than the corridor. But all he can pick out are the ghostly shapes of the furniture – chairs and sofas, empty and sinister-seeming. Then he hears someone coming up the stairs to the second floor. He steps quickly into the sitting room and stands behind the wall as still as a sentry. He tightens his grip on the gun. It's David – he can hear him quietly calling his name. Matthew waits while David searches this side of the staircase – passing the sitting room, peering in, seeing nothing – and then walks slowly down the hall on the other side of the stairs. After a short while, Matthew decides David must have gone down the servants' staircase.

Matthew follows in his footsteps, to the other end of the hall. The door to the housekeeping closet is unlocked and opens beneath his hand. He steps inside, turning the weak torch on briefly. He turns it off again. Continuing down the hall, he reaches the back staircase and pushes the door open and finds himself on the narrow landing. The door closes behind him, and he stands motionless, listening. Satisfied that David is no longer on the back stairs, he switches the torch back on. He ventures slowly down the staircase to the first-floor landing, all senses on alert.

He turns the torch off again and cautiously opens the door to the first floor. He doesn't hear David calling him any more; he's probably given up and gone back to the lobby. Here, on the first floor, is the room that he and Dana were sharing.

He peers down the first-floor hall, listening. It's so dark that without the torch on he can't tell if anyone else is here. He walks quietly down the corridor, peeking into the housekeeping closet and the sitting room, then returns to the back staircase and finds himself once again on the ground floor. The servants' staircase opens into the dark hallway outside the kitchen. He makes his way silently along the hallway at the back of the hotel and turns, finding himself outside the library. He steps inside. The faintest sliver of moonlight falls now through the French doors. For a moment he just stares around the room.

He spies a large book open on the coffee table. He switches the torch on, and sees a picture of a nineteenth-century ship locked in the ice. He wonders who was reading it. He sweeps the torch around the room and turns it off again. Losing interest, he pauses at the doorway. If he goes right, he knows he will find another sitting room and wind up back in the lobby. He doesn't want that. Instead, he turns to his left, and moves back along the rear of the hotel. This time he recognizes the door to the woodshed. He hesitates, then pushes open the door.

Chapter Twenty-six

RILEY IS GLAD that David is gone. She thinks he's reckless, and she's glad he's gone. Maybe he'll get himself killed.

She hears the muffled sound of a door closing somewhere in the hotel and her nerves jump.

'What was that?' she says, frightened.

Henry answers nervously, 'It's probably just Matthew, or David.'

Straining to hear what's happening outside their little circle, all she can hear is the wind drumming against the windows. Whether the storm subsides tomorrow or not, they must try to make their way – no matter how slowly, or with how much difficulty – out to the main road and try to get help.

She thinks of her therapist, Donna – the woman who has been helping her regain a sense of control over her life, or at least trying to. With Donna's help, she's been trying to learn how to manage her negative thoughts. She certainly wouldn't be happy with the way Riley's using alcohol to cope this weekend. But she's trapped in a remote inn with a bunch of strangers, and people are being murdered. She imagines being in Donna's office, telling her all about it. She would say, *You have experienced some terrible things.* Yes, she has. She would say, *Because of this, your mind will sometimes play tricks on you.*

'Are you all right?' Gwen says suddenly. Somehow Gwen is standing right in front of her. She doesn't remember seeing her move from the sofa. But Gwen is squatting down in front of her now, looking intently into her eyes, concern stamped on her face.

'I don't know,' Riley whispers. Gwen stares back at her, alarmed. 'I don't know,' Riley repeats, more urgently. She's in a strange place. Hell isn't imaginary; it's real. It's a real place and it's also a state of mind. And she can feel herself slipping into the pit, she can feel the fear taking over, the paranoia, the need to react. She doesn't want that to happen. God, not here. Not now. She grabs Gwen's hand tightly. 'Stay with me,' she says.

'Of course,' Gwen says, and sits down beside her, the tension between them seemingly forgotten, at least for now. 'I won't leave you,' Gwen promises.

Inside the woodshed, a sudden rattling sound coming from the direction of the outside door startles Matthew. He whirls towards the sound and trips over something, dropping the torch before he can turn it on. Completely blind, he senses something in the darkness, something moving. Matthew fumbles from cold and nerves, clutches the gun and raises it. He fires wildly in the dark.

*

David followed Matthew as best he could. He felt his way up and down the first-floor corridor, and then made his way up the main staircase to the second floor. He walked down the west side of the hall, quietly calling Matthew's name, and then the east side, finally finding himself outside the servants' staircase.

He pushed open the door and listened carefully. It was dead quiet. It was also dark as pitch in the back staircase. He wished fervently that he had a light. He had to find Matthew. Matthew didn't know what he was doing. He was liable to shoot at anyone.

He called softly, 'Matthew?' There was no answer. But he could be there, in the dark stairwell. Perhaps he'd turned off the torch. 'It's David.' He waited and listened, but there was no answer. He stepped cautiously into the stairwell. He felt around clumsily for the handrail. He searched for the first step with his foot, found it. He started down the stairs, moving slowly, feeling for each step, listening carefully. Where the hell was Matthew? David was frustrated at how difficult it was to know what was going on in the dark. The darkness was so absolute that it was disorienting. It was like floating in space, with nothing to mark where you were. He felt unmoored; he'd felt that way since they'd discovered Dana dead that morning.

He found his way to the first-floor landing and hesitated. He had a pounding headache. He thought longingly of the bottle of aspirin that he had in his bag in his room at the other end of the corridor.

David opened the door onto the darkened first-floor hall. He made his way to his own room at the other end, ears sharpened for any sound. When he got to his room, he fumbled with his key and opened the door with relief. His room was not quite as dark as the corridor. There was the briefest glint of moonlight coming in through the open curtains of the windows – and then it disappeared. David closed the door behind him. He felt around for his bag and found it on the floor, by the bedside table. He searched for the aspirin and then made his way to the sink. He poured himself some water into a glass by feel, and took the tablets, relieved to be alone, if only for a few minutes. Spending so much time with all the others, under so much strain – he wished it were all over. He was so tired. He wanted to lie down on the bed, burrow under the covers, and never get up. Instead – despite the cold – he spent a couple of minutes splashing icy-cold water on his face.

Feeling a bit better, he left his room and returned to the servants' staircase, intending to resume his search for Matthew in the ground-floor hall along the back of the hotel. He could be in the kitchen, the cellar, or in any of the other rooms on the ground floor.

David is coming down the back stairs when he hears the gunshots.

He feels the shock through his entire body, a spurt of fear. He freezes. Tries to focus on where the shots came from. He thinks from somewhere on the ground floor. From the woodshed, maybe. He stumbles down the rest of the stairs as quickly as he can. His breath is ragged. What if something has happened to Matthew? What if he's too late?

Matthew feels the kick in his hand from the pistol and whirls and flees. He's not sure what he saw, doesn't know what he shot at. He doesn't want to stay and find out. He clutches the gun tightly in his hand and bolts out of the woodshed and down the dark hall. He stumbles his way back into the library and stops, breathing heavily, trying to listen over his own noisy gasps.

The sound of gunfire finally sends Riley over the edge. She springs up abruptly, flinging Gwen off. Gwen tries to calm her but Riley is too agitated; she takes off suddenly towards the front door, as if she needs to escape. Riley doesn't know what she's doing, Gwen realizes – she's just reacting, running blindly.

'Riley!' Gwen calls after her, pointlessly. 'Stop!'

But Riley pulls open the door and flees into the blustery night, leaving the door open behind her.

Gwen hesitates for only a second, casting a desperate look at the others for help, and then grabs her coat off the coat hook and follows Riley outside. She's wearing her sneakers. She has no light, and she must feel her way. It's pitch dark, the moon hidden behind the clouds. She hurries after Riley. Gwen is terrified of going out into the darkness, but she can't let Riley go alone. She wishes David were with her.

She can hear Riley somewhere ahead of her in the cold, can hear her scrambling on the ice, falling and picking herself up again, can hear her panicked, heavy breathing. Gwen follows her out over the icy lawn, barely able to stay upright. She slams hard into the broken tree branch that she'd forgotten was there and falls, her bare hands scrabbling at the ground. Gwen realizes Riley is running aimlessly, like a frightened animal – she's running and that's all. She may not even be aware of where she is. She must reach her and calm her down. Persuade her to come back inside, where it's safe.

She hears voices behind her. She stops briefly and looks back. She can see James and Bradley dimly outlined in the doorway; they are coming to help. The door closes and all is dark again. She can hear them behind her, quickly catching up. She glances over her shoulder and sees nothing until Bradley and James are almost upon her. Then she sees them, looming towards her in the darkness. She feels intensely grateful that they've come after her. They don't have a light either; they are all swimming in the dark.

'Which way did she go?' Bradley asks.

'I don't know. She was ahead of me, but I can't hear her any more. I don't know where she went,' Gwen says anxiously.

The front door of the hotel opens again, and Gwen barely discerns, in the faint light of the open door, Lauren and Ian coming out to join them. Gwen thinks of Henry and Beverly sitting alone in cold animosity back in the lobby. What if something happens to them? But she doesn't really care. They're not her problem – her first duty is to help Riley. The killer might be out here somewhere and Riley might run right into his arms. She turns away from the hotel and looks out into the darkness.

'Riley!' Gwen screams. They all hold still, ears cocked.

But all they can hear is the lashing of the trees in the wind.

'We should spread out,' Bradley says. He moves off to her right; James moves off to her left.

Gwen moves forward over the ice, towards the drive, the tree line looming to the right. She's slipping and falling, her ungloved hands freezing from contact with the icy ground. Where did Riley go?

She can't see anyone any more. They're there, but they've all slipped away again into the darkness. The trees and shrubs are menacing shapes in the dark. We have to find her, Gwen thinks, as she slides precariously forward.

Chapter Twenty-seven

DAVID'S HEART IS pounding so loudly, his breath coming in such short, loud rasps, that he can't hear anything over his own fear. He feels his way, touching the wall of the ground-floor hall with his right hand as he makes his way to the door of the woodshed. When he reaches it, he takes a deep breath and pushes the door open. He curses himself again for not having a light.

'Matthew?' he says. 'Are you there?' He's met with absolute silence. And he can't see a thing.

Riley runs wildly into the cold, icy dark. The terrible fear has taken over, driving her. She runs and slides, falls and picks herself up again, instinctively searching for somewhere to hide, some low place where she can crouch unseen. She needs to take cover. She senses the forest ahead of her and heads for it. Somewhere in the recesses of her mind, she knows to stay hidden, not to make a sound. She reaches the edge of the forest and crawls into some brush. She crouches on the ground, turning herself into a tight ball. She squeezes her eyes shut and rocks back and forth, her hands over her ears, trying to block out everything.

Gwen has never been so frightened in her life.

There's some comfort in knowing that the others are out here with her, even if she can't see them. It's like she's alone in a dark void. She can't bear to think about David, what the gunshots might mean. Is someone else dead? She wonders if soon there will be no one left at all. She wants to live, but she hopes that if she has to die, she isn't the last one. She doesn't think she could bear it. She is defenceless. She thinks of the small, sharp letter opener that had been lying on the writing desk in their room. She wishes she had it with her now.

She keeps going, past the lawn to the drive, every footstep treacherous on the ice. 'Riley!' she calls. 'Where are you?' She takes a few more steps down the drive and stops to listen. She can see nothing, hears nothing ahead of her. How she wishes she had a torch! Suddenly she hears a wild howling. Coyotes, she thinks. Or wolves. She stops in her tracks, overwhelmed with terror. How has it come to this?

She suddenly realizes that she can't hear anyone else. 'Bradley?' she calls urgently. But Bradley doesn't answer. No one answers. Perhaps they can't hear her over the furiously gusting wind. Gwen's heart pounds frantically; she can hardly breathe. She turns around, looks back towards the hotel, where she last heard the others. 'Bradley? Lauren?' she cries again, more loudly, her voice infected with panic. But no one answers. She can't think. She is all alone.

Gwen stops moving. She doesn't know where anyone else

is, whether there's a killer out here. There's a crushing pain in her chest.

She thinks she hears a sound like something falling heavily, but she can't tell where it's coming from. With the darkness like a void and the wind swirling around her, everything is distorted; she doesn't trust her senses. For a moment, she does nothing. She doesn't move, for how long she doesn't know. She has lost all sense of time. Maybe a minute, maybe ten. She's so frightened, so cold, that she doesn't think she *can* move. She has to wait for the ache in her ribs to subside.

She begins to feel her way back towards the hotel, body low, arms outstretched, looking for Bradley or James, Lauren or Ian – anyone who can make her feel less alone. Less terrified. Even as she does so she's aware that she's abandoning Riley to her fate. Riley, her friend, who is afraid, and vulnerable, and irrational. Riley, who needs her.

But she doesn't care. Right now, she can't think of anyone but herself. She stops for a moment in the dark, trembling violently, listening, convinced now that the killer is nearby, that he has murdered the rest of them without a sound. And then she is fleeing back to the hotel, reckless on the ice, slipping and sobbing, terrified that she will be next. She aims for the hotel, which is hulking in the dark, desperate to get back to the lobby, to the light of the fire.

Alone in the lobby, Henry and his wife sit frozen in silence and fear. He watches her stare into the fire, which is starting to falter. He needs to add another log.

Somewhere out there David is searching for Matthew, who is armed and possibly a killer; Riley and Gwen are outside.

207

He can understand why James and Bradley felt they had to go after the two women, but once they did, he doesn't see why Lauren and Ian had to go after them, too. He's angry at them for choosing Riley and Gwen over him and Beverly. Now he and Beverly have been left to fend for themselves. What if the killer comes for them?

He watches his wife carefully. He no longer feels a shred of affection for her. He loves his children, that hasn't changed. But something about her – something about her fills him with revulsion. He thinks of her flabby white thighs, the veins that run in little maps along her legs. Her breasts that are too heavy. The perpetual look on her face of being fed up. As if life is only to be endured.

But it's more than that. It's the way she views *him*. Overweight family man. A bit of a fool. Someone whose life is mostly over, who will never do anything interesting or exciting again. Just her presence near him, knowing that she believes this about him, makes him hate her. What had she said to him? – *It's just a phase*. She diminishes him; she always has. Jilly doesn't do that. She admires him. She finds him interesting, attractive. She told him she wants to spend the rest of her life with him. She won't get tired of him, as Beverly says.

His wife doesn't *want* to spend the rest of her life with him, but she would. If this hadn't happened. All she thinks about is duty. The tyranny of the shoulds. I should do this, or you should do that. *You should be at home more. You should spend more time with the kids. You should try for promotion.*

He gets up to stir the fire. He reaches for the poker with his right hand. Oddly, time seems to slow down. He grasps the poker very tight. She's sitting right there. It would be so easy. There's no one here to see it. He could run outside after the others, make up some story . . .

He grips the poker tight.

David feels his way across the woodshed floor, sliding his feet along in case Matthew is there, somewhere, on the floor. He calls his name, but gets no response. He forces himself to get down on his hands and knees and feel around on the sawdust-covered floor for Matthew. He reaches the stump they use for chopping wood, feels its rough surface with frantic hands.

All he finds is the torch.

Riley huddles in the forest, her entire body shaking with fear and cold, reliving some of the worst moments of her life. Memories of victims – screaming, suffering, dying – bear down on her. She presses her hands to her ears to try to block out the noise, but it doesn't work because the tumult is inside her head. She closes her eyes tight to stop seeing, but it doesn't help, because the images are in her mind's eye.

Matthew hears someone approaching the library. Someone who is trying not to make a sound. Without warning, outside the French doors, the clouds part to reveal the moon, and a glimmer of ghostly light filters into the library. Matthew stands facing the door. He has his gun in his hand, and he knows there are several bullets remaining.

209

And then he sees David appear in the doorway. 'Oh, it's you,' he says. He explains. 'I thought I heard someone, in the woodshed . . .'

'You'd better give me the gun.'

Matthew hands the gun over.

Sunday, 1:45 AM

When Gwen opens the door and stumbles into the lobby, she's almost surprised to find Henry and Beverly still there, exactly where she'd left them, except that Henry is standing near the fire with the poker in his hand. He starts and drops the poker suddenly, and it rattles as it strikes the floor.

She half expected to find them dead.

David appears suddenly from out of the dark near the staircase. Matthew is with him. She almost faints with relief.

Henry turns from her to David and Matthew and asks, 'What's happened?'

'Nothing. We're fine,' David says bluntly. 'Where the hell is everybody else?'

Gwen whispers, 'Outside.' Her entire body is shaking.

Henry says, 'Riley ran outside when she heard the gunshots. The rest of them went out after her.'

'We can't find her,' Gwen says. 'She won't answer us. It's so dark – the others are still out there, looking for her.' She can't stop trembling.

'Jesus,' David says. 'We'd better get out there. We need to find her.' He sounds desperate. He turns to Gwen and says, 'You stay in here with Henry and Beverly.'

'No! I'm coming with you.' She will stay close to David. She'll be safe with him. They have to find Riley.

'Are you just going to leave us here?' Henry splutters.

Nobody answers him.

Chapter Twenty-eight

MATTHEW SLIPS OFF the porch and vanishes into the night. David watches him go, wondering about the wisdom of all of them tearing off in different directions. But they have to find Riley, and time is of the essence. They can cover more ground if they spread out. It's freezing out here.

'Is she wearing a coat?' David asks Gwen.

She shakes her head. Mumbles, 'Just a sweater.'

David swears under his breath. They make their way along slowly. David can hear nothing but the howling of the wind. 'Is anybody out there?' he yells. The wind tears the words from his mouth and they are lost.

'Anyone?' he tries again, cupping his hands around his mouth.

'I'm over here.' It's Ian's voice coming from somewhere in the direction of the drive.

'Anybody else?' David yells.

And then less faint, from not so far away, Lauren answers. 'I'm here, on the east side, near the trees. I haven't seen her.'

This is impossible, David thinks wearily. He can't see the hand in front of his face without the torch, and the rest of them have no light at all. He can barely keep his footing. He turns to Gwen, 'What do you think she'd do? Where would she go?'

Gwen looks at him blankly, her face close to his. 'I don't know. I don't think she's thinking at all. I don't know if she'd run down the driveway to the road or hide in the trees. I have no idea.'

'There are trees everywhere,' David says miserably.

He cups his hands around his mouth and calls, 'Bradley? James?'

'I'm here,' James shouts back. It sounds like his voice is coming from David's right, west of the hotel. 'I haven't seen her either. But you can't see anything out here. She's not answering. Where the hell is Bradley?'

David suddenly feels anxious. Why hasn't Bradley answered? Maybe he's already made it into the woods and can't hear them. He and Gwen make their unsteady way forward, towards the forest.

They're almost across the lawn to the trees when David hears a muffled cry and the sound of someone falling down. And then it's a penetrating cry of pure pain. Coming from somewhere behind them to their right.

'James!' David calls wildly. He turns and tries to hurry towards the sound. He hears Gwen panting and scrambling behind him.

'Bradley!' It's James's voice. The desperation in it makes a chill run along David's spine.

David stumbles and slides faster and faster, frantic to reach them, leaving Gwen struggling to keep up. But when he finally sees James, he wants to close his eyes and block everything out. His weak torch picks out the dark shape of James bending over Bradley, who is lying still, apparently lifeless, on the ice-covered snow.

David comes closer until he is almost upon them. Bradley lies face down in the snow. He'd run out without a hat, and there is an ugly, vicious gash at the base of his skull. Blood is spattered all over the snow.

James looks up at him, his face almost unrecognizable in his grief. 'Help him!' he screams. 'You have to help him!'

David kneels in the snow beside him and shines the feeble light on Bradley's face. His eyes are closed, his lips are blue. He looks dead. David feels for a pulse – he can feel nothing, but for a moment he hopes that's because his hands are shaking, frozen and numb. But it's no use. There's nothing. Bradley is dead.

James begins a terrible keening. It's the most dreadful sound that David has ever heard – a loud, despairing wretchedness, the sound of a father mourning the loss of his only son. He can't bear it. He looks up at Gwen and sees fear reflected back at him. He sits back on his heels and wants to weep himself.

He hears others approaching noisily. He shines the light towards them. He sees Matthew, and behind him is Lauren.

'What happened?' Lauren cries before she reaches them, before she can really see.

'Stay back,' David warns.

He rises unsteadily to his feet, and splays the light around. He spots something dark, dropped in the snow. He lurches towards it. Some dark shape, with blood on it. He's seen it before. It's familiar. He looks at it for a bit longer and then he recognizes it. It's the iron boot scraper from the front porch. Someone picked it up and must have used it to murder Bradley. Who? When? A stranger? *Or one of the people who came out here to look for Riley?*

He whirls around again to face them.

Lauren steps closer into their little circle of light and stops abruptly. She looks down at Bradley in the snow, his father crouching over him.

'Oh, God,' she whispers, taking it all in. 'Is he . . . ?'

'He's dead,' David says dully.

'Oh, God, let me—'

'Stay back,' David says again. 'There's nothing you can do for him. It's too late.'

'Are you sure?' She's hysterical. 'He can't be dead! He can't be!' She tries to get past him to Bradley. 'Maybe he's still alive! Maybe we can still help him!'

He shakes his head and stands in front of her, blocking the way. She begins to cry and beats her hands against David's chest, sobbing. 'There's nothing you can do,' he says.

He hears someone coming closer, his breathing heavy as he approaches. Ian looms into view, takes in the scene.

'Oh, no,' he says.

Ian watches James weep, collapsed onto his son's body. His shoulders jerk spasmodically as he sobs. It reminds him of his mother's endless weeping, her relentless grief. He turns away.

'We can't leave him out here,' David says finally, his voice low.

He doesn't have to say what they're all thinking: if they

215

leave him out here overnight the animals will get him. The coyotes, the wolves. *And God knows what else,* Ian thinks to himself.

Finally James slumps back in the snow, his eyes vacant.

'Does anyone have any charge left in their phone?' David asks. 'I'd like to take a photo before we move him.'

They all shake their heads.

'Damn,' David says.

'What are we going to do with him?' Ian asks David quietly.

'I think we should take him to the icehouse,' David says. 'It will be easier if we take him through the hotel, rather than all the way around the building.'

Ian nods wearily and turns to Lauren. 'Help James back inside. We've got this,' he says, indicating him and David and Matthew.

She nods, and waits as David slowly nudges James back to his feet.

Once they've gone ahead, Gwen trailing miserably after, the three men try to pick up Bradley and carry him. But it's impossible. They can't carry him and remain upright on the ice. They end up dragging him. They leave a smear of blood along the snow. Then they lift him onto the porch and inside, into the lobby.

They put him down on the floor for a minute to rest. Ian straightens, catching his breath, and looks up to see Beverly and Henry staring aghast at Bradley's body. They are both speechless with shock. Ian looks away, back down at the body.

David tells them, 'We're taking him to the icehouse.'

*

They go back out again to look for Riley, for as long as they can stand the cold. This time they all stay very close together; they are afraid of one another. But Riley is not answering their desperate pleas. It's bitter cold and pitch dark and the going is impossible. They can't find her. They will never find her. She doesn't want to be found.

Sunday, 3:10 AM

Beverly watches them return, silently, without Riley. One by one they shrug off their coats and boots and slouch towards the fire in defeat.

Beverly thinks Riley must be dead, like poor Bradley. She's almost glad they haven't found her because she doesn't think she can stand the sight of another corpse. She has never been so close to death. It feels as if death is standing over her, just waiting for the right moment. It's an awful feeling.

Beverly thought she caught an odd look on Ian's face in the shadows, when they brought Bradley in. Something cold in his eyes that she hadn't seen before. It gave her a chill. She's not sure – the expression was so fleeting. She might have imagined it.

Gwen slumps on the sofa, numb. Riley is out there, dead, or dying. It's all Gwen's fault; they shouldn't have come. She looks down at her hands; they're shaking. She's beginning to realize that almost any one of them could be the killer.

Henry stares moodily into the fire. Three people are dead – and maybe Riley, too – but his wife is still here.

217

He failed, interrupted at the last moment. He had hesitated for too long. Coward! But they might have come back just as he'd finished bashing her brains out, and then they'd have been on him like a pack of hyenas.

His wife appears silently at his side, kneeling down by his chair, making him jump. It's almost as if she's read his mind.

'Henry,' she whispers, her voice so low that he has to lean his ear down next to her lips to hear what she wants to tell him. He can smell her breath. He wonders if she can possibly know what he's thinking.

'I think I know who the killer is.'

He raises his head and looks at her frightened eyes, gleaming in the dark.

Chapter Twenty-nine

IAN DOESN'T LIKE the way Beverly's been looking at him. She's gone over to her husband and is leaning close to him, whispering something in his ear. That's interesting, seeing as usually she's stayed a good distance away from her husband lately. He wonders what she's saying. Maybe something about him.

Ian sits in the dark, thinking in the shadows.

Henry would like to figure out who is responsible for these murders. He really thought it was Matthew and David. Two unconnected murders. But Bradley's murder changes things.

His wife has been whispering in his ear, has almost persuaded him now that it's a madman who is doing the killings. And she thinks Ian is the killer. She thinks there's something wrong with him. But if he committed the murders, Beverly thinks Lauren would have to know. They're always together. She would have to know.

Henry gives this some consideration. His wife has a lot of

irritating qualities, but stupidity isn't one of them. He looks at Ian now with narrowed eyes, trying to see what his wife sees. Trying to imagine him killing someone.

He finds that he has no difficulty imagining Ian as a killer, because Henry has learned a thing or two this weekend. He's learned that he himself has it in him to be a killer. He finds it's not that big a leap, after all, to imagine anyone else as a killer either.

He wonders if Lauren is covering for Ian. He studies her from across the room with a new interest. He doesn't know how far she would go for love. Love is so much harder to understand – and predict – than hate.

Lauren shifts uneasily in her spot on the sofa. The wind still howls and slams against the windows. It's gloomy in the lobby, the oil lamp guttering softly on the coffee table, and the fire needing attention again.

How long will it be until the police come?

She surveys them all sitting around the fire. How different it is from when they first arrived, Lauren thinks, remembering cocktail hour Friday evening. How cheerful everyone had been, how relaxed. She thinks of Bradley gaily mixing drinks. She thinks of the handsome Matthew – now so changed – and his bright, shiny girlfriend, who is lying in the icehouse. She thinks of Candice, with her scarf wound around her neck.

She would like to know who David thinks the killer is.

She doesn't know what's going to happen next.

James reels with shock and grief. He keeps turning things over in his mind. He remembers how a couple of years ago

Bradley had begun dealing drugs. He thought he'd seen an opportunity to make some easy money, but it hadn't turned out the way he'd expected.

Suddenly, James shakes off his apathy, and springing up out of his chair, cries, 'Who did this? Which of you killed my son?' He feels an overwhelming grief and rage. 'Why? Why in God's name would anyone kill my son?' His voice is wild, accusing, as he looks at each of them in turn. He can see that he has frightened them.

David rises and approaches him, tries to calm him, but James doesn't want to be calmed. He wants an answer.

'I don't know, James,' David says. 'I'm so sorry. But we will find out. You will know who murdered your son.'

'One of you killed him!'

'Unless there's someone else here,' Lauren reminds him shakily.

'*There's no one else here!*' James screams. Then he collapses back into his chair, puts his face in his hands and sobs.

Sunday, 3:30 AM

Despite how late it is, Lauren is wide awake. Everyone is glancing uneasily at everyone else and then looking away again. Everyone but Henry and Beverly. Henry and Beverly are sitting side by side now and watching her and Ian intently. She finds it unnerving. She wonders what they're thinking.

'Why are you staring at us like that?' she says to Henry at last, her voice sharp.

'I'm not staring,' Henry says, quickly averting his eyes.

221

'Yes, you were,' Lauren accuses him. 'Is there something you want to say?'

The air is sharp with tension. She doesn't care. She wants to know why he's looking at them like that, and she wants him to stop.

But it's Beverly who speaks up, surprising her.

'I thought I saw something.'

David turns to Beverly. 'What? What did you see?'

'I saw something on Ian's face,' Beverly says.

'What are you talking about?' David asks impatiently.

'I saw Ian looking at Bradley when you brought him in.'

'We were all looking at Bradley,' Lauren says sharply. 'So what?'

'It's the *way* he was looking at him,' Beverly says nervously.

'What the hell do you mean?' Ian asks.

Now Beverly looks at Ian more boldly and says, 'You were looking at him – as if – as if you were glad he was dead.'

'What?' Ian looks shocked. 'That's ridiculous!' he protests.

'How dare you!' Lauren exclaims, turning from Ian to glare at Beverly. 'I was right there beside him. He did no such thing.'

Beverly turns on her, and says with conviction, 'I know what I saw.'

'You were imagining things,' Lauren says. She flicks her eyes towards Ian.

'My wife wouldn't make something like that up,' Henry says in her defence. His face flushes in the firelight, and he sounds belligerent. 'Why would she?'

Lauren can't think of an answer.

*

222

David is startled at this outburst of Beverly's. He doubts the reliability of what she says. No one knows better than he how notoriously unreliable eyewitnesses are. They see a black car and think it was red. They miss things that are right in front of them and see things that aren't there at all. How much is she projecting her own fear? Beverly had seemed fairly solid until now.

Yet he had himself been suspicious of Ian, ever since he sensed he might be lying about the death of his younger brother. He'd wondered about the sleeping pills, how much they could rely on Lauren even knowing where Ian was the night Dana was killed. He too would like to know more about Ian. He would like to press him.

Gwen watches this exchange, appalled. Beverly seems to be accusing Ian of being the killer. It seems impossible – he's so charming, so easy to get along with, and he has that wonderful smile. She thinks suddenly of that line from Shakespeare – where was it from? – *One may smile, and smile, and be a villain.* Her body has gone rigid, every muscle tight and stiff. Ian could have done it. He could have killed Dana while Lauren was knocked out with her sleeping pills. He was upstairs, with Lauren, when Candice was murdered. And he was running around in the dark like the rest of them when Bradley was killed. It was so dark – he could have done it. Lauren might be lying for him. Gwen clenches her hands tight.

She looks across the coffee table at David but she can't tell what he's thinking.

'Something's been bothering me,' David says. And now they all turn to look at David, who is watching Ian. 'Something about the story about your brother.'

'What's that got to do with anything?' Ian asks sharply.

'It's just that something didn't quite ring true,' David says.

'What makes you think that?' Ian asks, licking his lips nervously.

Gwen, watching, feels sick.

'I can usually tell when someone is lying,' David asserts. He leans forward, out of the shadows. 'Was there something more to that story? Something you aren't telling us?' He waits a beat and adds, 'If there is, maybe you'd better share it with us now.'

Ian swallows nervously and considers his position. David had caught him in a lie. He *had* lied about his brother. He feels cornered.

'Okay,' Ian says, his voice low and distraught. He looks up at the attorney. 'You're right. I didn't tell the whole truth about my brother.'

'I don't see how that matters much, right now,' Henry says. 'Who cares about your brother?'

David sends Henry a look to shut him up. 'I want to know why he was lying.'

'I've never told anyone this before,' Ian says nervously. He glances at Lauren. 'I was thirteen. And Jason, he was ten. He could be difficult. I didn't like hanging out with him, keeping an eye on him. Jason wanted to go to the pond that day. He wasn't allowed to go by himself. So I went with him. But when we got there we got into a fight about something stupid. He was so stubborn. I got pissed off and I left. I left him there alone. I didn't think he'd go in the water. He knew better.' He pauses, takes a breath, and exhales heavily.

'When I got home, later, and we couldn't find him, I went

back to the pond. He was floating there, dead. And I knew it was my fault for leaving him. I never should have left him there. I've had to live with that my whole life.

'I lied to my parents. They didn't know we'd gone to the pond together. I let them believe that he'd gone on his own. That it was just a fluke that I was the one to find him. All these years, I've been living with the guilt. And my parents still don't know.' He looks up at the rest of them. 'I don't know if I'm guilty under the law. I left him there alone, and I've been lying about it ever since. I probably knew he'd go in the water. I told you the same story I've told everyone, even my parents.' He looks at David – he's afraid to look at Lauren. 'This is the first time I've told the truth about it.' He slumps back in his seat, exhausted. 'Now you all know.'

225

Chapter Thirty

LAUREN WATCHES IAN, her lover, through startled eyes. Then she glances at the attorney, tries to gauge what he's thinking. He looks as if he believes Ian now. But she doesn't know what to believe. Maybe it happened the way Ian says. Or maybe Ian pushed his brother in. Maybe he held him down.

He'd told her about his younger brother before, the original version – the lie.

He's sitting close to her, their bodies touching, but now she pulls away. He looks back at her in consternation.

'Why didn't you tell me the truth?' she says, her eyes glancing off his.

'I didn't even tell my parents! I couldn't tell you – I was afraid of losing you.' He looks back at her imploringly. 'I didn't mean for it to happen. Do you think I haven't blamed myself every single day since then? Do you think I don't feel guilty every time I think about my parents? Every time I talk to them?'

She turns her eyes away from him.

'C'mon, Lauren. Don't let this come between us.'

She doesn't answer him for a moment. Then she turns to him in the dark. 'You should have told your parents the truth.' It comes out sounding a little too pious.

'I was a kid,' he says defensively.

Lauren shifts further away from Ian on the sofa, and speaks nervously, without looking at him. She feels everyone staring at her. She takes a deep breath and says, 'You're not a kid now. And we have to tell the truth, Ian. It will come out eventually.'

'What?' Ian says, startled.

'What is it you want to tell us?' David asks.

She says reluctantly, 'When we went upstairs after lunch – I know I said that we were together, but – I went to the little sitting room on the second floor to be alone for a bit, to read. Ian said he was going to have a nap. I wasn't with him.' She feels Ian stir on the sofa beside her uneasily. 'We weren't together all afternoon like we said.'

'Why did you lie?' Beverly says.

'Because I didn't think' – Lauren's voice falters – 'I *still* don't think that Ian had anything to do with this.'

Ian says, 'It's true that Lauren went to read in the sitting room in the afternoon while I was alone in our room. We probably should have said so. But I'm not a killer. That's ridiculous. It's not me!' He turns to Lauren. 'You don't think it's me, do you?' He sounds a little worried.

'No.' She shakes her head but she sounds uncertain, and she knows it. She can hear it in her own voice. Perhaps they all can.

'Why on earth would anyone think it's me?' Ian asks. He looks nervously at the others seated around the fireplace. 'Why me? It could be anyone.'

'It *might* be you,' Lauren whispers suddenly. 'Maybe I've just been too blind to see it.'

'What?' Ian splutters. 'Lauren, come on.' He looks genuinely alarmed now. 'This is insane.'

'When Dana was killed, I just assumed that you were with me all night.'

'I *was* with you all night! I never left the room. I swear.' He runs his hand through his hair nervously. 'And how would you even know? You were asleep.'

'That's just it, Ian.' She looks doubtfully at him now. 'You know I take sleeping pills. I took two on Friday night. You knew I took them. You could have left our room for hours and I wouldn't have known.'

'But that doesn't mean I did!' He runs his hands up and down his thighs. 'So you can't vouch for me being in the room all night.' He looks uneasily at the others. 'So what? None of you can prove where you were all night. Why are you pointing the finger at me?' He says, 'I think we all need to take a step back here. We're all getting a little paranoid.'

Lauren glances at the others in the room. Their eyes are all trained on Ian. She shrinks further away from him. 'But I wasn't with you in the afternoon, either.'

'So now you think I might have killed them?' He shakes his head furiously. 'No. No. Why on earth would I kill three people?' He looks around at the others as if for validation. 'You'd have to be crazy!'

'Maybe you *are* crazy.' Beverly has spoken and Lauren

turns to look at her in surprise. 'I saw the way you looked at Bradley when you brought his body in here.'

'What? I don't know what you're talking about!' Ian protests. 'You're mad,' he says, glaring at Beverly.

'I'm not the one who's mad!' she cries, her voice shrill, as Ian shrinks back into his chair, a look of fear on his face.

Lauren watches it all, her eyes wide.

Ian sizes up the situation and doesn't like it at all. He doesn't like the way everyone is staring at him. 'I'm not a killer,' Ian says, more quietly. 'Lauren and I weren't together for part of the afternoon. It doesn't mean I murdered three people in cold blood. You have no reason to suspect me.'

Lauren looks at him, her face pale, and says, 'But how could you lie to your parents like that for all those years? How could you do that? Maybe you're not who I thought you were.' She lurches up suddenly and moves to the other sofa a few steps away. She sits down beside Gwen and looks back at him with something like fear in her eyes.

'Lauren,' he begs her. But she turns her head away. She won't even look at him.

Gwen watches all of this feeling like she's going to be sick. She wants to vomit up all her fear and grief and guilt and get it all out of her. She doesn't know what to believe. She doesn't want to believe that Ian may be the killer. But she has to admit it's possible.

They must survive until the police arrive; let them figure it out. But God only knows when they'll get here. She's even more frightened now. She no longer feels there is safety in

229

numbers. She thinks of Riley out there in the cold, probably dead. She wonders if anyone else will die.

Matthew broods in the dark, staring malevolently at Ian. Suddenly he leans forward and says, 'Why should we believe you?'

'Believe what you like,' Ian growls back. 'The police will get here eventually, and they'll believe me. There's no evidence at all that I killed anyone. Because I *didn't kill anyone*.' He turns to Lauren. 'And you'll know I didn't do it, too.'

Matthew sees Lauren looking at Ian, as if wanting to believe him.

'You lied about your brother,' Matthew says.

Ian doesn't answer.

Matthew lets his voice grow quieter, and more menacing. 'Maybe it still didn't happen the way you said. Maybe you killed your brother. Maybe you drowned him on purpose. Because maybe you're a killer. Maybe you're just made that way!' Matthew glares at him accusingly. Everyone remains frozen, watching.

'No.'

'I don't believe you,' Matthew says. 'I think you killed Dana. And I have no idea why.' He stifles a sob. 'I'd like to strangle you myself.'

David stirs, as if ready to jump in.

Matthew finds himself standing now. David rises, too, and steps in front of him and puts a hand on his chest. Matthew is taller, and broader, but David's hand is firm against him.

'I didn't kill her!' Ian protests. 'I didn't kill anyone!'

230

'Sit down, Matthew,' David says firmly.

Matthew hesitates. And then, grudgingly, he sits.

David slumps back down into his seat, his heart beating fast. For a moment, it looked like Matthew was going to attack Ian. Emotions are running dangerously high. People who are frightened can be unpredictable, and dangerous. David knows he must not let his guard down for even a minute.

Beverly shivers beneath her blanket and watches the others carefully. She's convinced that she saw something odd cross Ian's face when he looked at Bradley's body on the lobby floor. And now Lauren herself has said that she wasn't with Ian the afternoon that Candice was killed. And that story about his brother – that gave her the chills, too. What kind of person can lie to their parents about something like that for years? He's cold, that's what he is. Matthew obviously believes Ian is the killer, too.

Beverly asks herself what Ian – or anyone – has to gain from these murders. If there's a connection here, none of them can see it. Whoever is doing this is mad. And that's what scares her the most. Because if someone is killing for the fun of it, because they *want* to kill, because they can't help it, rather than for a real reason, then all bets are off. You can't know what they're going to do, where they'll stop. You can't know how much risk they'll take. Perhaps Ian is planning on killing them all. Perhaps at some point, before first light, he will start laughing and slaughter the rest of them.

Maybe, Beverly thinks, it's finally dawned on that foolish Lauren what might happen. She looks scared out of her wits.

*

Gwen wants to close her eyes and sleep. She wishes she were home safely in her own bed. She wishes the police would come. She's exhausted by fear and grief and guilt. She can't stop thinking of Riley, out there alone in the freezing cold – and she's the one who's responsible for bringing her to this terrible place. Furtively, she watches the others through tear-swollen, half-closed eyes. Her heart breaks for James, who has just lost his son. He looks like he will never recover. Well, that makes two of them. She tries to feel sympathy for Matthew, but she doesn't trust him. Ian looks frightened; he doesn't look like a murderer at all. But perhaps that is all for show.

She must not fall asleep. She gives her head a little shake, trying to stay awake.

Gwen catches David's eye across from her, but she cannot tell what he is thinking. Does he think Ian is the killer? If Lauren was in the sitting room, then they can't be sure where Ian was when Candice was killed. But then, they can't really be sure where any of them were at the time of the killings. That's the problem, it's all so confusing and unclear, and she's so tired she can't think it through . . .

She drifts off for a moment and then wakes with a start. She shifts her position, fighting to stay awake. This is her second night of almost no sleep. She wishes again that she had something to protect herself with. But the truth is, even if she had a knife, she doesn't think she could use it. If the killer came for her, or for someone else, could she plunge a knife into his neck? She looks at Ian, staring moodily into the fire. Could she plunge a knife into *Ian's* neck? She studies his neck, the Adam's apple that protrudes ever so slightly. She watches him swallow in the firelight, unaware of her scrutiny, of what she's thinking.

She doesn't think she would have the guts. She shivers beneath the thick wool blanket that covers Lauren and her. She reaches for Lauren's hand beneath the blanket and holds it. Lauren squeezes her hand back.

Sunday, 4:05 AM

'We should kill him,' Henry says into the dark without warning, 'before he kills us.'

David feels the small hairs on the back of his neck stirring. It's as if everyone has stopped breathing. He takes a deep breath and says, his voice outraged beneath the evenness, 'Don't be ridiculous, Henry – we don't know that Ian killed anybody.'

Henry says recklessly, 'It's him or us!'

He's in no mood to listen to reason, David realizes. They are all reaching breaking point; perhaps Henry has just reached it first.

David glances quickly at Ian; he looks petrified.

David gets angry then, at the recklessness of it. 'We can't just murder him.'

'Why not?' Henry says. 'It would be self-defence!'

David shakes his head at Henry. 'You fool,' he says, raising his voice. 'It would be murder in cold blood. We don't know that he killed anyone. Look at him, cowering in his chair. There are seven of us, and only one of him. Do you really think you can kill him and get away with it? You want to be judge, jury, and executioner all at once?' He can't help it; the outrage has taken over, and comes through loud and clear.

Henry grudgingly settles back into his chair, his face hidden in shadow.

Sunday, 4:59 AM

Henry's eyes flutter. He's having a dream, a very unpleasant dream, that he is paralysed, that he can't move, can't act. He's had this dream before – it's symbolic of course, but it has never seemed so real. He's held fast inside this nightmare. He can't move his arms, or legs, not even his fingers or toes. He cannot move his tongue, which feels thick in his mouth. The only thing that is alive is his brain, his mind.

He realizes now that something is terribly wrong. He'd been sleeping, but this isn't a dream. He tries to speak, but he can't open his mouth, can't form any words. It's difficult to swallow. He thinks his eyes are open, but he can't move his eyelids, and all is darkness. He can't see anything – it's as if a black film has fallen over his eyes, like that moment before you pass out. He knows he's dying but he can't tell anyone. He wants to flail and thrash to get their attention, but he is unable to. He knows where he is, even though he can no longer see. His sense of smell is still working, and he recognizes the scent of the logs burning in the fireplace; it reminds him of Christmases as a boy. He's still in the lobby of Mitchell's Inn, and the murderer has got him, too.

Chapter Thirty-one

OUTSIDE THE HOTEL, wild things scurry and howl in the forest. The wind has dropped to a whimper. The sky is just beginning to lighten in the east, but inside, it is still dark, and quiet as the grave. Suddenly the chandelier overhead flickers and turns on, flooding the lobby with light. The remaining guests stir and look up in surprise. There are sounds of whirring and clicking as various parts of the hotel come back to life. The power is back on.

David, who hasn't closed his eyes all night, glances first at Gwen, who appears to be asleep, her dark lashes a smudge against her pale face. She's breathing peacefully, for the moment at least. Lauren is curled beside her. He shifts his eyes next to Beverly. She's looking at him, blinking in the sudden brightness.

'The electricity's back,' she says with feeling. 'Thank God.'

At the sound of her voice, Gwen stirs, opens her eyes.

Lauren straightens up suddenly on the sofa. 'Hallelujah,' she says.

Matthew and Ian shift beneath their blankets; David doesn't know if they were ever really asleep, but they're wide awake now. James is slumped in his chair; his eyes are open, and David can't tell if he's slept at all.

Now Beverly gives a startled cry, and they all quickly turn her way. She's staring at Henry.

'Henry!' Beverly cries. Her face is aghast, and she shakes his arm.

But there's no mistaking that Henry is dead. He's perfectly still in his chair, his head thrown back, his eyes closed, his mouth open. In the light of the chandelier his face has a hideous pallor.

'Henry!' Beverly shrieks again, shaking him harder, panicking.

David rises swiftly and goes over to Henry, but there's nothing to be done. Beverly is now sobbing hysterically. David looks up and meets Gwen's eyes, and sees pure fear.

James slowly gets up and makes his stumbling way to the reception desk. David watches as James dials the number, his hands shaking, and realizes he's holding his breath. To his profound relief, the phone appears to be working. At last.

James speaks into the phone, his voice breaking, 'We need help.'

Sunday, 6:45 AM

Sergeant Margaret Sorensen, fortyish, stocky, blonde hair going grey, always an early riser, is enjoying her Sunday morning coffee at home in her favourite, least flattering flannel pyjamas when she gets a call from one of the officers at the station.

'Ma'am, we've got a situation out at Mitchell's Inn.' Officer Lachlan sounds tense, which is unusual. He's generally a laid-back sort, especially good with community events.

'What kind of situation?' she asks, putting her coffee cup down.

'We just had a phone call from the owner there. James Harwood. He said at least three people have been murdered, maybe more.'

'Is this a prank?' she asks in disbelief.

'I don't think so, ma'am.'

She can tell from his voice that he doesn't believe the call was anything but genuine. *Good God*, she thinks, shocked.

'We need to get out there, ma'am.' He's breathing quickly, shallowly down the line.

'Who've you got there?'

'Perez and Wilcox. We'll get the snowmobiles ready. No other way out there at this point.'

'I'd better let the chief know. I'll be there in ten minutes.' Good thing she lives so close to the station; it's just around the corner.

Sunday, 7:35 AM

Sergeant Sorensen pushes the snowmobile hard over the ice-covered snow up the long, winding drive to Mitchell's Inn. She has gunned it as fast as she can all the way from town.

A triple homicide. Things like this are rare up here. They

don't even have a detective at the station. She will have to do until New York State Police can send someone. Officer Lachlan had briefed her more fully when she arrived at the station, but the facts are sketchy. Three guests and the owner's son are dead, and another guest is missing. She is shocked. She doesn't know what they might be walking into. She's familiar with the hotel, and with the family. Young Bradley – dead. She can hardly believe it. Her adrenaline is pumping fiercely as they approach the final curve in the long drive.

She cuts the engine outside the hotel on the brittle, glittering lawn. She reaches for her gun and gestures to the other officers parking their snowmobiles to do the same. They approach the front entrance cautiously, their heavy boots sliding on the ice. It's so cold she can see her breath.

Sorensen notices a smear of blood on the ice near the front porch, and silently points it out. She creeps up the side of the porch steps and looks in the window. Finally, she pulls open the front door, her weapon ready. It opens easily. She steps inside the lobby and her eyes automatically turn towards the group around the fireplace. She sees pale faces peering out from blankets, staring back at her. She thinks, *I will always remember this moment.*

She hears the three officers coming in behind her. She takes in everything with her quick eyes. The people sitting around the fire look haggard and dishevelled, as if they haven't slept. As if they've survived some kind of siege. She recognizes James, blindsided by the loss of his only son. She feels a stab of pity for him. She counts eight survivors sitting around the fire. No, make that seven. On closer inspection, one of the chairs is holding a corpse.

She approaches the small gathering, holstering her weapon.

'I'm Sergeant Sorensen, and these are' – she indicates each with a nod of her head – 'Officers Lachlan, Perez, and Wilcox. We're here now, and we're going to help you.' She tries to sound authoritative and reassuring at the same time. Sorensen steps forward to look more closely at the dead man. She can't tell from looking at him whether he was murdered or died of natural causes.

She takes in the pallid faces looking up at her and wishes fervently that the medical examiner and the forensics team were here with her. She has no idea how long it will be until the roads are passable. She's on her own here.

'For now, I'm afraid everybody has to stay put,' she tells them. 'There's no way to get you all safely into town. We're going to take a look around, then I will have questions for all of you. When the roads are clear, you will be taken into town to the station to give official statements. In the meantime, I need all of you to help me as much as you can.'

She gets a few weary nods in response. 'Before I look around, I need someone to put me in the picture here. Just a quick overview for now.' Her eyes light on a man in his late thirties with an intelligent look about him. 'What's your name?' she asks in a friendly way.

'David Paley.'

She pulls up a chair and sits down beside him. 'Maybe you could tell me who everybody is, and then tell me what happened.'

She listens grimly as he gives her the story. When he's finished, she says to them all, 'We'll look for Riley, just as soon as we can.'

*

239

After that, Sergeant Sorensen instructs Perez and Wilcox to remain in the lobby to ensure the safety of the survivors. She keeps Lachlan with her, to take notes, and as a second pair of eyes and ears. She does a quick walk through the hotel and its environs, with Lachlan by her side.

They start in the lobby. She pulls a pair of latex gloves out of her pocket and puts them on, then walks over to the bottom of the staircase, feeling the eyes of the survivors on her back. She squats down, notes the blood on the edge of the stair. She looks up to the top of the staircase, and back down again.

She motions Lachlan to follow her. She climbs the staircase, hardly making a sound. How quiet the stairs are, she thinks. All she can hear is the squeak of her boots. She continues to the second floor, Lachlan behind her. They arrive at the room to the left of the stairs across the hall, number 206. Taking the key that James had handed her, she opens the door carefully with her gloved hands. She flicks on the overhead light. Inside she sees the body of the second victim, slumped on the floor, her scarf still wound tightly around her throat. She and Lachlan take a close look, careful not to disturb her.

Next they visit room 202, the room that had not been made up. She takes in the messy bed, the unwiped sink. She glances wordlessly at Lachlan, who purses his lips. Forensics will go over this room with a fine-tooth comb, when they get here.

The two of them make their way back down the stairs and out through the woodshed and the bitter cold and down the path to the icehouse. When they step inside, the first thing she sees is Bradley's body lying near the back wall, the only colour in the glittering, translucent interior. She stops, takes a deep breath. She knew what she was going to find, but still, it's hard to see Bradley stiff on the snow floor, dead. She takes a closer look. Such a fine-looking boy. Such an awful blow to the head.

Beside him, another body has been placed on the floor against the wall. It's wrapped tightly in a white sheet. 'Might as well unwrap her,' she says. Lachlan puts on a pair of gloves and carefully pulls the sheet partly away. They look down at the woman's frozen face, distorted by death. She can see that she was beautiful. She's dressed in a negligee and a navy satin robe. Seeing her there, dead, lying in an icehouse so scantily clad, Sorensen shivers involuntarily.

'Christ. What a horror show,' she says, with feeling.

She leans down and studies the head wound.

Eventually she stands up. 'I want to see where Bradley was killed.'

They head back inside and then go out again through the front door. Outside, they follow the smears of blood. The spot where Bradley was killed is about thirty yards from the hotel. There's an impression in the icy snow, and a dark red patch of blood where Bradley fell. She sees the boot scraper in the ice a couple of feet away. She gives it as thorough a look as she can with her bare eyes, and then turns away, sick at heart. She looks back at the hotel and says to Lachlan, 'What the hell happened here?'

Lachlan shakes his head.

Back in the lobby again, Sorensen pulls Perez and Wilcox aside and explains the situation. 'The two of you need to search this hotel thoroughly, from top to bottom. Check all the nooks and crannies, the closets, the cellars, the attic, if there is one. Take James with you, if he's up to it. Treat him gently; he's just lost his son. Check outside, too, and all the doors and

241

windows, every outbuilding. We need to be absolutely sure there is no one else here. And that no one else *was* here.'

'Will do,' Perez says.

'Meanwhile, Lachlan and I will search the area in front of the hotel for Riley.' She adds grimly, 'She can't have got far.'

Outside, she and Lachlan stand at opposite sides of the broad lawn where the scrub begins and start their sweep, working towards one another and out again as they proceed. When they reach the edge of the woods, they must move more carefully, looking for signs that someone has passed this way. Sorensen remembers other searches in woods like these, looking for lost hunters, sometimes for lost children. Occasionally searches end happily; she's under no illusions about this one. A woman alone, not dressed for the elements – it wouldn't have been long before hypothermia set in. Unless she knew something about how to survive alone in the winter woods, and Sorensen doubts that. To make matters worse, Riley was in a panic, not thinking clearly. And the first rule of survival is to not panic.

The branches snap beneath her boots, and the cold, sharp air makes her chest feel tight. She scans the forest, always aware of Lachlan's carefully moving presence to her left. She usually loves walking in the woods, but not today. Along with the urgency she always feels with a ground search – the simultaneous hope and fear – she knows that there might be a killer here somewhere.

When they've been at it for a while and Sorensen is really starting to feel the cold, they enter a little clearing where the snow is deeper. She lifts her eyes across the clearing for signs of human trespass, noticing nothing, but then Lachlan calls, 'Over here.'

Just from the tone of his voice, she knows.

Nevertheless, she hastens over to him as fast as she can, clumsy in the deep snow. Lachlan is standing over something darker against the white, a shape huddled up against a large boulder. As she comes closer, she sees that it's a woman, approximately thirty, face an eerie white, lips blue, eyes open but crusted in ice. She's dressed in jeans and a grey sweater. Running shoes. No coat, no hat. She's crouched up against the boulder, stiff as a board, her knees to her chest and her arms around them, as if hiding, or waiting for something inevitable. Her hands are tucked into her sleeves. It almost breaks Sorensen's heart, but she's careful not to show it. Instead, she bends forward to examine her more closely. There are no visible signs of violence. She pulls back again.

'Shit,' Lachlan mutters.

Crows gather and fly overhead, dark against the pale sky, and Sorensen watches them for a moment.

'No signs of trauma,' Sorensen says finally, glancing at Lachlan.

'But who was she running from,' Lachlan says, shaking his head, 'out here without a coat?'

'I don't think she even knew.'

Chapter Thirty-two

Sunday, 10:05 AM

SORENSEN AND LACHLAN return to the hotel and deliver the bad news. Sorensen doesn't think anyone expected Riley to still be alive, but it is difficult nonetheless. Predictably, her friend Gwen takes it the hardest. She sobs loudly and begins to rock, wailing uncontrollably. Sorensen sits beside Gwen, a hand on her shoulder until she calms down.

Finally, she and Lachlan leave the group and go to the privacy of the dining room, where Perez and Wilcox soon report that they are certain there is no one else in the hotel other than the people they know about. There are no signs of anyone having left. They tell her about the broken window and the branch, but they feel the branch likely broke the window on its own. Which means, Sorensen realizes, that it is highly likely that one of the people here is a murderer. For now, each one of them is a suspect. 'I'd better caution all of them,' she says to Lachlan. 'To be safe.'

Sorensen's first interview is with the hotel owner, James Harwood. She calls him into the dining room, where she has set up an interview table. Some of the warmth from the kitchen filters through. It's taking a while for the heating to come back up. The shutters have been opened so that the room is filled with daylight. In the natural light, James looks terrible. She wonders how he will be able to go on without Bradley. He sits down in front of her. Beside her, Lachlan has his notebook out. She advises James of his rights, and he indicates that he is willing to proceed.

She begins gently. 'James, I'm so sorry about Bradley.'

He nods, his lips firmly together in a deep frown, fighting back tears. She knows he's no stranger to misfortune. His wife died of cancer some years back, and he's raised Bradley these last few years on his own. He's had his struggles with Bradley.

She leans forward a little and says, 'This might be difficult to talk about, James, but you know I've known you and Bradley for a long time.' He looks up at her with red-rimmed eyes. 'You know I liked Bradley.'

He nods. 'You've been good to us,' he says, his voice a broken whisper.

'So don't take this the wrong way.'

He hunches his shoulders warily, as if he knows what's coming. Of course he knows what's coming. She's certain he's had these same questions himself, especially since Bradley was killed.

'Is there any way Bradley could have been involved with this – this situation?' She looks at him intently, with compassion.

He looks back at her tearfully. He takes his time answering. 'Bradley was a lot of things, but he would never be involved in

245

something like this,' James says, his lips trembling. 'He had his problems. You know that. You know what he was like. He was impulsive, he liked excitement – he thought he was invincible. Driving too fast, running with the wrong crowd. The drugs.' He sighs heavily. 'He liked money, and what it could buy. He didn't want to have to work too hard for it. And he didn't always know when he was crossing the line. But he was a good kid.' His eyes flood with tears. 'He wouldn't do anything really bad,' James says.

'James, I don't mean to suggest that Bradley could have had a hand in these killings,' she says. 'But perhaps he stuck his nose in, perhaps he knew something, something that got him killed.'

'I've wondered that,' James says at last, exhaling heavily. 'He had this look that I recognized, the look he had that time he got caught dealing drugs. Remember? He was always so cocky, but he knew when he was in over his head. That's the way he looked after we found Candice's body.' He shakes his head. 'And I thought he looked tired, like he hadn't slept that night, the night Dana went down the stairs.' He looks up at her. 'What if he saw something? What if he saw who did it?'

'Did you ask him about it?' Sorensen asks. James nods, tears running freely down his face now. He wipes them away. 'What did he say?'

'He said he was just freaked out about the murders, like everybody else.' He looks down. 'I didn't push it.'

She puts her hand on his shoulder. 'James, I doubt there was anything you could have done to make things turn out differently.'

He sniffs loudly. 'Maybe if I'd tried harder to talk to him. I should have. And now he's dead!'

She lets him cry, her hand resting on his shoulder. Finally, he wipes his eyes and blows his nose. He looks up at her and says, 'Room 202, with the unmade bed.'

'Yes?'

'There's no way that room was missed,' he says. 'There's no way it wasn't made up properly after the last guest left. That has never happened before. And once you can talk to Susan, the housekeeper, I think you will find that she says the same thing.'

'So what do you think?'

'I don't think there's anyone in the hotel we don't know about. I never did. I know this hotel like the back of my hand. If there was someone else here, I think I'd sense it somehow. Or Bradley certainly would have. And he was certain there was no one else here. Maybe he knew who the killer was.' He chokes back a sob. 'I think that one of the guests is the killer, and whoever it is got into that room and messed it up to make us think there was someone else in the hotel. Bradley thought so, too. He told me.' He looks at her harshly. 'One of them killed my boy.'

She's already come to that conclusion herself.

'Thank you, James.' She looks at him sympathetically as she stands up. 'We'll find out who did this.'

She dismisses James and calls in David Paley next.

'Sergeant,' David Paley says courteously to her, as he takes the seat across from her and Officer Lachlan.

'Can I get you anything? Water?' she asks.

David shakes his head. 'I'm fine.'

She's pretty certain he is the same David Paley who was charged and released a few years back for the murder of his wife. She remembers the case; it remains unsolved. She's not going to ask him – yet.

She has already had his brief account of what happened. Now, after cautioning him, she leads him through all of it again, each painful step, each awful detail.

'Had you ever met Dana Hart or Candice White before this weekend?'

'No, never.'

'Ever heard of them?'

He shakes his head. 'No.'

'Ever met anyone else who was here this weekend?'

'No.'

Finally she tilts her head at him and asks, 'What do you do for a living?'

'I'm an attorney.'

So, it is him. 'Who do you think committed the murders in this hotel?'

He hesitates, and then says, 'I don't know.'

She remains silent, waiting for him to continue.

'The others – Beverly and Henry and Matthew, especially Henry – seemed convinced last night that it was Ian. They were looking at him as if they thought he was going to murder us all.' He rubs his eyes tiredly before going on. 'Perhaps it was relief at finally having someone to blame. They desperately needed to know who it was and they thought they did.' He looks up at her. 'In my experience, the human mind doesn't like to deal with uncertainty.'

He tells her, then, what he hadn't told her before, the way they turned on Ian.

'Jesus,' she says, imagining it.

'They calmed down. I'll never forget how relieved Ian looked.'

'You may have saved his life.'

'I don't think it would have actually come to that.' He shrugs and looks up at her cynically. 'But that's me, protector and defender of the accused, no matter how heinous the crime.'

Next, Sergeant Sorensen invites Beverly Sullivan into the dining room. Officer Lachlan, who has an excellent bedside manner, sympathetically offers the bereaved woman a glass of water. She accepts it, takes a sip.

'Mrs Sullivan,' she begins, having advised her of her rights. 'May I call you Beverly?' Beverly nods. 'I'm so sorry about your husband.'

'Thank you,' she says quietly, tears pooling in her eyes. Lachlan delicately pushes a box of tissues towards her. He'd found them in the kitchen.

'We don't know the cause of death yet. It looks like he died of natural causes, but there will have to be a postmortem.' Beverly nods, wiping fiercely at her eyes with a tissue. 'I know this must be very difficult,' Sorensen says, 'but I'm sure you understand that I must speak to everyone who was here this weekend, to try to determine exactly what happened – and why.'

Beverly nods again, blows her nose. 'Of course.'

She asks Beverly to give her account of what happened over the course of the weekend. When she gets to the part about bringing Bradley's body into the lobby, Beverly leans forward slightly and says, 'Something odd happened then.'

'What do you mean?' Sorensen asks. She knows what's coming – she has already heard about this from David.

Beverly looks at her for a moment, and then explains. 'It was Ian. He was looking at Bradley . . .' She hesitates, as if unsure how to describe it.

249

'How was he looking at him?'

'He had this look on his face, but only for a moment. It was there, and then it was gone. But it gave me the creeps. I didn't trust him after that. I whispered to my husband that I thought Ian was the killer. Right after I'd seen that look on his face.' She sits back again in her chair. 'Henry hadn't seen it. Then, when Lauren told the truth – that she'd been shielding him, that he hadn't been with her all afternoon . . .'

'Go on,' she says, when Beverly stops.

'When Lauren said she'd been covering up for him, it all began to make sense. He denied it, of course. He was desperate that we believe him. The situation was – indescribable.'

'And what did you think?'

'I know what I saw. I think Ian is the killer, although he was doing a convincing job of denying it. But he's probably a good actor.' She leans forward intently and says, 'All those years he lied to his parents about his little brother. Who could do that? He must be a psychopath.' She stops, takes a deep breath. 'I've never met a psychopath before. I was terrified of him then. We all were.'

Sorensen interviews Gwen next. She is obviously deeply traumatized by what's happened, and very distraught over the death of her friend.

When Gwen has given her account of what happened, she asks, 'So Riley wasn't murdered? She died of exposure?'

Sorensen says, 'We won't know for sure till the team gets here, but that's what it looks like.'

'So she didn't have to die at all,' Gwen whispers.

Sorensen comforts her as best she can.

When she finally sends Gwen back out to the lobby, Sorensen

feels slightly overwhelmed for a moment by the situation she finds herself in, but she thrusts the feeling aside and refocuses on the job in front of her.

When Sorensen calls in Matthew Hutchinson for questioning, she watches him get up stiffly from his chair and make his way to the dining room.

Normally they would separate witnesses into different rooms, but it's easier to have them stick around the fire. She relies on the vigilance of her officers, Perez and Wilcox, to make sure they don't talk among themselves.

After advising him of his rights, Sorensen takes her time going through what happened over the weekend with Matthew. She can tell how upset he is. His fiancée is dead. But he answers all of her questions willingly. He has nothing to say that contradicts what the others have told her.

She asks, 'You had no reason to kill your fiancée?'

'What?' He looks wary now. Afraid.

'Beverly says she heard you arguing earlier that night. Tell me about that.'

He drops his head, but he doesn't deny it. She thought he might. It's only Beverly's word against his.

'Yes, we did argue that night, but it was nothing serious. Just a bit of tension, wedding jitters, you know? She was finding it stressful.'

'She was finding what stressful, exactly?'

'The wedding preparations. Dealing with my family. They can be a bit . . . difficult. Intimidating.'

'Your family wasn't happy about the wedding?'

'I wouldn't say that, exactly.' He looks away. 'My mother

wasn't one hundred per cent on board, but I loved Dana. And she knew I was going to marry her.'

'Okay.'

'I didn't kill her, or anybody else,' he says truculently.

'But you could have.'

'What?'

'You could have committed all of the murders. There is no one who can swear to being with you when any of the victims were killed.'

'Why the hell would I do that?'

'I don't know. You tell me.'

He stares at her in dismay.

'Why would your fiancée have left your room in the middle of the night?'

'I – I don't know.'

'You admit you had an argument. You didn't go after her, and perhaps – in a moment of anger – push her down the stairs? And then – in for a penny in for a pound – when you saw that she wasn't dead, you didn't grit your teeth and smash her head against the bottom step?' She knows she's being rather harsh. She wants to see how he'll react.

'God – no!' He looks appalled. 'I didn't kill her!'

'And then, perhaps someone here knew. Maybe someone found out. Maybe Candice knew what you'd done, or suspected it, at least. Or maybe Bradley saw something. Did one of them try to blackmail you? Were they *both* trying to blackmail you?'

'No! That's outrageous!' he manages to splutter.

'Is it?'

'Of course it is! I didn't kill my fiancée! I loved her.'

She gives him a long, thoughtful look.

He looks back at her, uneasy.

'Candice was writing a book. Was that book about you? Or about Dana, perhaps? Something that would be damaging?'

'No. I'd never heard of her. We didn't know anything about a book. And Dana and I have nothing to hide. Why would anyone write a book about us?'

She waits, lets him squirm. 'Okay. That's all for now.' She gets up and opens the glass dining-room doors. 'You may go back to the lobby.'

Chapter Thirty-three

Sunday, 12:45 PM

SERGEANT SORENSEN RETURNS Matthew to the lobby and asks for Lauren.

She watches Lauren rise and walk past her into the dining room. Lauren takes her seat at the table. Sorensen sits down across from her, cautions her, and they begin.

Sorensen gives her a small smile. 'You okay?' she asks.

Lauren nods. 'I guess so, considering.' She accepts a glass of water from Officer Lachlan and takes a sip. She adds, 'It will probably all hit me later.'

Sorensen nods. 'Shock.'

Lauren nods back. She seems tense. They have all been tense.

'You discovered Dana?'

'Yes. I went down early to see if I could find some coffee. I didn't even know if anyone would be up yet.'

She says, 'Go on.'

'When I got to the landing, I saw Dana lying at the bottom.' She glances at Lachlan, as if embarrassed. 'I'm afraid I screamed. I could tell she was dead. She was so still. I ran down to her and – then the others came.'

'Did you touch her at all?'

'Yes, I did. I felt for a pulse.' She hesitates before going on. 'Then the others arrived. We were all very upset. You don't expect something like that to happen. We thought she'd fallen down the stairs. And then David – later, David said he thought it wasn't an accident.'

'When did he say that?'

'It was after lunch. He said that she had to stay where she was until the police came. That it might be a crime scene.' Lauren looks up at her. 'I don't think anyone believed him at first – we thought it was an accident, that he was overreacting. Until Candice was killed.'

Sorensen has her go through the rest of the day, the discovery of Candice's body, what happened that night. When Lauren is finished, Sorensen says, 'Some of the others think that it might have been your boyfriend, Ian, who was committing the murders.'

'I don't know,' Lauren says tightly, looking down at the table.

'Do you think it's possible?'

She hesitates before she answers. 'It's possible.' Lauren looks up at her, clearly uncomfortable. 'I spent some time in the afternoon in the sitting room on the second floor, reading. I wasn't with him. I suppose – I suppose he could have done it.' She looks back down at the table.

'What about you, yourself?' Sorensen asks.

'Pardon?'

255

'You could have killed Candice yourself. You don't have an alibi either. You were alone in the sitting room. For that matter, you could have killed Dana, and later, you could have killed Bradley.'

'Oh. Well. I can assure you that I didn't. What possible reason could I have had?'

'I don't know. Had you ever met Dana Hart or Candice White before?'

Lauren answers firmly, 'No, of course not.' When Sorensen says nothing, Lauren leans forward earnestly. 'You have no idea what it was like, being trapped here with all this going on. Last night, when everyone ran off into the dark – David running after Matthew, the rest of us running outside after Riley . . .' She shakes her head, as if in disbelief that it ever happened. 'It was so dark, you couldn't tell where anybody was. But then I heard Gwen – she must have been nearby, I could hear her breathing, sliding on the ice. She sounded like she was panicking, as if she thought someone was after her.' Lauren pauses, as if reliving the memory of those awful moments when everything was falling apart. She whispers, 'I heard her calling my name. But I didn't answer. I thought maybe, if the killer was there, he would follow her, instead of me. So I kept very quiet.' A sob escapes from her throat. And then she is crying in earnest.

Sorensen gives her time to recover. She's patient. She offers the box of tissues. Officer Lachlan waits, his pen poised above his notebook.

Finally, Lauren says, 'I'm not proud of that.' She looks up at her. 'But I certainly didn't kill anybody.' She reaches for a drink of water.

Sorensen notes that Lauren's hand is shaking as she brings the glass to her lips. 'Take your time,' she says.

Lauren continues. 'I've been trying to think of signs that I might have missed, signs that Ian might be insane, but honestly – there weren't any.' She stares across the table at Sorensen with dark, disbelieving eyes. 'He seemed completely normal to me. He charmed everyone. He was so . . . likeable. People warmed to him, just like I did. It's so unnerving, to think that you might be so wrong about someone, so . . . taken in. I certainly never saw any cruelty in him. I thought – I thought that he was someone I could become serious about.'

'True psychopaths can be very convincing,' Sorensen says.

Lauren looks back at her, her face bleak. 'I don't think you have any idea how frightening it was, sitting in that room all night knowing there was a murderer somewhere nearby, waiting to see what was going to happen next.'

'I can't imagine,' Sorensen says.

As Lauren is leaving, Officer Perez taps at the dining-room door. Sorensen turns and asks, 'What is it?'

Perez enters the room and speaks to her in a low voice. 'I've just remembered something. It might be important.' She nods. 'You wanted to know if I or Wilcox had ever heard of the author Candice White. I thought the name sounded familiar but I couldn't place it. I thought maybe it was someone my wife read. She reads a lot of books.'

Sorensen nods her head again impatiently. 'Yes?'

'But actually I've read one of her books. She wrote a true crime book a few years ago that I quite enjoyed. That's pretty much all I read.'

'Is that so?' Sorensen says. 'What was it called?'

'I don't remember exactly, but it was about that school principal who murdered one of his students.'

Perez leaves the dining room and Sorensen glances at Lachlan, who is pursing his lips at this new information.

She rubs her hands together and walks to the dining-room windows to look out at the forest. She thinks about what might be hiding in that dark wood – bears, wolves – things that kill. She thinks about the human killer she has in this very hotel.

She hears someone enter the dining room. She turns away from the window and sees James carrying a tray with coffee and sandwiches. The sight of James doing what Bradley would normally do almost breaks her heart. It must be lunchtime already. She wants to say thank you, but doesn't trust her voice. He places the tray on the side buffet table, nods, and leaves the room.

She walks over and pours a cup of steaming coffee. Then she takes a sandwich and her cup, goes back to the window, and looks out thoughtfully at the forest.

David has returned to the dining room, summoned again by Sergeant Sorensen. He wonders wearily what she wants with him. He's told her everything he knows. What he wants right now is sleep.

'Mr Paley,' Sorensen says after a long pause.

Her voice has changed. It's not quite as friendly as before and his body tightens automatically, as if expecting a blow.

'I know who you are.'

The blow is delivered, exactly the one he was expecting. 'I've told you who I am,' he answers coldly.

258

She nods. 'You gave me your name, yes. You didn't tell me everything, did you?'

'Why would I, when it's not relevant?'

'Perhaps it is relevant,' she says.

'I don't see how.'

'Candice White was writing a book.'

'Yes,' David admits. 'That's what she said.'

'Do you know what it was about?'

'I have no idea,' he says, feeling uneasy. 'She didn't say.' He adds, 'None of us had ever heard of her.' He feels his heart sink. Here it comes, he thinks.

'You are still under suspicion for the murder of your wife, are you not?'

'No.'

'That's not exactly true, is it?' she prods.

He looks at her angrily. 'I don't know what you expect me to say. I was arrested and the charges were dropped, as I'm sure you know. There was insufficient evidence to proceed. As far as I'm concerned, that's the end of it. I don't consider myself under investigation any longer.'

'Oh, but you are, of course. These investigations don't just stop, do they? Just because they don't have enough to nail you now, doesn't mean they won't have enough to nail you down the road.' She pauses. 'A good police officer never gives up. You must know that. They just go about it more quietly.'

'What's your point?' he asks angrily.

'I'm just wondering if you might have been in mortal fear of someone writing a book about you – and what Candice might have had to say about the murder of your wife.'

'That's ridiculous. I told you – I'd never heard of her. She wasn't writing a book about me.' His head feels light, and his heart is beating far too quickly. He knows he didn't murder Candice. Or anyone else. She's barking up the wrong tree.

'I hope not.' She adds, 'But it's been brought to my attention that Candice White is known for writing true crime books.'

David feels himself go pale.

'In any case, it's just a matter of time until we get into her laptop, and then we will see,' she says. 'That's all for now. You may go.'

Chapter Thirty-four

Sunday, 1:45 PM

SERGEANT SORENSEN SITS back heavily. She doesn't know how much longer it will be until the crime team gets here. She looks impatiently at her watch. After spending hours in chilly rooms, drinking endless hot coffee, she's starting to appreciate what it must have been like to be trapped in this godforsaken hotel for the weekend with no power. She can't even imagine the rest of it.

But the evidence is there. At least three people have been murdered. Another has probably died from exposure, having fled the hotel in terror. And a fifth has died under suspicious circumstances. The survivors are clearly traumatized.

She calls in Ian Beeton, the one they're afraid of, the one some of them seem to think might be the killer. Ian appears pale and apprehensive as he enters the dining room. He regards her warily. She wonders what he thinks is worse – being accused by the others in the middle of the night when their fear and paranoia were at their greatest, or being questioned by the police in the cold light of day.

He must be under the most terrific strain, she thinks. She says, 'Please have a seat.'

He sits down and looks at her as if he's expecting to be arrested. She wonders if he will be the first one to refuse to talk to her after she cautions him.

But he nods assent and glances nervously towards the lobby where the others are gathered; the glass doors are closed. Haltingly, guided by her questions, he gives his own account of the weekend. He denies ever having met or heard of Dana Hart or Candice White. He tells her he's as shocked by the murders as everyone else.

'The others think you did it,' she says.

'They're crazy. I didn't kill anyone,' he says defensively. 'It could have been any of them.'

'Who do you think did it?'

He's silent for a moment, and then says, 'I don't know.'

She raises her eyebrows deliberately. 'No idea at all?'

'I'm not a detective,' he says stubbornly. 'But whoever did it must be crazy. This whole situation is crazy.' He licks his lips nervously. 'Honestly, last night I was scared for my life. If it wasn't for David – if it hadn't been for him, they might have murdered me. That asshole Henry suggested it. David managed to calm him down.'

She looks back at him impassively. 'And now Henry is dead, too.'

He looks up. 'I had nothing to do with that, either, I swear!'

'We don't know how he died yet,' she tells him. 'There will

262

be an autopsy, of course. That's all for now. You may go back to the lobby.'

Sunday, 3:30 PM

Sergeant Sorensen and Officer Lachlan move to the ground-floor sitting room, where James has made them a fire. It's more comfortable than the dining room. The others remain in the lobby, under the watchful eyes of Wilcox and Perez. Perez reports that they've been fed, but are getting restless. Sorensen knows there isn't much she can do about that. She's feeling impatient too – the police chief, the medical examiner, the forensics team – and the detectives – will get here when the roads are navigable, and not before.

She has looked at the physical evidence as best she can herself; until the forensics crew arrives, there is not much more she can do on that front. She has interviewed everyone present as far as she dared without them all clamming up and starting to ask for legal counsel. She's not happy about being in this remote hotel without the techs to quickly and expertly secure the evidence the way it should be secured. She wishes they would hurry the hell up clearing the roads.

There's nothing to do but watch her charges – keep them safe and make sure no one tampers with the evidence. Trapped here, without the forensics team, she has only her wits to work with.

'At first glance,' she says to Lachlan, sitting across from her by the fire, 'none of these murders seems related to one another.

The victims didn't know each other until they arrived at this hotel. At least, not as far as we know. Maybe something will come to light as we dig deeper. What we don't have right now,' she adds, 'is any kind of motive.'

Lachlan says with obvious frustration, 'I hate sitting here with our feet up and our hands tied.'

She sighs and says, 'It's Bradley who's bothering me.' She continues to think out loud, but in a lower voice. 'I knew Bradley. He was always up to something – very enterprising, always had some scheme going. He's involved with this some-how, I'm certain of it. He saw something, or knew something, and it got him killed. What did he know?'

'Up to a bit of blackmail, perhaps?' Lachlan suggests.

She looks up at him and nods. 'That's what I'm thinking. I wouldn't be at all surprised. But who was he blackmailing? Which one of them is our killer? Or do we have more than one?' She looks into the fire for a moment, and then says, 'Any one of them could have killed Dana. Any one of them could have killed Candice. Any one of them could have killed Bradley, except for Henry and Beverly. They're the only ones who didn't go outside when he was killed.'

'Yes,' Lachlan agrees.

'And any of them could have slipped something into Henry Sullivan's drink, for instance, if in fact he was murdered somehow and didn't die of natural causes. They all admit they periodically warmed themselves in front of the fire, and Henry was sitting right there.' She adds, 'Not to mention, it sounds like Henry was making himself a bit of a pest with his snoop-ing and his theories, and our killer had to be getting nervous.'

*

David aches all over from sitting in the chair with his muscles tensed all night. He longs to go home. But he knows it's going to be a while before any of them can leave.

He passes the time watching Gwen – wondering if there is any possible way she might be willing to see him when this is all over – and thinking about who the murderer is. The rest of them seem convinced – or had at least seemed convinced last night – that Ian was the culprit. But he doesn't think so.

There is only one person here who knows the truth, he thinks, and that's the killer. And he has a pretty good idea who that is. He just doesn't have any proof. And he doesn't want to share his theory with Sorensen. At least, not yet.

Gwen desperately wants to know who the killer is.

She thinks uneasily about what happened in the early hours of the morning – when Henry had suggested killing Ian. How dangerous people can become when they're scared, she thinks. She's grateful to David for putting a stop to it. Surely a man who maintains his reason while others around him are losing theirs – surely such a man could never kill his wife or anyone else?

She needs to know who the murderer is because she has to know for certain that David didn't do it.

Ian paces back and forth in front of the windows of the lobby, ignoring the others as best he can, but he can feel them all watching him. He's glad there's a police officer in the room, watching everybody, protecting him. Even so, he's frightened. He's insisted to all of them that he didn't kill anyone. They don't seem to believe him. What matters is what the police believe. He might need a very good lawyer. He thinks about David Paley, sitting over there with the rest of them. David probably saved his life. Perhaps he will represent him, if it comes to that. If he's arrested.

Chapter Thirty-five

Sunday, 4:10 PM

THE FIRE HAS burned low in the grate, and James arrives in the sitting room to build it up again. Sergeant Sorensen and Officer Lachlan are still in front of the fire when they hear a sound in the distance. The sound of heavy machinery out on the drive.

'The road crews must be out,' Lachlan says, standing up eagerly.

'Thank God,' Sorensen says with relief, rising from her chair. 'It won't be long before everybody else gets here then.'

They leave the sitting room and reach the lobby, where everyone's attention is turned towards the windows. The sound is louder out here. Through the windows, she sees a big yellow snowplough coming slowly and laboriously up the drive.

She turns away from the window and looks back at the survivors in the lobby. James has come out of the kitchen at the sound of the plough; the rest remain where they are, as if

267

frozen in place. Sorensen looks at each one of them in turn: James, Beverly, Matthew, Gwen, David, Ian, and Lauren.

Sorensen turns back to look out of the window. She sees then that there's a truck following behind the snowplough – and she recognizes the crime team. She feels her face break into a relieved smile.

Gwen watches as the forensics team disperses and gets to work. Officers Wilcox and Perez remain in the lobby, as if afraid that someone might try to make a run for it.

Gwen wonders what the crime team will find.

She has spent so much time with these people over this appalling weekend. She has learned their secrets – at least some of them. They have all been scraped raw. And yet, she still feels she knows them hardly at all. She has survived this weekend only to take something ugly away with her – she's learned that you never *really* know anyone else. That is terrifying. Because you can't tell, can you? When she leaves here and goes back out into the world, she will think of everyone she meets as having the potential for evil deep inside.

Sergeant Sorensen gets a call saying that the detective has been delayed. For now, she is still in charge. She watches the techs as they work, quickly and efficiently. No matter how careful someone is, she knows, it's very hard these days to get away without leaving a trace of evidence of what they've done.

She follows the technicians around the hotel as they put out their careful little markers and take their laborious photographs. She hovers over them while they study the bodies, one after the other, and mutter to each other as they work. It will be a while yet before the bodies can be moved, although they are working as quickly as they can.

Now she's outside, watching them pore over the area in the snow where Bradley died. Bright floodlights have been set up in the late afternoon; the effect is almost blinding.

'Looks like he was hit once, on the back of the head,' one of the techs says. 'The blow was strong enough, and heavy enough, to kill him.'

Now one of the other techs waves her closer. 'Look at this,' he says.

She looks closely as he bends over and points at something in the snow. But she can't see anything. She adjusts her glasses upwards a bit, to get the full effect of her trifocals. 'I don't see anything,' she says.

The tech bends forward again, and using a pair of tweezers, removes something tiny from deeper in the snow and holds it up for her. It's a small diamond earring. No wonder she couldn't see it.

'Are you telling me that that was underneath the body?' she says.

The technician nods. 'It was frozen into the snow, so it can't have been here long. Only since the snowfall on Friday night. And it's a pierced earring. Ought to be able to get some satisfactory DNA off of that.'

'So it's a woman,' Sorensen says, unable to hide her surprise.

'Looks like it.'

'Good work.'

Back inside, Sorensen asks Ian Beeton to come with her into the dining room to answer some more questions. She doesn't look at him when she asks for him. She notices the others stir in expectation.

Ian, pale and shaken, lurches his way into the dining room.

She asks him to sit, reminds him that he is still under caution, and he drops as if his knees have buckled beneath him.

'I've got a couple of more questions for you, Ian,' she says.

He looks at her, his eyes wide with fear.

She holds up a little clear plastic evidence bag and places it on the white linen of the dining table. 'Have you ever seen this earring before?'

He looks down at it, as if struck dumb. Whatever he was expecting, it obviously wasn't this.

'Do you recognize it?' she asks.

He nods slowly. 'It's Lauren's. I mean, it looks like the ones she was wearing . . .'

'When was the last time you saw her wearing it?'

He sits back in his chair, aware now of what is being asked of him. 'Where did you find it?'

She doesn't answer; she waits.

'She was wearing that pair yesterday, I think.'

'You think?'

'She was wearing them yesterday.'

'Okay.' Sorensen made a point of noticing when she came through the lobby that Lauren isn't wearing any earrings now. But Beverly and Gwen both are. She knows that none of them would have had the opportunity to go back up to their rooms to get another pair, if they'd lost one. 'Did you happen to notice when she stopped wearing them?'

He shakes his head and whispers, 'No.'

*

They all watch warily as Sergeant Sorensen returns to the lobby. They've been on tenterhooks since Ian returned, white and silent, to the lobby and sat down, clearly shaken.

Lachlan stands beside Sorensen, ready with a pair of handcuffs.

David notices how still everyone is, how alert. He feels his heartbeat escalate as they come to stand in front of Lauren.

'Please stand,' the sergeant says to Lauren.

Lauren rises, visibly trembling.

The sergeant says in a firm voice, 'Lauren Day, you are under arrest for the murder of Bradley Harwood . . .'

David tunes out the rest; as they read Lauren her rights, he's watching her. She opens her mouth to protest but it looks as if she can barely breathe. She throws a panicked glance at Ian, but he's unresponsive; he seems too shocked to react.

Then Lauren turns to David, her eyes full of panic. She needs someone in her corner; she needs an attorney. But when she looks at him, he meets her eyes only briefly, then turns away. He sees the others' faces, stunned at the turn of events.

When Ian hears the handcuffs click as they lock around Lauren's wrists, he feels physically sick.

This can't be right, Ian thinks, his heart pounding in his chest. He can't believe it. This can't be happening. He runs his hands agitatedly through his hair.

She seems so normal.

He thought it was Matthew who had killed everyone – born with a silver spoon in his mouth, maybe he'd killed his fiancée after an argument and then tried to cover it up with the natural arrogance of the born rich. Maybe Candice and

Bradley knew something, and he'd had to keep them quiet. But it hadn't been Matthew at all. Matthew is a victim; he has lost the woman he loves. Ian looks at him now and feels terrible for him; he will never be the same.

Ian will never be the same either. None of them will ever be the same.

He has a sudden bout of dizziness, fights another wave of nausea. Maybe the police have made a mistake. Surely Lauren did not kill all these people. *What possible reason could she have?*

He looks at her again, her lips now pressed in a tight line, her eyes closed. And suddenly he knows it's true. He can't stop staring at her, wondering what's going on behind those closed eyelids. He realizes that he does not know her at all.

He tells himself that he has made a very narrow escape. He shudders. They have spent months together. He'd thought he was falling in love with her.

Matthew watches the police arrest Lauren. He doesn't know what evidence they have, but he trusts the police. They must have good reason for arresting her. He is filled with inexpressible grief and rage, but also relief. Relief that he is no longer suspected of killing his fiancée. He takes one instinctive step towards Lauren and stops. *She's* the one who murdered Dana! It was *her*. He can hardly believe it. *She's* the one who pushed Dana down the stairs and hit her head at the bottom to make sure she was dead. And then, for a time, she allowed everyone to believe that he had probably done it. He'd almost wanted to kill himself out of despair and fear.

'Why did you kill her?' he demands, his voice loud with anguish.

'Please step back, sir,' the sergeant says.

Lauren's eyes fly open and she looks back at Matthew with desperation. 'I didn't kill her!' she cries. 'I didn't kill anyone! They've got it wrong. This is all a mistake. It wasn't me!' She turns frantically to Ian. Surely he will help her. 'Ian, tell them! Tell them it's not me!'

But he looks back at her strangely, as if he's afraid of her. What did he say to the police just a few minutes ago, when he was in the dining room? What does he know? He can't know anything!

David steps forward and cautions her. 'Don't say anything. Not a word.'

Chapter Thirty-six

LAUREN LOOKS INTO David's eyes – and they aren't the eyes of someone who believes her, someone who will protect her. She collapses to the floor, handcuffed, and closes her eyes again. They let her stay there on the floor, leaning against the sofa; she hears them talking in low voices in the background.

She's not going to tell them anything. She has the right to remain silent and she's going to use it.

When Ian invited her up here for a naughty weekend, she had no idea what was going to happen. None of it was planned.

She thinks back to that first night. She'd taken a dislike to Dana right from the start. She thought it was because she reminded her of someone, but she couldn't think who. It wasn't until after cocktails, when they were having dinner, that she realized who Dana reminded her of. It wasn't until Dana's comment, *It sounds like someone fell off the roof,* and her laughing about it, that she realized exactly who Dana

274

was. And then Lauren's heart began to pound and she could feel herself turning hot and cold and breaking into a sweat.

Dana – she had been Dani when Lauren knew her – had given no sign of recognizing her. Not until that comment. Then she knew for certain that Dani had recognized her, but had pretended not to. Dani always was a good actor. But Dani obviously wanted Lauren to know that she knew who Lauren was.

They'd both changed. At least on the outside.

It was a long time ago. Fifteen years. Half her lifetime. Lauren had been a plain, sullen, overweight teen then, and Dani had taunted her relentlessly. But she had recognized her.

Dani looked different now, too. At fifteen, she'd worn her hair very short. She had a tough, mean look. She was a tough, mean girl. Now, fifteen years later, she was completely different. This new version – *Dana* – was very feminine, polished, expensive-looking – no wonder Lauren hadn't recognized her at first. But Lauren was certain that the scrappy Dani was still there – Dana was a fake. *Dana* didn't look like she'd ever spent a single night in a miserable foster home, taking her frustration, rage, and fear out on others more vulnerable than herself.

Lauren, too, had put her past behind her. She didn't want it to come out now. She had Ian now. She couldn't let Dana ruin everything. She had to be sure that Dana wouldn't say anything.

For the rest of the evening, her mind was in turmoil. She let Ian fuck her on the back staircase, but her mind was on other things. *Would Dana tell?*

She told herself that Dana also had a lot to lose. She was about to marry, and obviously into money. Lauren was certain Matthew didn't know about Dana's past. Dana would keep that from him, surely. She wouldn't want a man like Matthew to know what she'd come from. But Dana knew something about Lauren that Lauren couldn't allow to get out.

Of all the shitty luck.

How easily it all came back to her that night. That horrible time in her life. She was full of rage. She'd been removed from her family's house and sent to that wretched foster home on the other side of the city. Her parents had found her unmanageable and she thought they wanted to teach her a lesson. She hated them for it. Her father had had enough of her, but her mother – her mother thought Lauren was just unhappy. Her poor, long-suffering mother. She never really understood who Lauren was.

The foster home was awful. She didn't even have her own bedroom, but had to share with two other girls. One of them was Dani, tall and skinny and vicious. She never knew what Dani's situation was – they never talked about home, and how they ended up in that shithole. The bathroom was shared among six of them. No one ever seemed to clean it. The food was barely edible. But she ate it anyway, and hated herself for shovelling it in, looking for comfort wherever she could find it.

They would go up onto the roof. It seems unlikely now, unbelievable, that when they were in care, they would climb up the TV antenna tower in the backyard and get onto the roof. The house was at the end of the street, and if they stayed on the back of the roof, no one saw them. They would hang out up there, smoking cigarettes that Dani stole from Mrs Purcell, the woman who was supposed to be looking after them. One afternoon, one of the kids, Lucas – he was thirteen, but seemed younger – climbed up after them and asked Dani for a smoke.

Dani told him to fuck off.

He stayed. He kept pestering them until Dani told him his parents were drug addicts and they were never coming back for him because she'd heard the social worker telling Mrs Purcell that they'd overdosed and he was an orphan now. She really could be a cold-hearted bitch.

'You're lying!' he shouted, furious tears streaming down his face. 'I'm going to tell on you!'

'Go ahead,' Dani said, flicking her cigarette ash. Then she added, 'God, you're such a baby.'

Getting nowhere with Dani and stinging with hurt and the need to hurt someone else, Lucas turned on Lauren and said, with a contempt beyond his years, 'You're fat and ugly!'

And Lauren stood up suddenly and pushed him off the roof, just like that.

Dani turned to her in shock. 'Jesus! Do you know what you just did?'

They looked down at the boy on the patio stones below. He wasn't moving; his head was split open and leaking. They bolted off to the mall and didn't come back until suppertime.

It was assumed he'd fallen, or jumped. He was a troubled boy, the child of drug addicts, with probable fetal alcohol syndrome and poor impulse control. No one even questioned where they were. But Dani knew what Lauren had done, and for a few days she held it over her, threatening to tell whenever she felt like it.

Dani left, no more than a week after Lauren pushed the boy off the roof. She stuffed her things in a bin bag and said, 'See ya, loser.' And then she was out of the house, slamming the door behind her. Lauren didn't know if she'd gone back to her parents or to another foster home.

Lauren wanted to go home. She hadn't thought she would be there long. But it dragged on, week after week, until she wondered if her parents would ever ask to get her back, and no one told her anything. Lauren's rage grew and grew.

When Lauren was finally reclaimed, her mother came for her alone. Her father was gone; she never saw him again. Her mother took her home and things went back to normal, with Lauren doing whatever she wanted. A couple of years later, her mother remarried. Her stepfather adopted her and she changed her name to his.

And then Dani showed up at Mitchell's Inn.

That night, Lauren didn't actually take her sleeping pills. She waited until Ian was asleep, and then, when all was quiet except for the bluster and rattle of the wind, she slipped out of her own room and padded quietly down to the first floor and knocked lightly on Dana's door. She was all alone in the hall; everyone was asleep, the storm crashing outside their windows. She didn't have to knock twice.

Dana answered the door, looking guardedly at her. Lauren said that they should talk. Dana glanced back at the sleeping form of her fiancé, slipped the room key into the pocket of her dressing gown, and stepped into the hall without a word. She followed Lauren down the stairs to the landing and then stopped. 'Wait,' she said, her voice low. 'We can talk here.' And she stopped as if she wouldn't go any further. So, at the top of the stairs, Lauren looked Dana in the eye and said, 'We need to clarify a couple of things.'

Dana stared, her eyes wide, the same way she'd stared at Lauren in the dining room when she made the crack about someone falling off the roof. They had a fraught, shared history. The only question was, *what happened now?*

A cool, blank expression settled over Dana's face. 'What is it, exactly, that you want to clarify?' she asked. And then she simpered and said, 'Oh, wait! I know. You want to be sure I'm not going to tell anybody that you're a *murderer.*'

'Shut up, Dani,' Lauren snapped, her voice low. 'Don't think you can push me around any more. Things have changed.'

Dana snorted. 'Oh, I don't think they've changed that much. I think I've still got the upper hand here, given what I know about you.'

'But I don't think you want Matthew to find out about *your* past, either, am I right?'

'Oh, I don't know. My past may be sad, but it's not *criminal,*' Dana said.

Lauren reached out and grabbed Dana's robe and yanked at it. There, over Dana's left breast, was the small, telltale tattoo. A viper. 'You didn't get rid of this?' Lauren almost laughed. 'You can get those removed, you know.'

Dana looked at her and spat, her voice low, familiar, '*You always were a little sociopath. What are you going to do – are you going to push me, too?*'

And with one sudden, violent thrust, Lauren pushed Dana down the stairs. Dana fell clumsily to the bottom, her descent muffled by the thick carpet. She let out one short scream that panicked Lauren. She froze. But she was committed now.

Dana lay completely still at the bottom of the stairs. Lauren had only moments before others might come running. She ran lightly down the staircase. At the bottom, she felt Dana's pulse still beating in the soft curve of her throat. She grabbed a fistful of Dana's shiny hair and pulled up her head and smashed it – as hard as she could, with all her rage – against the edge of the stair. Lauren's heart was pounding violently. She looked up towards the top of the staircase, expecting someone to come at any moment; someone must have heard the scream. She was getting her story ready. But still no one came. She felt again for a pulse. Dana was dead. Glancing around, certain that no one had seen her, but not wanting to run into anyone who might have heard something, Lauren ran quietly along the back hall and made her way up the back staircase to the second floor and let herself back into her room. Ian was sound asleep.

She'd killed her. She'd killed Dani, the one person who knew what she'd done all those years ago, and all she felt was relief. And to know that she killed her before she could marry a rich man and have everything she ever wanted was especially satisfying.

They would think Dana fell down the stairs.

Lauren crawled back into bed and lay awake all night thinking about what she'd done. She felt no remorse.

But as the long night wore on, she started to worry. It had all happened so fast. She worried that Dana might have already said something to Matthew about her, that they might be able to tell it wasn't an accident, that Dana wasn't really dead.

Finally, she rose very early in the morning – having not slept at all – and crept downstairs before anyone else. She went quietly, careful to wake no one. Her heart was pounding as if it had grown to fill her entire chest. She stood on the landing at the top of the stairs and looked with cold relief down at Dana, so clearly dead. She swept down the stairs and bent over her, and confirmed that she was dead as a stone. She was so relieved she almost laughed.

And then she let out her unholy scream. People came running then, and she made sure they found her feeling for a pulse, in case the police found traces of her touch. She hoped it looked like an accident. And if anyone thought it didn't, there was Matthew – the obvious suspect. She thought she was in the clear.

But then David, the attorney, had suggested that it wasn't an accident at all, that it was murder. Still, she thought she might be all right. She thought they might think Matthew did it. And even if they didn't, there was nothing to pin it on her. She was certain they wouldn't find the connection between her and Dani.

But then after lunch she found the note in her book. The book she'd left in the lobby after breakfast. She took the book back upstairs with her after lunch and opened it and saw the small slip of paper inside, not folded, with her bookmark. And written on it, in big block capitals, in an obvious attempt to disguise the handwriting, was: *I saw what you did to Dana.*

She felt her heart jump in her chest like someone had jolted it with electricity. Someone had seen her! The note was unsigned. But she'd seen Candice in the lobby with the book in her hand, and she'd put it back down in a hurry. It had to be her. Was she going to try to blackmail her? Lauren thought uneasily about the hotel, how someone could have been hidden, behind a chair, in an alcove, how she might have been seen, or heard, after all. How rash she had been, how cocky, to take a quick glance around and assume that no one had been there! But

Candice had been watching. She must have been. And now Candice was going to try to blackmail her. The bitch. But Lauren was not the kind of person to be blackmailed.

She knew what she had to do. It didn't bother her to kill. Not if it was necessary. She's always been able to do whatever is necessary. She's different from other people. She's always known this, ever since she was a little girl.

She has also known the importance of hiding such a fact. And she's been clever enough not to have been discovered. It gives her a certain freedom that other people seem to lack. She can do things that they can't. But she's learned how to hide it by watching what other people do and pretending to be like them.

After finding the note, she told Ian she wanted a bit of time to herself and went to the small sitting room on the second floor with her book. She knew she couldn't confront Candice in the library – it was too risky. Candice would probably come up to her room at some point. She'd already noticed that Candice had been wearing a silk scarf around her neck that morning.

After a while, she heard a sound in the hall. She got up from her seat by the window where the light was good enough to read, and moved quietly to the door and looked out. It was Candice, unlocking the door to her room across the hall. Candice opened the door and went inside, leaving the door open. Lauren crept down the corridor towards the open door. She looked quickly up and down the hall; no one was there. Candice was standing at the desk, her back turned to her. Lauren wasn't going to negotiate. There was only one way to deal with a blackmailer. It was easy to sneak up behind Candice, her feet sinking noiselessly into the carpet. She quickly grabbed both ends of the scarf around Candice's neck and pulled with all her strength. She didn't let go until she was sure. She let Candice slump to the floor. Once Lauren was absolutely certain she was dead, she left, using her sleeve to close the door behind her. And then she retraced her steps to the sitting room, where she took up her book again.

Problem solved.

And then she had another idea. Checking that no one was coming, she slipped across the corridor and, picking the lock – a skill she'd learned as a troubled teenager – slipped quietly into the empty room at the end of the hall across from Gwen and Riley's room. She had to be very quiet, so that they didn't hear her. She messed up the bed a bit, made it look like it had been slept in. She went into the bathroom, and taking a towel, turned on the tap and sprinkled some water on the sink. Then she slipped carefully out of the room and returned to the sitting room feeling rather clever. She was sure no one had seen her this time.

She thought it would end there.

When Candice's body was discovered, she found it easy to dissimulate, to pretend a horror, a fear, she did not feel. She behaved like the others, mirroring their emotions like a chameleon. She's been doing this all her life. It was easy.

They'd all crowded around Candice's room, messing up the murder scene. She deliberately bent down over Candice and made a show of touching her in front of everyone, trying to loosen the scarf, just in case. So she wouldn't have to worry about trace evidence.

But by then she'd already realized that she'd made a terrible mistake.

283

It was when they'd returned from the icehouse, before Candice's body had even been discovered. Bradley had gone off to the library to look for her. Lauren had stood in front of the reception desk and reached across, using her iPhone to search for a pen. She wanted to do a crossword by the light of the oil lamp. Her eyes fell on a small white notepad with paper the same size as the disturbing note in her book. She held the light closer. She could see the faint imprint of block letters. Even upside down, she could make out the words *saw* and *Dana*, clearly enough.

It was Bradley's desk. She'd never seen his father – or anyone else – behind the desk. Bradley might have written the note and put it in her book. Maybe Candice had nothing to do with it. It might have been Bradley who'd seen her kill Dana. She quickly grabbed a pen and turned away from the desk, her heart pounding in her chest.

Still, she thought, settling down and pretending to work on a crossword, Candice may have seen the note – *I saw what you did to Dana* – inside the book, which was in her hand. And Lauren told her the book was hers. It was probably just as well that Candice was dead. Snoopy bitch. But Bradley . . . He must be the one who'd seen her.

Later, after Candice was found, she realized that Bradley must be afraid that she had also killed Candice. She thought that maybe he'd lost his nerve, was too afraid now to approach her and ask for money. He knew what she'd done. She knew she had to kill him.

When Riley ran outside into the dark, and Bradley followed, she saw her opportunity. She grabbed her coat. Her leather gloves were inside the pockets. Ian was with her but she urged him to go after Riley quickly, pretending to struggle with her boots. Alone on the porch in the dark, she picked up the boot scraper and slipped quietly in the direction she'd seen Bradley take. When she finally came upon him she let her rage take over – she struck him with everything she had.

Then she froze in the night, listening, worried that someone had heard him fall. But it was too windy to hear much of anything. No one came. She could just hear, faintly, Gwen calling for Riley, panic in her voice. Lauren stayed in a crouch and moved away from Bradley, abandoning the boot scraper by his body. She headed for the other side of the hotel, far away from the body. Soon after, she saw the light appear at the front door and saw David and Matthew coming outside to join them.

When she heard the shouting, she made her way over to where she'd left Bradley dead. But then things didn't go the way they were supposed to. David was there, holding the fading torch, Gwen beside him. She saw James hovering over Bradley, and she tried to go to him, to offer help, to check Bradley's pulse, to see if he was really dead. But David wouldn't let her near him. He stopped her. He wouldn't let her go to Bradley, even when she pummelled his chest and sobbed. She thought she seemed pretty convincing. But she hadn't been able to get near the body. He wouldn't let her help carry Bradley inside, either.

She wondered then if David was on to her.

It was unfortunate that she'd had to reveal the truth about her and Ian. That they hadn't been together that afternoon, after all. She'd undermined him, suggested he was the killer without looking like she was doing it. It was lucky, that lie about his brother. She loved Ian as much as it was possible for her to love anyone, but ultimately, he was disposable. It was necessary. She would find someone else.

Of course, they have no motive. She's not worried they will be able to find the connection between her and Dana. They'd been in the same foster home for only a couple of weeks. People came and went there in a constant, sad procession, with their pitiful plastic bin bags holding all their worldly possessions. They were in foster care, not in the criminal system. And it was in another state. Lauren's life since has been a clean slate. She's never been caught for anything she's done.

She's been so careful. She touched Dana in front of everyone – that's why her DNA will probably be on her. Candice, too. If they find trace evidence of her it will be meaningless. And Bradley – she'd been wearing gloves, and there were so many of them around him, and they'd moved him. The evidence must be hopelessly contaminated.

But they must have something on her, she thinks anxiously, something definitive. Maybe they found her earring. That must be why they brought Ian in again, to identify it. She feels little prickles of moisture rise on her skin.

She'd noticed, in the dark, early hours of the morning, that she was missing an earring. She could have lost it anywhere, long before she went outside after Bradley. There had been no struggle. She'd lifted the boot scraper and brought it down on his head and he'd dropped without a sound. But she was worried: what if she *had* lost the earring when she killed Bradley?

Just in case, she removed the remaining earring when no one was watching, and slipped it onto the end table beside her.

Now she's glad she thought ahead. If they do have her earring – if they found it near Bradley – she will insist that she took both of them out before Riley ran outside, and put them down on the little end table. The killer must have seen her do it. The killer must have taken one, and deliberately planted it near Bradley's body.

It's perfectly plausible. Especially as they won't have any other evidence against her. It should be enough for reasonable doubt.

They won't get anything out of her.

Chapter Thirty-seven

Sunday, 6:00 PM

THE ROAD CREWS are out in force, ploughing, sanding, and salting the roads. They will soon be able to let the survivors drive to the station in town to give their statements. Sergeant Sorensen has been advised by telephone that a detective will be arriving any minute. They've done pretty well so far, she thinks, without one.

A technician approaches her holding up a laptop. 'I was able to get past Candice White's password. I pulled up what she was working on.'

Sorensen raises her eyebrows. 'And?'

'It looks like a romance novel. About two women who fall in love and adopt a baby.'

'Really?' Sorensen says, surprised.

He nods. 'Yup. Have a look.'

Sunday, 6:30 PM

Ian has been outside for the last half-hour, running the cars, warming them up, and trying to scrape the ice off the windows. It's already dark outside, but the hotel is brightly lit.

Gwen stops on the front porch, looking out. Her car has just been pulled out of the ditch and brought back to Mitchell's Inn.

It seems wrong to get back in the car without Riley. So horrible to leave without her, to abandon her here. She's still in the forest, with various people photographing her, examining her, under floodlights. Gwen is sure she'll never forgive herself.

She becomes aware of David coming up to stand beside her. She doesn't know what to say to him. Is there any future for the two of them? Immediately, she feels disloyal to Riley, to her memory. How resentful she would be.

'Gwen,' David says. It's just the two of them on the porch. 'Are you okay?' His genuine concern almost makes her break down. She wants to press her face into his chest, but she doesn't. Instead she just nods quickly, blinking back tears.

She turns to him suddenly. 'Did you suspect it was Lauren?'

'Yes,' he admits. 'She touched Dana, and she touched Candice, too, in front of everyone. It's a smart thing to do if you're worried about the possibility of having left trace evidence. It's very difficult to *not* leave forensic evidence. And she tried to get to Bradley, too, but I stopped her. Physically stopped her. That's when I suspected her. But I didn't *know*, not for sure.'

289

'I had no idea it was Lauren,' Gwen says. She'd been shocked by Lauren's arrest. Ian whispered to her and David afterwards that they'd found Lauren's earring outside, and that he figured it had to have been near the murder scene, because they'd quickly arrested her.

David says, 'She didn't get near Bradley after we found him. So if they found her earring near him—'

'I liked her. I trusted her,' Gwen says. She looks up at him in disbelief. 'Why would she do it?'

'What her reasons were, I have no idea. I imagine it will come out in the investigation. I suspect Bradley knew what was going on, and that he was killed for it.' He looks down at her, his face serious. 'I think Lauren is probably a psychopath – and very good at pretending that she isn't.' He hesitates. 'They're different you know – not like you and me.'

She looks at him more closely. He seems different to how he did the first night they arrived. More weary, less sure of himself. They're all different. She wonders how she seems to him now, how she's changed. She knows that when she gets into her car, Riley will be in the passenger seat beside her, saying, *He killed his wife. Stay away from him.*

Beverly walks slowly and sadly out of the front door of the hotel past David and Gwen and down the steps. But Henry is still in the hotel, in his chair by the fire, as if he will never leave. It feels strange to leave without him, to leave him stuck there. But of course the coroner will have him taken away for an autopsy. There must be an autopsy. There will be arrangements to make, a funeral to see to. She thinks about how to tell the kids that their father is dead. It will come as a shock. You don't expect your parents to go away together for a weekend and only one of them to come back.

But first she must stop at the police station and give her statement. Then, they've been told, they will all be allowed to go home. All except Lauren.

Matthew is getting into his car. His grief weighs him down. David and Gwen are still talking on the front porch. Beverly gets into her car, backs up, and then turns slowly down the drive, towards town and the police station.

What a difference a weekend can make. She'd come up here in hopes of reconnecting with her husband. Now she is going home a widow.

She checks her rear-view mirror to see if anyone is watching her. There's no one behind her, and no one can see her in the dark. Even so, she waits until she is around the first curve of the drive before she smiles.

She feels so light it's like she's floating.

She thinks back to when they were searching the hotel, when she helped search the others' bags. She saw the drugs that Lauren had, the sleeping pills. An entire vial of them. Full. After holding it up for all to see, no one had noticed her spill part of the bottle into her hand inside the overnight bag and then slip the pills into her pocket. It was dark, and no one was paying much attention.

She hadn't known for sure that she would do it, not until Bradley had been killed, too. And she hadn't known for sure if it would be enough, but she sneaked the pills into her husband's Scotch in the dark and hoped for the best. Perhaps, combined with all the Scotch he'd been drinking, it would be enough. It was. She knows that the autopsy will show the

291

sleeping pills, that he was murdered. But he will be one of four people murdered at Mitchell's Inn this weekend. And Lauren, the murderer of the other three, can't exactly say anything without implicating herself. She can't say, *But I didn't kill Henry!*

She can't say a thing.

Shari Lapena worked as a lawyer and as an English teacher before writing fiction. Her debut thriller, *The Couple Next Door*, was a global bestseller. Her second thriller, *A Stranger in the House*, was a *Sunday Times* and *New York Times* bestseller. *An Unwanted Guest* is her third thriller.